# THE DIVERSITY
# CALLING

# THE DIVERSITY CALLING

## CALLING

Building Community One Story at a Time

# The Diversity Community Exchange Group (DiCE Group)

**To order additional copies of this book, contact:**
Xlibris Corporation
1-888-795-4274
www.Xlibris.com
Orders@Xlibris.com
89588

# CONTENTS

# DEDICATION

Dedicated to our dear friends,
Marvin and Sonny

# INTRODUCTION

APPROXIMATELY NINETY-THREE MILLION miles away from the sun, its third planet—the one with the abundance of *intelligent* life—wraps up yet another record-breaking trip around the life-sustaining orb. Its inhabitants (the intelligent ones) have again managed to avoid heaping unbearable misery and destruction upon one another during this last circuit, but for some reason, it doesn't seem to get any easier. After each celestial circuit, the planet seems to return bristling with a few more energy sources, a few less forests, a slightly bigger ozone hole, a few more people, and a lot less peace. Why is that?

We, the Diversity Community Exchange (DiCE Group), can confidently assure you that we *do not* know the answer to this question. However, we can just as confidently affirm that we do know where the answer lies. The answer lies in the very same place that the problem originates from—the human spirit. And while we cannot claim to know the solution to the dilemma that our tendency toward conflict presents to our quality of life (not to mention our continued survival as a species), we are absolutely convinced of where the solution lies: in the process of dialogue.

The authors of the following chapters make up the membership of the DiCE Group. We are a diverse group of professionals from multiple sectors; community based, consulting, corporate, education, engineering, psychology, religion, and so on. What we have in common, and what has brought us together, is a personal and professional commitment to diversity. In each of our respective fields, diversity work is referred to differently. Be it diversity and inclusion, multicultural education, equity, social justice, or other current nomenclature, our goals are much the same. Collectively, our work addresses root causes of societal ills such as workplace discrimination, hate crimes, educational disparities, gang violence, human trafficking and modern day slavery.

DiCE was born of the conviction that we, as human beings, can benefit tremendously from being willing to respect one another's personhood and common humanity enough to engage in respectful dialogue. We are talking here about more than mere polite conversation within our small group. Rather, we feel that if we (collectively) sincerely solicit, hear, and value one another's views, perspectives, and experiences, the synergy resulting from this intellectual, emotional, and spiritual exchange will allow us to successfully cross the divisions between us and overcome our collective challenges.

The nine autoethnographic stories contained in this book represent but a small slice of the spectrum of human experience in the vastness of our world today. This point is worth repeating. We are nine ordinary people. We have nine different birth narratives, nine families of origin, nine (or more) coming-of-age experiences, nine most embarrassing moments, nine fondest memories, and nine hopes for the world.

The joys, laughter, tears, and epiphanies we've shared during the process of discovering and sharing one another's stories have helped to convince us of the richness and deep satisfaction that awaits all who are willing to take the courageous step of creating community through dialogue. While there are a fair number of terminal-degree holders in the group, arriving at this position and point of view was not simply the result of a dispassionate academic exercise for us. Rather, the inspiration that called forth the birth of this book stems from the totality of our life experiences.

As a result, the book unfolds very much like an invitation to take a leisurely walk in a garden, occasionally pausing to ponder some subtle but wondrous example of nature's beauty that you may have seen hundreds of times but only noticed just now! The landscape you will view on this walk happens to be that of our DiCE family. But the really exciting part of the whole experience is that other similar excursions await you and other fellow travelers—in your own communities—that you may have seen many, many times but perhaps have not yet noticed or even been fearful of approaching.

We invite you then to come along for the ride. Join Marvin as he flies with the angels and Sonny as he reflects on his unique journey of progressive discovery and passionate conviction. Experience the enlightenment of Santalynda's multiple realities and defining moments, and help Tommy choose the right path at the crossroads. Take a deep breath and a long satisfying drink as Sidalia reveals a view of diversity infused in the air we breathe and the water we drink, and listen in as Simma ponders the meanings of the tapestry of her life and mosaic of her experiences. Pull up a chair and listen as Juan recounts the birth of a movement, and hang on as Nadia shares a literal and figurative round-the-world journey of discovery and realization. And be sure, on your way out, to look in on Dr. Joe-Joe to witness firsthand the making of a diversity champion.

We realize that we have promised much in this introduction, but we are confident that we have neither oversold nor overstated our case. What gives this book such promise is not us, the subjects, but you, the reader. We have merely shared nine regular stories. But in doing so, we hope and believe that we will spark an interest and longing in you to do likewise. Our belief is that if you ponder the subject long enough, you will agree that there is nothing quite like the promise, excitement, and fulfillment that result from taking a peaceful journey in an open human mind. The wonders of joy, acceptance, and affirmation that result from nonjudgmental sharing with just one other person are overwhelming. Multiply this by as many people who are willing to be open and honest with each other, and you soon begin to see the tremendous potential that we as a species have for blessing one another's lives.

While we come from a variety of religious and spiritual traditions, the ancient text of Genesis recounts a story about mankind's beginnings that seems apropos. The story alleges that God instructed mankind to spread out over the face of the earth and repopulate it. However, after having recently experienced a flood, mankind decided instead to stay put and instead build a tower that would go up to heaven. The story goes on to say that God came down to inspect the tower and commented that "because the people all speak the same language, there is nothing that they won't be able to do." Finally, to force mankind to cease building and to disperse, God confused their languages. Whether one chooses to view this story as history or myth, it suggests a profound truth: *that humanity that is able to access each other's minds and perspectives through language and understanding can (according to God) accomplish anything!*

Building towers up to heaven may still be a long way off. However, building a common understanding within a community or a shared commitment among coworkers or a peaceful settlement to a family feud just might be within reach.

A final note before you begin. We have mentioned a couple of times that we are a family of nine. We still are, but two of our members have transitioned beyond this realm. Marvin R. Smith departed this life on January 30, 2006, and Floyd "Sonny" Massey III followed him on January 20, 2009. Our lives have been undeniably and permanently blessed through the time we were fortunate enough to share with Marvin and Sonny, and we have them to thank most for this book's existence. We mention this for two reasons: first, to honor and laud them for the beautiful, intelligent, and compassionate men that they were and their tremendous contributions to us as individuals and as the DiCE family. The second reason is to gently nudge and remind you, our readers, that time is of the essence. Life is a wonderful gift that we don't know how long we'll be able to enjoy. We urge you therefore to, while you're here and while you can, step across borders and boundaries to exchange stories and develop shared narratives.

Tommy Smith, on behalf of the DiCE Family

# "I LOVE WHAT I DO!"

### Floyd "Sonny" Massey III

M Y NAME IS Floyd "Sonny" Massey III, and I love what I do! It has actually taken me twenty-five years into my professional life to be able to make that statement. My dad used to quote the scripture that read, "Happy is the man that has found his work; there is no greater joy." That is one piece of scripture that I now understand.

I never really thought about why I love diversity work until I began to piece this story together. Upon reflection, I see that there are at least four areas that have helped me come to really love what I do. The first one has to do with being willing to take a deep look at the "early messages" that I received in life. Messages that were both positive and negative and how those messages impacted my life.

The second area has to do with continuously looking for those experiences in my life that challenge the way I do things and then using those experiences to help myself and others. This is the area in which I constantly force myself to hold up the mirror and ask myself what are sometimes some uncomfortable questions.

Surrounding myself with people who do the work is the third area that has given me tremendous support. I have been blessed with diversity colleagues that "walk the talk." They have become my salad bowl of partners that continuously celebrate life.

The fourth area speaks about the involvement of my family in the work I do. I know that their love and support has sustained me over the years and continues to fuel my fire and passion for the work. My name is Floyd "Sonny" Massey III, and I love what I do!

Before I go on, I should probably pause and say, in all fairness, there were some special moments during those first twenty-five years of my professional life. Moments that have helped to shape how I do the work I do today. As a sales manager for a major communications company, I was able to help develop, support, and influence the lives of a very diverse workforce. Some of these mentees are still very much a part of my life today. I am happy to report that they have become very successful in their careers. Being one of the only Black men to do sales skills instruction enabled me to try to establish a positive role model for many of the Black employees who were redeployed to sales positions. Many of them came to me at different points in my career to let me know how I had influenced their careers. That kind of positive feedback never failed to lift my spirits.

As I look back, that special feedback always seemed to come at just the time I needed it. In my position as the curricula manager responsible for the development and delivery of sales skills training, I was able to influence the training that was given to the entire the sales force. I made it my business to make sure that diversity concepts and awareness were integrated into every aspect of the training. My greatest joy came at the end of my career when I was given the opportunity to direct the diversity program for the company. This assignment gave me the opportunity to influence everyone, from senior leadership to the individual contributors across the company. I was able to bring people in to deliver diversity messages to the various organizations and departments in the company. As I observed these diversity trainers, it became clear to me what I wanted to do with the rest of my life.

I like to call myself a diversity facilitator. My workshops are delivered to businesses and companies throughout the United States. My greatest joy is taking a group of people through a workshop and having them self-discover things about themselves. Things that speak to the way people behave toward one another, particularly when they are different from one another. My goal is not to have people change their values. My goal is to facilitate people to understand what kind of behavior they are demonstrating toward one another. As people take a deeper look, hopefully they will begin to see what kind of impact their behavior can have on their performance, the performance of others, and the overall performance of the company.

It is always my hope that this exploration extends outside the four walls of the workplace. I do not come into my workshops as a six-foot-tall Black man ready to beat up White people. I am usually outnumbered. I come to my workshops ready to help people explore the many differences and similarities that exist in our lives and the impacts that are made as a result of how we behave day in and day out.

I believe that you cannot do the work unless you are willing to take a deep look at the early messages you received in your life. In working with Barnes, O'Neale & Associates, Rosalyn Taylor O'Neale introduced me to an exercise that I have found to be useful not only in the sessions but also in my personal growth as a facilitator of diversity work.

During the introductions, I ask participants to reflect on the nicknames they received before age ten. Most participants share the humorous nicknames they received from their parents, other family members, and friends. This serves as a kind of icebreaker and almost always relaxes the class. However, on one occasion, a Native American woman named Debbie stood up and delivered a long list of ugly and hateful nicknames she received as a young person. I can't remember the nicknames, but what I do remember is the pain that young woman revealed to us that day. When she finished, you could have heard a pin drop. Her brave participation in this exercise took the whole workshop to a deeper level. The group began to talk about how something as seemingly innocuous as a nickname could mean something very different to an individual based on their life experience. The group began to reach out to her in a way that they had never done before.

When I returned to this company to do the next group of workshops, I looked for Debbie. I wanted to let her know the effect she had on me. I had not been able to stop thinking about her nicknames and her courage. When I saw Debbie, I asked her how she was doing, and she replied that as a result of the workshop, she felt more included than she had ever been before. She also shared that not only did the nickname experience open other people up to her but it also opened her up to other people. She was quick to add that as painful as the memory was, she didn't ever want to completely erase it from her memory bank. She said that those early messages helped her to keep her edge and maintain an ever-present awareness of just where she had come from.

Debbie's statement to me about keeping her edge was, indeed, very powerful. It is something that I try to do so that I won't ever forget the challenges of my life's journey. So often we get so caught up in where we are today that we forget how we got there and who helped us to get there. Whether I am speaking to a room full of people or having one of my daddy-daughter conversations, I never hesitate to speak to the challenges of how I got to where I am today. I continually celebrate those people in my life who have helped clear the path so the journey would be a little easier for me than it was for them.

I liked the way my colleagues Sheila Barnes and Rosalyn Taylor O'Neale described the concept of nicknames. Nicknames were those things you were given at a very early age before you had a chance to say "No, thank you." And like the nicknames, we were given early messages before we had a chance to say "No, thank you." Messages that came from family members, friends, teachers, and others in our lives. Messages about people, places, and things. Sometimes the messages were positive, but many times they were not. Particularly if the people, places, and things were different than what we were used to dealing with on a daily basis.

I remember as a young boy of eight years old playing with my best friend, Eddie. I was crazy about his mom. In fact, I think she was my first crush. I can still remember the fragrance of the perfume she wore to this day. One day, she came into the house and stormed right through the living room without speaking to us and went into the kitchen. She started talking to herself, and this is what we heard her say: "Old people should not be allowed to drive. They are going to get me killed. They should have their licenses taken away. They are all dangerous and should not be allowed behind the wheel of a car." I looked at Eddie and was confused. I had never heard his mother go on like that. But she was, after all, his mom and someone that I looked up to (and had a crush on), so I took the information she inadvertently shared and stored it in my memory bank.

Two months later, my grandmother came to live with my family for the summer. One Saturday morning, she asked me if I wanted to go get an ice cream cone from the Dairy Queen. (An ice cream cone from Dairy Queen was second only to a White Castle hamburger.) Of course I said yes. I saw her go to my mom's purse and take out the car keys. I asked what she was going to do with those keys. She said that she was going to drive us to the Dairy Queen. My memory bank kicked in, and before I knew it, I was saying the following to her: "You can't drive, Granny, because you are old. Old people shouldn't be allowed to drive. In fact, they should have their licenses taken away from them." Well . . . I didn't get my ice cream cone.

I do remember what I did get. My dad was standing behind me and thought I was being very disrespectful. Even with the nonverbal early message that my father delivered to me on that particular day, it took me some time to shake off the early messages about senior citizens and driving. I imagine that I am not the only person that fights the demons of negative early messages. But that is why it is important to continue to take a look back to find out just where some of those early messages may have come from.

As I grew older, it became clear to me that regardless of the negative messages I received about people, places, and things from television, newspapers, and other people, there were people in my life who would turn those negatives into positives. This would not happen without experiencing some painful situations.

Growing up in St. Paul, Minnesota, provided me as Black person many other, often painful, early messages. And yes, there were Black people in

Minnesota back then! As an example, my parents really wanted me to learn how to swim. So they sent me to the YMCA at some degree of financial sacrifice to them (I found that out years later). I remember that first session like it was yesterday. I was eleven years old and both excited and nervous. I walked into the pool area and didn't see anyone who looked like me. Everyone was White, and no one spoke to me. Needless to say, my excitement began to quickly dissipate. What I remember was how strange and disconnected I felt. For some reason, we had to swim in the nude. Now that really is an odd early memory. One of the boys in the class pointed at my "stuff" and started to laugh. I remember wanting to run and hide, but something stopped me dead in my tracks. I turned to the boy who had been laughing at me and asked him why his "stuff" was so itty-bitty. He turned a whiter shade of pale because some of the other guys started to laugh at him. I was so busy enjoying the fact that I had scored some points that I didn't see him come at me. The next thing I knew, I was in the deep end of the pool and terrified. I could hear the boys laughing and calling me the n-word. It wasn't the last time I would have that word directed my way. I could not swim and began to panic. The next thing I remember is being pulled out of the pool by a guy whose name I learned was Steve Nelson. It was a name and a person that I would never forget.

After I coughed up enough water to fill a bathtub, he took me into the office, and we talked. He explained that he was a junior instructor and apologized for what had happened to me. He also had the kid who pushed me come in and apologize. He then offered to give me private lessons during his lunch hour to help me learn to swim. I told him that I thought my parents could only afford group lessons, but he told me not to worry about that because he would charge me at the group rate. It took me a couple of lessons before I asked him why he was doing this for me. He told me that learning to swim was hard enough without also having to deal with the pressure from the other boys. He also said that I was going to need all the help I could get if I was even going to learn how to tread water! The final thing he said about his helping me was that at one time in his preteen life, a Negro (that was the word at the time or at least one of them) had helped him out of a pretty serious situation in Chicago. He never shared the details of that situation, but he didn't have to. His words may have fallen on young ears but definitely not deaf ears. What began as an ugly early message was turned into something positive.

You know, I never did learn to swim very well. However, I did learn not to be afraid to speak up and out for myself as well as others. My colleague

Rosalyn Taylor O'Neale calls it not being afraid to say ouch. It helps in this work called diversity and in this thing we call life. I know that to live in this world, I can't always play it safe and stay in the middle. I was going through old papers and found a note that came from one of the participants in a workshop I facilitated in Clearwater, Florida. The note simply stated, "If you are not living on the edge, you are just taking up space."

As you can see, early messages mean a lot to me. They come in all sizes, shapes, and colors. But none mean more to me than the messages that came from my father. Some of the messages came from him when he wasn't even around.

I can't remember the date or what the weather was like on the day I ventured down into our basement to explore my dad's "study" without his permission! That was many years ago, but I remember the feeling as if it were yesterday. I had been in the study before, but it was always at his invitation. My dad was a Baptist minister, and this was the place away from the church where he solved people's problems, reconciled marriages, brought families back together again, counseled people on career decisions, and secured scholarships and jobs for young people. He also encouraged those who needed it, mapped out his strategies to protect the rights of Black people, and provided spiritual leadership to his parishioners.

My parents were away for the day, and I had the chance to fully experience being in this special place . . . alone! I remember the smell. My father smoked a pipe, and the rich smell of his special brand of tobacco lingered in the air. I sat in his beautiful black leather chair and took in the feeling of the room and of my father. I looked at the weathered bookcase that housed his books and oh, what books. Books about the struggles of Black people over time. Books by and about W. E. B. DuBois, George Washington Carver, Frederick Douglass, Harriet Tubman, Sojourner Truth, and Mary McLeod Bethune. I smiled as I saw the book that my dad had used to explain "the birds and the bees" to my brother and me. He had invited us into the study to have THE TALK, but as my dad began to explain things to us, my brother and I started laughing and couldn't stop. That session lasted all of five minutes.

I walked around the office and touched the oak paneling that framed the study. I remember seeing a stack of newspapers behind a cabinet in the corner. As I pushed back the cabinet to get a closer look, I had no idea how seeing those newspapers would affect me for the rest of my life. The newspaper was called the *Pittsburgh Courier*. I later found out that it was one of the only Black newspapers being printed during that time that told the stories of what was really happening to Black people across the country and particularly in the South. It was around 1958, and horrific things were happening to Blacks. I don't know how long I spent reading those newspapers, but I do know that when I left my dad's study, I wasn't the same person. There were many terrifying stories that I read that day, but the one that stood out was about a young teenage boy named Emmet Till. He was visiting his cousins in Mississippi. The only son of a Chicago schoolteacher, he was described as a brassy citified boy. He didn't say "Yes, sir" and "No, sir." Till had been in Mississippi three days when he made his mistake. He stopped at a store where he was alone for a moment with the store owner's wife. His cousins later testified that they heard him give a wolf whistle. I would later learn in life the ugly details. Three days after the wolf whistle incident, the store owner and his brother burst into the house where Till was staying. They took him to a barn, beat him, shot him, weighed his body down by tying a seventy-five-pound fan from a cotton gin to his neck with barbed wire and threw him into the river. They were arrested the next day. They were acquitted by an all-White jury. A year later, they confessed to a *Look Magazine* reporter who paid them $4,000.

What I do vividly remember as a young boy about this horrific murder was the description of Till's body after they fished him out of the river. His face was monstrously distended with one eye hanging from its socket. I later learned that his mom left the coffin open during the entire service so that everyone present could see what had been done to her son. Reading that story cut to the very core of my soul. I remember crying like a baby and wanting to find a way to do something about it. I really believe that it was the result of reading the story about Emmett Till that laid the foundation for my participation in this work.

And then, as if on cue, the phone rang in my dad's office. What happened next was beyond my twelve-year-old level of understanding. I answered the phone, and a raspy and ugly-sounding voice asked to speak with my father. I told the person that he was not at home and asked if I could take a message. What the voice said next to me will always be with me. He said to tell my father to get out of town before someone kills him!

I remember slamming down the phone. I ran out of the study and up to my room where I stayed until nightfall. I had just read about threats like that happening all across the country, but how could this be happening in St. Paul, Minnesota? Yet another early message. It took me a week to work up the nerve to tell my father what I had done on the day that I had ventured down into his study. I expected the worst. My father told me to go down into the basement and wait for him. That usually meant that a whipping was going to take place.

It seemed like an eternity before my dad came down. When he finally did, he put his arm around my shoulder and guided me into his study. He told me that he was disappointed that I had disobeyed him and entered the study without his permission. But then he quickly added that he wasn't surprised because that was just the kind of son I was. He said that I had always been incredibly curious and had an insatiable hunger for learning. My dad told me that the articles in the *Pittsburgh Courier* were true and that he and Mom didn't think I was ready to hear about those horrible stories. But now that I had read them, he would answer any questions that I had about the stories.

We talked for hours about the racial injustice that was so pervasive in the country. He talked about his dedication to making things better for the Black people in the Twin Cities. He told me that he wanted all people to come together in a peaceful and respectful way. That led to a discussion about the threatening phone call I heard on that life-altering day. My dad's comments were very succinct. He said that it would take more than a phone call to keep him from doing what God had led him to do.

As I look back on our time together, I realize that it was probably one of the longest conversations that I ever had with my dad until I became an adult. I also know it was one of the most meaningful. My dad spent twenty-one years in St. Paul, Minnesota, as the pastor of the largest Black Baptist Church in Minnesota. (And yes, one more time, they did have Black people in Minnesota!) As a young person, I was often jealous of the time he gave to helping others, particularly on the weekends. Perhaps I thought that I could steal my dad's attention away on Saturdays by playing peewee-league football. I actually hated football, but I could run pretty fast so I gave it a shot. I did everything possible to avoid being tackled. I would run out of bounds in a second unless I saw the opening that would take me across the goal line. I actually had to wear a gold helmet (everyone else's helmet was blue and white, but they didn't have one that fit my big head). Talk about diversity! I finally got a chance to start at running back. That day, I ran like Dobermans were chasing me. My dad missed that game because some family needed help. I was angry then; after all, I scored three touchdowns in that game. I didn't then fully understand my dad's calling in life. As I grew, I began to truly get it. After all, he told me in his study what God had called him to do.

There are some other life experiences that I know have helped me to hold up the mirror and discover some things about myself as well as help others self-discover things about themselves. These are things that help us to grow so that we can create the kind of world in which I want my daughter and, perhaps someday, her daughter or son to live. A world where as Dan Zadra expresses, "If there must be a stereotype let it have nothing to do with race, creed, sex, color, or advantage . . . but rather let it have everything to do with effort, energy, ideas, commitment, and capabilities."

I suppose I could tell you about the time in my life when I was sixteen and was invited by a Jewish friend of mine named David to attend his brother's bar mitzvah. I was excited to experience this sacred ceremony, but he called me two days before and informed me that we would not be going. I asked him why, and he said that his dad didn't think it was a very good idea for me to be there. I remember telling David that he couldn't miss this very special event because of me. He told me that if I couldn't attend, then he wouldn't be there. He called me the next night and said to me that his parents had reconsidered and told him it was all right to bring me.

I remember entering a synagogue for the first time in my life and feeling like everyone was staring at me, and they probably were. I also remember looking at my friend and feeling very proud to be his friend. As I reflect back on that time, I now truly appreciate the courage it took for this young boy to stand up to his family in this particular situation. We have talked about this over the years, and he always tells me that he had no choice. It was what he believed was the right thing to do. It is a relationship and experience that has helped to shape my own personal journey. Flash forward thirty-five years later to the bar mitzvah for the son of my daughter's godparents, Bruce and Laura Presnick, in Walnut Creek, California. My wife, Kathy, and I were invited to participate in the service by doing one of the readings. It was indeed a high honor. We were also asked along with our daughter, Kia, to light a candle at the reception. I remember that Bruce asked me to sit near the family at the front of the synagogue to give him support. I remember being the one needing the support. Indeed, the tears did flow that day as I remembered David and his brother's bar mitzvah many years ago and the beauty and love that flowed through the ceremony for Jordan Presnick on that beautiful Saturday in June 1998. What a difference over three decades makes.

Perhaps I could tell you about the time in high school when I was selected to attend Boys State. This was a three-day experience where over three hundred boys gathered to play "government." I was the only Black person at the conference, and the first twenty-four hours were not a hit! (Yes, I know I told you there were Black people in Minnesota. There were just not a whole lot of us!) No one talked to me, and that made me uncomfortable as my confidence started to dissipate. And these boys were supposed to be the best of the best. However, at lunch, another Nelson stepped into my life. If you remember, the teenager that rescued me at the YMCA was named Steve Nelson. This Nelson's first name was Paul. He saw me eating alone and asked if he could join me. I said yes, and he sat down.

I can't tell you what Paul managed to do with me and for me in the span of fifteen minutes. He took me from a place where I was feeling sorry for myself and ready to head home to a place where I began to feel comfortable and confident once again. We still maintain a friendship to this day. Only now as I looked back did I remember that Paul and Steve shared the same last name. I don't know what the significance of that may be or if there is any significance. I do know this. I do everything I can to make sure that everyone is included in any group setting in which I find myself.

I remember the work I did for MTV years ago and the feedback that I received after those workshops. The groups were larger than normal, but many people thanked me for making them feel included. In any group, be it large or small, I always try to make contact with everyone in the room. It could be a handshake, eye contact, or directly addressing the individual. I remember how good it made me feel to be included, and I want to do my best to create that feeling for others whether in workshops or anywhere else. If I am truly holding up the mirror, I realize at this very moment that I could be doing a better job in the eye contact arena with those closest to me. I want to say more, but that could be another chapter. Never forget that recognition is the first step!

I want to encourage you to continually use the greatest resource you have: your life. If you stop and reflect, you will be amazed how many deeply rich experiences have played out in your life. The question you need to ask yourself is, How will I use these riches to make my life the best it can be? I have chosen to use these riches as I facilitate people of all sizes, shapes, colors, genders, orientations, geography, religions, ages, nationalities, professions, disabilities, and on and on and on to self-discover how they behave toward one another based on differences and similarities.

One of those deeply rich life experiences that I constantly celebrate is surrounding myself with some very special people who do this work. They are the family I go to for the tune-up I need to keep my diversity engine oiled and lubed. People often talk about the melting pot, but that has never appealed to me. It feels like everyone is working toward being the same. I prefer the "salad bowl." In order for me to have a truly delicious salad, I need many different ingredients all mixed together. I am blessed to be a part of a spectacular salad. As you read on, I challenge you to compare your salad to mine. Ask yourself if there are people in your life that help to make your salad spectacular. As you make your discoveries, speak their names and don't forget to take the opportunity to thank them.

Here is my salad. Sid is the romaine lettuce. Fresh and crisp, she never disappoints. She gives the salad its foundation. But don't be surprised if every now and then she tosses in some arugula in the form of her wisdom to keep the salad interesting. She is also like the sister that I never had, and that is indeed special.

Santalynda provides the spices for the salad. She is unafraid to pepper up the dialogue when it needs it and often does. But she always checks in to see if perhaps she may have applied too much pepper. If so, she stands ready to apply the salt or whatever other spice is needed. And there is indeed the beauty of maternal love she possesses for her son who is an Aries, and what better sign on this planet could there be than an Aries!

Nadia embodies the cherry tomatoes. I once had a friend come visit me on my side of town. This was during high school, and she was Jewish and she wasn't supposed to be in my neighborhood. Her name was Lisa, and she brought me a gift. It was a small basket of baby tomatoes. I had never eaten a baby tomato before. I remember the surprise and joy when I put the tomato in my mouth and bit into it. It was like a miniexplosion, and I loved it. That is exactly what Nadia brings to my salad. She makes any gathering in which she is involved an explosion of agape-type love. She is always full of generous and amazing ways to make people feel unexpectedly surprised and joyous.

I do like some meat in my salad, be it chicken or turkey. It can often be tender or tough, rare or well-done, but meat regardless. Joe-Joe is the meat in my salad. Sometimes tender and oftentimes tough, he brings his true self to every situation. His take on things can be cooked rare one day and well-done the next, but what you see is what you get. I do believe there is a Black man inside this White man just screaming to get out!

I love sunflower seeds. Salted or unsalted, they bring a certain je ne sais quoi to my salad. You are never quite sure what Simma is going to bring to the work, but you can be sure it will be something worth thinking about. She is not afraid to bring the seeds of her life's experience to the table.

Whether salted or unsalted, you know that Simma will unabashedly leave the seeds of her own personal journey for those she loves to digest and to learn from. She is yet another example of how much a mother can care for her son.

Croutons make that crunchy noise that make people pay attention. Juan can make that crunchy, often-meaningful noise that make people take notice. He is my brown brother that is not for sale. Croutons come in different sizes and different flavors, and the messages and experiences that come from him have that same range and diversity. He has also taught me how to "breathe!"

Every salad needs dressing. I can think of no better dressing for my salad than that which Tommy brings to the table. He has a way of always being able to top it off. His words, his voice, and his presence give the salad the flavor that is needed to make it ready for consumption. This is one beautiful Black brother.

Finally, I need a container for my salad. I see a bowl made of beautiful teakwood that has gracefully weathered over time. The bowl had a crack or two. The color of the wood has a certain richness that only time can make more beautiful. The bowl is large. The bowl is deep. The bowl will beautifully present my salad. The bowl is our colleague who died in 2006. The bowl is Marvin.

I cannot end this journey without celebrating the rest of my family. I introduced you to my dad earlier in the chapter, and I hope you can see the deep impact he has had on my life and the work I do. This magnificent man passed away some three years ago, and not a day goes by when I don't think of him.

Standing right beside my dad is my mom. She is a beautiful symbol of what is true and good and right about this world. Like my dad, my mom is a wonderful storyteller. One of her favorite illustrations is about the quilt that her mother made when she was young. She talks about how her mother would collect scraps of old material from almost anything she could get her hands on. My mom would look at these tattered old pieces and wonder just what her mother was going to do with them. From these eclectic scraps, Mama Sophie would create beautiful quilts. I remember one of my only visits to my grandmother's house at an early age and being covered by Mom by one of these diverse masterpieces as I went off to sleep.

We took one of those amazing quilts with us when we left my grandmother's house, but the quilt was not all that we took. Later in life,

I realized how that quilt symbolized the beautiful differences that exist in all our lives if we just take the time to lovingly piece them together. One more wonderful thing about my mom, although I could go on and on, has to do with the fact that she missed her calling as an actress. I can remember inviting friends over to the house. She would come out on the stoop (we didn't have a porch) and reenact scenes from the films of Ingrid Bergman, Susan Hayward, and Joan Crawford. She was magnificent and would hold my friends in awe. In fact, we would often watch the actual movies and be very disappointed because my mother's performance on the stoop was so much better than those of the aforementioned movie stars on the screen. I mention this because I am very proud of my fabulous mom, and I must credit her (along with my dad) with what I hope are not the over-the-top theatrics that I manage to infuse into my diversity workshops. What joy . . . what joy!

As you can see, I have been blessed in life to have parents that walked the talk and were incredible role models for me. But the blessings don't stop with my parents; my wife and daughter continue to be excellent models and people that love, value, and respect what is good about the people they meet in life. My wife, Kathy, is a truly beautiful woman (inside and out). We have loved each other for over thirty-four years. Earlier, I mentioned the concept of holding up the mirror to keep yourself in check as you experience day-to-day interactions with people both different and similar to you. Kathy holds up that mirror for me, and I don't believe I could do this diversity work the way I do it if I didn't have her in my life.

We made the decision to adopt our daughter, Kia, in 1994. We had no idea what incredible joy she would bring to our lives. Nor did we know what new elements of diversity would come our way as she became a part of our family. Elements that would include parenting, dealing with kids of many different races, elementary school life, work-family balance, and finding other Black kids to be a part of her life in a community where not too many kids looked like her, just to name a few.

I am happy to report that in the midst of differences and similarities, the results have been off the hook! At my sixtieth birthday party, I received a special gift from both my wife and daughter. My wife sang an Anne Murray song to me. (And yes, some Black people like Anne Murray!) The song was called "You Needed Me," and it moved me very deeply. It occurred to me then as it does now that in doing this work, we need to find connections at a much deeper level if we are going to move this planet forward. My daughter's gift came in the form of a card she read that she had given me for Father's Day several years ago. Permit me to share the words read to me by my daughter.

## To the Man Who Stepped into My Life and Became My Dad

Janet Kostelecky Nieto

You'll never know how important you are to me.
You stepped into my life at a time when I really needed someone
I could look up to . . .
You didn't try to overwhelm me.
You didn't try to take anyone's place.
You never demanded anything of me.
You never let me feel threatened by you.
You just loved me.
You were patient with me.
You became whatever I needed you to be; most of all that was my friend.
You gave of yourself and asked nothing in return.
In the process, you earned my respect, my love, my trust and admiration.
You gave me a firm foundation on which to build my life.
I will never be able to tell you how very much I appreciate all that you
are and all that you have enabled me to become, and how grateful I am
that God picked you to be my special dad and to share my life.

I am sure you can imagine there was not a dry eye in the house when Kia finished.

I believe that we are all given goals to shoot for, and that is what my daughter gave me that magnificent evening. I really believe that if we are going to do this work called diversity, we have to aim high and set examples that encourage others to do the same. Will it happen overnight? I don't think so. I am sixty years old, and I still have miles to go before I can rest. I keep remembering that diversity is a process and not a one-time event, and that is what keeps me going. To my family and extended family, I say thank you, and I love you.

There is a story that I once heard, and I use it in all my workshops. I wish I could remember where I heard it and who told it, but I know it stuck! There was a guy waiting to check in his bag at the airport. He noticed that the customer in front of him was yelling at the airline agent. He was complaining about an upgrade and was really assailing the airline gentleman with some pretty harsh language. What the guy also noticed was that whatever the guy said, the agent just smiled and continued to provide good customer service. Finally, the irate customer yelled one final time and stormed off.

When the guy moved up to check in his bag, he felt compelled to ask the airline agent how he had handled the irate customer with such calm and poise. The airline agent looked at the guy and smiled and simply said, "That guy is going to Los Angeles . . . I just checked his bags to China!" I don't know about you, but I don't want my bags checked to China. And believe me, there are many different ways to get your bags checked to China! Are you feeling me?

Let me end this journey with the following reminders for those of you who just might think about involving yourself in diversity work.

1.  Be willing to take in-depth looks at the early messages you received in life. These looks can often assist you in telling your life's story.
2.  Be willing to hold up the mirror. This often helps you to ask and answer what are sometimes uncomfortable questions.
3.  Be willing to surround yourself with people who do the work. Everyone needs a support system. And everyone should love a good "salad"; after all, it's good for you.
4.  Be willing to involve your family and friends in the work you do. Their love and support can sustain you in the work. And what fantastic ideas you can gain just by watching and listening to family and friends.
5.  Be willing to live the kind of life that won't "get your bags checked to China!" You have no idea how many people you will meet in life that just may be able to help you get to where you want to go.

I have a dear friend named Frances Emerson who is eighty-five years young. We have been friends for over forty years, and she has given me some wonderful things to think about and learn from over the years. There are two I would like to leave with you.

The first says, "Is this heaven and am I there?!" Her aunt Julia used to share that with anyone who would listen when something wonderful, uplifting, or just plain old-fashioned good would happen to her. Frances remembers the times that Aunt Julia would hit for $60 on a $2 bet at the racetrack and say to the world, "Is this heaven and am I there?" I share that with you because that is exactly how I am feeling as a result of sharing a portion of my journey with you.

The other is "Best to be ready if you don't get to go." You never know when that window of opportunity may present itself to you. Keep your bags packed—mentally, physically, and emotionally—so that if your chance comes, you are READY. I sincerely hope that you discovered something along my journey that will enable you to be ready when you DO get to go!

My name is Floyd "Sonny" Massey III, and I love what I do!

*This chapter is dedicated to my brothers Ronny and Rickie who, like diversity, have differences and similarities and who I love very much. Thank you for your beautiful lifelong lessons.*

## In Memoriam

Floyd "Sonny" Massey, our joyful brother, passed on shortly after completing his chapter. His extraordinary spirit, great wit, and kind heart set Sonny apart. He wore his emotions on his sleeve, and they were genuine.

The poem that his beautiful daughter, Kia, read for him at his sixtieth birthday party expresses so well a daughter's love and appreciation. It also provides a glimpse into what a fabulous person Sonny was. It was his spirit and his love that made the greatest impact. We miss him dearly.

# MY DIVERSITY JOURNEY

Juan Lopez

## Embarking

I had the good fortune to be raised in a little steel mill and military town located in the East Bay of Northern California. The town was racially and ethnically diverse and too small to be divided by segregated communities. African Americans, Italians, second—and third-generation Mexican Americans, and poor Whites from the Midwest all lived in this community.

Growing up in this community was an exercise in community building. On most Sundays, Latinos gathered in the park for festivals. Since the park was huge, many of the other groups also frequented to play sports, eat, drink, and have fun. During the summer, when the kids got bored, we all met at the fountain in the middle of the park to swim and show off. Many relationships were formed around this time. As our friendships grew, we invited members of different groups to our traditional Mexican celebrations.

To my surprise, I discovered our fathers mirrored the same behavior. A number of them worked together at the steel mill. After their shifts, they gathered at the downtown bar to "pop a few." During the summer, employee connections were further strengthened when we attended company picnics to eat barbecue chicken, swim, play baseball or volleyball, and compete in potato-sack racing.

The little city of Pittsburg prospered when the steel mill was productive. However, every once in a while the strikes came, and I remember how the workers supported one another. The strikes were good for uniting people. It deepened the bonds across race and ethnicity for their common cause, and the men joined to fight on. As a little guy, I was with my dad when he bought food for friends who were short on cash. I remember he was concerned about the families and felt bad for the men who were embarrassed about not providing for their families.

Other significant events like first communion, weddings, and deaths pulled people together. Within the community, there was a constant movement as a result of community gatherings that felt natural over time. I remember as a child how my father seemed comfortable around the diverse community groups. I often wondered why he moved so easily within these various communities while my mother seemed less open to associating with people who were not Mexican.

When I was about seven years old, my dad would take me with him into the downtown area, and we would visit Black barbershops. We would hang out for a while, and the men would banter, and I would observe. Music always seemed to be playing in the background. James Brown had become very popular, and his songs were playing repeatedly.

When James Brown's song came on, my dad would say to the guys, "Watch my Johnny dance." Then he would say to me, "Johnny, get up and show them your moves" as he would stand back and watch me slide and glide. I loved James Brown; I studied him every time he was on TV, and my goal was to be as light on my feet as he was. The guys in the shop would laugh and give my dad kudos for having a son who could dance. I enjoyed the attention and, more importantly, learned that this was a good way to earn some coin.

When we moved to Oakland, things changed. The community was not so close, and Latinos and African Americans tended to look at each other more suspiciously. Unfortunately, fighting and sticking to your own neighborhood replaced celebrating, dancing, and listening to music.

These experiences forced me to think differently about the other groups. It was during this period of time that feelings of difference began to take on a negative association. In our part of Oakland, the Mexican community was small, and African Americans were large in numbers. There was a great deal of mistrust and dislike, and we all talked about each other's groups as inferior.

When we left Oakland and moved to the suburbs, I brought with me the experience of city life. I had developed a mistrust of people who were different from me. It didn't help that I fought with White and Black kids on the way to school, at school, and on returning home.

I'm sad to say that I didn't develop meaningful relationships with African Americans while I was in high school. There were few Black families in our suburb city. It wasn't until I was in college that I began to build close bonds with African Americans again while we worked together in convict-to-college programs. I was a codirector of a program at Sonoma State University called Getting Out, and there were a number of multiracial counselors and convicts in the program.

Working together in this program required from us significant emotional reprogramming. We had to unlearn racism and tribal thinking that was formed in barrios and ghettos and, for the convicts, in prison. Learning how to trust each other was big because many of the convicts had group affiliations when they were in prison.

My experience in this program was a reawakening. It reminded me of my earlier years growing up in the Pittsburg community. There was a spirit of being connected through work, prayer, and celebration of life. It was during these special moments that I felt the exuberance of a common humanity. On one such occasion, a group of the guys organized a surprise party for my twenty-first birthday. I think they broke into my house to decorate. When I walked into my house, the group was in the front room, and they blasted me with whoops and hugs. I was surprised and amused as I looked around the room at the collection of Blacks, Whites, and Chicanos hardened by difficult lives and rough experiences in jail. Yet our joy of being a community who cared for each other was transparent despite the messages of our upbringing.

## Finding My Diversity Vision

My professional roots are in community organizing and social work. In addition to running the convict-to-college program, I was involved in many social activism initiatives. I was inspired by La Causa and was compelled by a force within to build a community of respect and equality for Chicanos and Mexicanos.

Although I worked in the fields for only a few summers, it became apparent based on pay, health conditions, and length of service that the field-workers were not respected. I was shocked at how little dignity existed for the work we did. This sense of powerlessness haunts me today when I drive by groups of Latino workers who congregate on corners hoping to be hired as day laborers.

As a student at Diablo Valley Community College in the East Bay, I organized for the United Farm Workers. My job was to provide information on boycotts, educate consumers on health conditions for farmworkers, and recruit and train new volunteers. In addition, I was president of MECHA (Movimiento Estudiantil Chicano de Aztlan), a Chicano student organization. Once I entered college, I jumped into as many Chicano activities as I could. It was important for me because I was learning about my cultural history, and it was exciting new information. While growing up, I had a feeling of purpose that was related to my difference, but I was unclear about my own ethnic identity and place in the world. My passion to get involved in social change and increasing cultural awareness was also fueled by growing up Mexican American and recognizing that my group was not valued or truly understood.

Attending community college was a lifesaver for me. It was also an accident. Originally, my plan was to join the military. It was the summer of 1972, and the Vietnam War was in its last days. Within my circle of friends, many of us had perverted visions of going to war and engaging in battle. I had talked a few friends into going to the recruiting center to sign up, but I was not accepted into the military because I had to wait for six months at which time my court-ordered probation would expire when I turned eighteen. I was very disappointed and cursed the police for their prejudice and profiling behaviors even though some thought they had good reason to follow me. I also felt bad for my friends because they did get accepted into the marines and navy, and two of them were sent to Vietnam. It was at this time that I decided to go to college and kill time.

## Defining Years

For many of us who entered the diversity movement, our stories resonate with a deep sense of purpose created by individual and group experiences of exclusion. I realized early in my life that who I was and how I looked would be a reality that I could not escape in my lifetime. To quote Susan Faust, "Race shapes not only identity but also destiny, and so often adversely."

For me, the spirit of diversity was a twofold process. The first step was to understand all my diversity dimensions (i.e., ethnicity, socioeconomic background, and culture, to name some of them). The second step was to accept and honor my uniqueness and move beyond early messages of inferiority that were delivered by my parents (because of internalized oppression) and the White community. As I began to understand the psychological and social issues inherent in the individual and group diversity experience, I was moved to take action to help other Latinos address diversity issues that were contributing to a dysfunctional and powerless state for many of us.

When I was a graduate student at the School of Social Welfare at UC Berkeley, I had a chance to study the impact of racism on communities of color. It was my goal to focus on the Chicano community's mental health, and I interned at La Familia in Hayward, a Chicano-centered community mental health center. We had a five-year grant to study and create new Raza mental health practices.

In moving into the mental health field, it became apparent to me that I had reached a transition point in my life. Clearly, I worked my way through issues of criminal justice. I was now moving into embracing multiculturalism in general and Chicano diversity in specific. It was a good transition because it also marked a level of maturity on my part. I no longer felt constrained by my homeboy consciousness wherein the option of prison or death by thirty years of age was the only outcome of our path. The liberation was exhilarating, but the call of the barrio continued.

In truth, the first six months of graduate school at UC Berkeley had a tremendous impact on my life and forced me to make some significant life choices. I had moved back to Concord, California. My friends who were still alive or not in prison wanted to rekindle friendships and started to come around again. I found myself living in two worlds: I was a UC graduate student by day in Berkeley and into my old ways at night while away from campus. I lasted six months in Concord and then had to leave for my survival. In those six months, all hell broke loose. I was stabbed by a member of the Mexican Mafia. He had been released from jail because they didn't have enough evidence on him for a murder charge. Upon his release, he sought out his girlfriend whom I was dating.

We were at a concert when he accosted her. I intervened, and he tried to kill me. He was shocked after he stabbed me several times, and I chased him down. I was furious and bleeding profusely; nonetheless, I wanted revenge. Fortunately, the cops showed up before I could do anything. I remember lying on the operating table waiting for the drugs to kick in. I was in pain, but the real emotional angst was a feeling of betrayal. The three-hour surgery was successful and the multiple scars eventually healed, but emotionally, I was in a much deeper quagmire. I felt deceived because as a Chicano activist and social work student who dedicated my time to helping my *gente*, I failed to comprehend how a fellow Chicano could attack me. It didn't feel fair, and I became increasingly enraged.

Once I got out, it became obvious the problem with this guy was not going away. He was arrested and posted bail. I kept getting phone calls from his associates. The cops had charged him with attempted murder, and the case was still in court. He wanted to make sure that I was not going to press charges against him. Feeling threatened, I sought out a weapon. I also wanted to redeem my manhood and settle the score.

I recall visiting some friends and asking them for a weapon. As we sat in their little bedroom discussing the situation, it became apparent they did not want to give me a gun. When I asked what the dilemma was, the elder Chicano, who had been in and out of San Quentin most of his adult life, told me he had a different proposal. He looked me in the eyes and said that I was supposed to help Chicanos—my *gente* was in need of people like me who could improve the lives of kids and make a difference in the community. He didn't want me to go after the guy because he said we didn't need another Chicano in prison. So he and my other friend proposed that they would go after the man if it would redeem my manhood.

I was stunned. These two men were willing to take action on my behalf, maybe go to jail if I gave the order. All because they believed in me and wanted me to finish my graduate work and become a social worker that would do good in the community. These two hardened convicts believed in my future and my potential. The choice was mine. Did I want to go the way of the street, or did I want to follow the path of social welfare and help my community?

After three weeks of agonizing, I chose the Chicano community. The decision was made easier when the guy who stabbed me arranged a meeting at a nearby park. I was tired of the harassing calls, so I agreed. He had his crew who were lying in wait. When I got to the park, I asked him to get into my car, and I took off. I eluded his friends, and we ended up alone. I pulled over, and when he realized we were by ourselves, he freaked. Seeing the knife in my hand, he asked me if I was going to hurt him. At that precise moment, I sensed his fear, and I said to him that I would not hurt him but he had to stay out of my life.

When I returned to UC, I resumed my studies. I had rededicated myself to making a difference in the community. I knew that focusing on Chicano mental health was critical, and to be effective in communities of color, we had to establish cultural competency models. This sense of purpose helped me through the next big crisis. The following month, my younger brother, Jim, was involved in a gang shooting and was arrested for second-degree murder.

When I graduated from UC Berkeley, I found a job as assistant director of a program component at the Region Three Mental Health Center with San Mateo County. I provided community-based therapy to nontraditional clients and introduced prevention and wellness education. As a mental health practitioner, I was in a position to work with Latino youth who were experiencing problems because their diversity was not acceptable at their predominantly European American high schools in the county. It was clear that this young population had low self-esteem. Many of them came from different Central and South American nations. This group exhibited anger and frequently talked about how teachers and students often cast them stereotypically as dumb, gang oriented, drug dealers, loose women, passive, and ignorant. Additionally, many felt alienated or invisible in their schools and community. Over time, the racism caused many students to give up and stop applying themselves academically. No wonder many of them dropped out of high school by the time they were seniors. They felt excluded and were tired of fighting against stereotypical assumptions and discrimination.

My experience with the Latino youth made me think about my younger brother, Jim. It has been a painful reflection because he committed suicide when he was twenty-three years old after he got out of prison. Jim and I frequently talked about race, ethnicity, and culture from the time he was about fourteen and moved in with me while I was attending college. He did not relate to being a Chicano or Mexican American. I, on the other hand, was an activist and took every opportunity to expound on our magnificent culture. Jim was uncomfortable around Latinos, and on occasion he would share with me how he felt devalued by them because he did not speak Spanish or come across as exhibiting any traditional Latino cultural values. During a Cinco de Mayo celebration, Jim took offense to comments about his appearance made by some of the Los Angeles Chicano students. This resulted in a major conflict that further alienated him and, to some degree, me from the Chicano campus community.

This also created a dilemma for me. As a Chicano student leader, I believed Chicanos did not come in one package. As a third-generation Chicano, I was very much acculturated and was disturbed by the exclusionary behavior I witnessed of Chicanos who were different and could be dismissed so easily for being different from the norm. Jim was not interested in politics, social change, or working with other Latinos. He thought college was a waste of time. His only reason for being exposed to the Chicano students was because he lived with me and I was in college.

This experience was a lesson in understanding the complexity of our community. I belonged to an ethnic group that was working hard to help the university accept students who were racially and ethnically different, and at the same time, they were excluding members of their community for their difference.

I have a tremendous amount of sadness about Jim. I wonder if he had more clarity about his ethnic identity could he have found inner peace and made better life decisions. I think so. When Jim was incarcerated, he found himself aligned with other Chicano prisoners. I visited him frequently, and he was part of that community. He even involved himself in La Raza events and proudly wore T-shirts of Emiliano Zapata and Poncho Villa.

Yet during those times when we spoke honestly about life, it was clear that Jim had no place where he felt at home either inside himself, the family, or in the community. This cultural disconnect has been written about by Dr. Price Cobbs in his study of African Americans. He called his work ethnotherapy and addressed it in more detail in his book *Black Rage*.

Drugs continued to be his salvation, and when he died, I was angry. This anger unfortunately spilled into my work as a diversity trainer. It also prevented me from letting go when I worked with tough groups, and as a result, I brought the toxicity home. This state of reality carried on for some time until my wife confronted me. I remember her words vividly. She said, "If you can't let go of the anger, maybe you should quit doing the work. It is not good for our family, and it is not good for our relationship."

As was my ignorant pattern, I rejected Giselle's wise words. However, I could not forget the power of her message. Shortly afterward, as part of my ongoing personal work with a Mexican shaman and my father-in-law who was a well-known Chicano leader, I found the vision of working with love in my heart as core to my diversity practice. I continue to follow this mantra—in doing so, I find an incredible spirit that allows me to be in the right places and stay focused.

The love I have for Jim is one reason I continue to do diversity work. I want to make sure that individuals and organizations understand the impact of exclusion and "-isms" on other human beings. In educating others, I focus on increasing personal awareness that will ultimately change behaviors. Additionally, our ability to reach and teach youth is critical to building positive work environments. As I get older, it becomes important to aim my diversity practice in the direction of helping human beings and organizations value the diversity of every person. If Jim would have been in a school that could help him understand his diversity as well as be accepted for it, it might have made it easier for him to find a community. I also work with young adults so they feel good about their unique diversity gifts: race, ethnicity, gender, culture, sexual orientation, and all the other ways in which we experience being different.

We all have a story to share. Within our stories, there rests a spirit (life force) that compels us to act. I suggest we remember the power of our story and continue to evaluate lessons learned. In doing this, we keep the spirit of change alive within us to make a difference.

## Developing My Practice

To illustrate this calling of spirit, I will time travel into the past and share what moved me to do diversity work. As I continued to do mental health prevention and education, it became obvious that our services were not impacting the lives of elders, African Americans, Asians, Latinos, and the large Tongan/Samoan populations in the area. We created community-based programs that were culturally competent, but the institution didn't seem to embrace our efforts. The results were very good, and our programs were recognized by California's state mental health department. Nonetheless, getting the psychiatrist to practice differently was futile.

I had faced these kinds of barriers at UC Berkeley. Trying to move an institution and professors to think about how to incorporate multicultural practices into social welfare was challenging. Cultural competency was in its infancy, and there were questions about its authenticity. A group of us were so committed to the emerging field of multicultural approaches that we organized a conference entitled the New Majority Minority, and we invited thought leaders to share their best practices and research. It was very successful, and the School of Social Welfare reluctantly supported us because they recognized that demographic shifts were taking place rapidly.

I was fortunate to work for the County Mental Health Center. It allowed me to work with a diverse community and to continue to work with troubled youth. At the Mental Health Center, there was a group of Latinos who were engaged in community organizing and developing new service programs. We helped develop youth programs and Cinco de Mayo celebrations. This also helped us build a political power base that influenced the board of supervisors when it came to health care—funding decisions.

In 1982, our little group was asked by a prominent consulting firm founded in San Francisco by Price Cobbs, MD, to develop the first Hispanic career development seminar for Hewlett-Packard managers. I now had a chance to work with corporate America by accident. We were asked to create models that could help Hispanic leaders be successful in navigating work environments that treated people who were different as outsiders.

I continued to work with Pacific Management Services until 1985. During those years, we ran career development programs and began to do training in race relations that evolved into diversity when Digital

Equipment Corporation asked for a program that was inclusive of White men who felt left out of the mix.

The Bay Area was a dynamic location for diversity professionals; many were becoming national thought leaders driving this emerging practice. I had the opportunity to work with some of the best minds in the nation, and we were creating a new field called diversity that was being fueled by a government report called Workforce 2000. It was exciting because the various perspectives introduced new language, vision, concepts, and outcomes.

The diversity work was so compelling that I left a secure government position doing the work I had envisioned while in college, which was to develop innovative mental health programs for Latinos. At the time, my position paid well, provided me freedom to be creative, and gave me a chance to work with many community leaders. However, when I engaged in diversity work, it lifted my spirit and energized me because I recognized the potential for organizations to radically change and potentially operate differently when it came to valuing and respecting all employees who worked for them.

I wanted to work in an environment that appreciated the contributions of its employees who were committed to their vision. This was a dream worth pursuing because it spoke to a purpose that could change the fundamental nature of organizations and its relationship to the communities it served. So I created Amistad Associates, and my consulting firm was going to work with public and private organizations around diversity, team building, leadership, and organizational change. The spirit of hope consumed me, and I knew it could be an impetus for a new future.

## Where Does Spirit Take Us?

The last twenty-seven years of my life has been dedicated to the practice of diversity. Initially, my work focused on inclusion and education to eliminate "-isms." I have had opportunities to work in corporations, government, and nonprofit organizations. My role has been to help organizational leaders evaluate and question their institutional beliefs, norms, values, and practices.

During my quarter of a century-plus in the field, I have observed and worked with a number of organizations that have undertaken diversity intervention programs. Those organizations that have been successful recognize that change is a long and complex course of action and have treated diversity as a crucial initiative. For them, diversity addressed the importance of creating a work environment that encouraged employees to be themselves and build a culture that could tap the potential of each person. Additionally, there was a need to capitalize on the knowledge of its employees. In taking this approach, visionary leaders who demonstrated devotion, persistence, and deep intention to ensure the organization's diversity initiative was successful emerged within their organizations.

There is a body of diversity research that highlights successful interventions, citing benchmarks and established methodologies of successful programs. In addition, there is anecdotal data, and it speaks to diversity champions who used their personal power to drive diversity initiatives. These individuals influenced their organizations and positively created change. It is important to note that internal organizational diversity champions frequently had partners outside the organization to motivate, challenge, and guide them. These partnerships helped organizations achieve its diversity goals and ultimately developed models for best practices.

Understanding the power of diversity is important. Diversity of people, ideas, business strategies, and products are of significant value to organizations. This was confirmed in a study that Vice President Al Gore convened as part of his reinventing government initiative entitled Best Practices in Achieving Workforce Diversity. In this study, a number of corporations were involved as study partners. According to them, diversity was critical to their organizational success. I think this quote by John Pepper, former CEO of Procter & Gamble, sums it up well.

> Our success as a global company is a direct result of our diverse and talented workforce. Our ability to develop new consumer insights and ideas and to execute in a superior way across the world is the best possible testimony to the power of diversity any organization could ever have.

Our work in diversity has influenced how organizations manage their people in the United States and abroad. In fact, many organizations now implement global diversity initiatives using best practices and view it as an essential part of doing business. For those of us who have been in the profession for a number of years, it is a proud achievement to have established diversity as a core business norm. I find it remarkable considering the many detractors attempting to eradicate diversity in the 1980s and early 1990s. Back then, one could find frequent articles criticizing the diversity movement as a pseudo profession in the *Wall Street Journal*, *New Atlantic*, *Newsweek*, *Fortune*, and other magazines.

The power of diversity is that it could not be eradicated. Despite all the forces pushing for its demise, it continued to grow and evolve. I think many of us believed diversity was special because it was a conceptual practice that weaved in many other disciplines. It also reflected a convergence of many disciplines that recognized the importance of addressing race, gender, ethnicity, sexual orientation, socioeconomic status, and age as critical factors shaping our way of life. Given that many of us wanted institutional change, each discipline helped to shape the evolving nature of the diversity conversation and collectively developed a body of knowledge that was instrumental in the mainstreaming of our field.

As someone who has done diversity work in the basement of housing projects and in plush senior-level suites, I believe we have made progress and am relieved that diversity will be around for years to come. Nonetheless, we have reached a point where diversity is in need of a new spirit.

As I reflect on the state of diversity, it is clear that the original spirit that propelled many of us into the field has waned. Many of us were driven by a commitment to build a better world by instilling equality in the workplace and in our communities. This was a driving force moving us to act with a dedicated sense of esprit de corps. I think that diversity practitioners maintain some of this vision of change, but the battles and successes have forced us to compromise. When many of us started out doing diversity work, we were primarily trainers. Some twenty-eight years later, many of us have established businesses, written articles and books, developed web-based training programs, produced videos, and established an impressive list of clientele. As we become the elders in the field of diversity, the challenge of keeping and building business along with other considerations have forced us to pay careful thought to how we do our work and maintain our relationships in the business world. This is a delicate balance, and it does impact the degree to which many of us push for substantive change.

Is it time for those of us in diversity to revisit our purpose? I believe it is. We need to rekindle that spirit that directed us into a profession that was not yet defined. When I entered diversity work, it was viewed as illegitimate, opportunistic, and useless. At that point, many of us experienced a significant number of obstacles, yet we persevered because we believed our actions would create a better world. Our passion for diversity was amazing, and the autodidactic nature of our early efforts allowed us to innovate rapidly. We had no choice—diversity was new, and the body of knowledge available was minimal.

There is a need to rekindle our collective spirits. A reconnection with our vision to change the world will inspire and energize our field. For years, I have been seeking a breakthrough in diversity that could unlock the secret of success in helping people treat one another with respect and dignity. A small group of us created Diversity 2000, now entering its eighteenth year and renamed Diversity 2020. We were dedicated diversity practitioners and strongly felt that the collective knowledge had to be shared. We employed open-space technology to seek diversity breakthroughs and explore the broad areas of diversity. The three and a half days that we spend together is very powerful. And there are many ideas generated that have been prescient.

After numerous years of searching, dialoguing, and working with other professionals at Diversity 2000 and other think tanks, I am convinced that our future is to connect to the driving force of the past. What does this mean? I believe we need to rediscover the passion and love for this movement we created called diversity. We need to tap into that force within us that allowed us to believe we could change the world.

For this to succeed, we need to be part of a community. The D2K community has demonstrated that people can come together and engage in deep thought, conflict, personal pain, joy, and creativity. In doing so, individually and collectively, we reinvigorate the passion to do this work. For many of us, electing an African American president was a sign that diversity and inclusion has worked.

Something happens in a community that is transformative. Clearly, we witnessed this when Mr. Obama was elected. Images from around the world allowed us to see the joy and hope that many felt. These pictures presented a culmination of what I suggest is a calling of spirit. I am not talking about religion when I use the word *spirit*. There is a life force or substance that, when tapped, creates power. The emerging field of diversity is an example of many people collectively tapping into spirit to create and sustain a vision where people could learn to respect and treat one another with dignity.

Obviously this work is not done. We must persist and, in doing so, keep the passion and spirit that inspired many of us to change our life course and get into this work. As pioneers, our experience, knowledge, and leadership will help us move forward.

We have created a field of study called diversity of which we should be extremely proud. Albeit in its infancy, much has been learned through blood, sweat, and tears. I believe that diversity is to humanity what physics has been for science. Therein lies the gift—we have been at this for less than thirty years. Our job is to build the foundation and pass it on to the next generation. Each generation of thought leaders will need to call that spirit to keep them passionately engaged.

## Being Called into Action

When I began this work in 1980, it was called affirmative action training, cross-cultural training, and/or race relations. As a social worker, I was also working in the arena of cultural competence, particularly as it related to service delivery. During that period of time, I was excited to engage in conversations about culture and race relations. Many diversity practitioners felt there was an opportunity to define the differences in the populations we served and that this would allow us to change institutional practices of service delivery.

We, as change agents within our respective professions, strongly believed in the need for institutional restructuring when it came to how races and ethnicities were identified, assessed, and treated. This passion for serving and respecting the client community was linked to a strong belief in the potential to heal and transform the community.

What is the heart of diversity, and how does spirit fit within it? I think it is characterized by calling forth all our creativity, passion, and values in an authentic manner to challenge the nature of discrimination in a fearless way. In so doing, we must explore how we collude or act to change these discriminatory practices. For example, I have seen European Americans challenge White privilege. I have also seen cases where they have benefited from their race at the expense of people of color. In the spirit of diversity, we must take risks to stand with others who are treated unjustly.

A good friend of mine, Thomas Mitchell, and I used to spend a tremendous amount of time exploring diversity from the perspective of entrepreneurs. In doing so, we asked ourselves what was in it for leaders inside organizations who decided to take action on diversity. Our curiosity was driven by our inability to predict who would step up in the organization to drive diversity change. After working with a number of corporations, a pattern emerged, and people appeared driven by two motivations. We called one of the motivations the Vested Interest Model.

The leaders who emerged from this group recognized that diversity was a visible and sensitive project that had career benefits if accomplished. The initiative was an opportunity to drive an organizational goal that would demonstrate a basic commitment to diversity. Most organizations did not want to be at the front of the line, but they did want to send a message to their employees that it was important. Those who could promote diversity without significant change were rewarded and often promoted.

The second group was smaller in numbers. For them, it was about personal commitment to equality and a belief that change was required inside the organization that would allow talent, independent of the package, to move into top positions. This group tended to want organizational change that addressed culture and practices that had been viewed as barriers for employees and customers. They also wanted their organization to be at the forefront of best practices and link leadership commitment to executive pay. Leaders in the second group did not always find promotions. However, they pushed on even when it negatively impacted their careers.

As it turns out, it was the case that a number of the managers with whom we worked that were able to make diversity fit with the organization's goals, did indeed get recognized as diversity champions, thus helping their careers. On the other hand, leaders and managers whose focus was on changing norms and behaviors that violated the spirit of diversity found themselves in conflict with their management and were treated with suspicion. In my observation of these dynamics, European Americans were often rewarded, and people of color were viewed as too emotional about diversity.

Having a program that enhanced the careers of those who took a leadership role in diversity was a good incentive. It began a transition within organizations that moved diversity from solely an EEO issue to a much broader program that had some impact on the organization's operations.

The Vested Interest Model was a good strategy for its time; however, as we move into the twenty-first century, we need to move from an emphasis on the individual to one of team collaboration. Our thinking must expand to look at diversity as a unique opportunity to build a web of unity that works together to solve critical organizational issues and community challenges. A business cannot exist independent of a community. Clearly, the community includes the consumer and employees of the organization.

Furthermore, if we are to make diversity work, it can't be viewed as a North American problem. Unfortunately, many other countries see diversity as unique to US history and civil rights issues. It is time for us to promote diversity as an idea with concepts and language for engaging in deep discussions on differences of values, beliefs, norms, and practices. This is particularly important when there are practices that are destroying the value of human rights and planetary existence. Currently, there is much world anger toward the United States because of perceived western imperialism. Americans have been described as arrogant and severely lacking in cultural respect.

As practitioners, we have succeeded in developing an appreciation for diversity with business leaders. As we move forward, we'll need to do the same for our governmental leaders.

## Diversity for a New Millennium

Those of us in the diversity field have made a difference. Yet for many of us, there is an element of unrest. Certainly, we can be proud of our accomplishments to date. Diversity is a powerful force. It is a part of our everyday language, recognized in corporate vision statements, incorporated into academic, government, and corporate policies and training curricula, presented in advertisements to bolster images, and frequently used in surveys to measure which organizations have the right values and are places where you would want to work.

I am frequently involved in conversations about diversity with colleagues at various conferences, participants in our training programs across the country, and in think tanks with peers who have written books on the subject over a number of years. As I step back and look at our creation, it is obvious there is a need for a calling of the spirit, one that speaks to the complexities of the twenty-first century and recognizes that we can no longer function individualistically to address global complexities.

Our world is consumed by religious, economic, and political conflicts. At the heart of these conflicts are diversity tensions that are rooted in paradigms that seem impossible to change. However, if we cannot find a way to work through the diversity issues, we run the risk of falling back into a state of sanctioned discrimination that permits abuses in the name of national safety or some other ideology.

It is precisely in those times of great divide that we understand what is at stake. Violence in Rwanda, Bosnia, Serbia, Iraq, Somalia, Darfur, and other places around our world are critical examples of human meltdowns that can lead to the lowest form of hate and murder in the name of righteousness.

Why do we need something new? At this point in history, we are in the midst of major institutional collapse in the world because of leadership failures. Many of us started doing diversity work to change the world. It is safe to say that for many of us, the world we focused on was within our US borders. Today, globalism has changed how we look at diversity. There are far more complex dimensions added to the diversity mixture. Diversity now has moved beyond the workplace and into the world stage. As we begin to look at these diversity issues, the problems will have to be resolved among a number of stakeholders with competing interests.

The workplace may involve teams who work together across continents. Furthermore, when you operate in several countries, nationalism is always a factor as well as religion. Hence, diversity has expanded at an incredible rate, and world events have thrust this opportunity to take diversity to a deeper level on us, much faster than we anticipated. If ideas can change the world, then it is time for us to define a compelling vision that puts diversity practices into action at the highest levels of leadership within the United States and abroad.

The models, concepts, and principles we have established for diversity have introduced skills for working through difficult conflicts of interest (i.e., power, race, gender, age, and equality to name a few). These tools must not be restricted to the work environment; I think they are applicable in the larger arena. I want to see diversity professionals involved in strategies to help victims of natural disasters. A diversity perspective would be helpful when we look at issues related to domestic terrorism. Also, it is interesting to think what a diversity lens could teach us about how North Americans are seen around the world.

As professionals, we have been able to introduce diversity skills into the workplace when issues as volatile as sexual orientation and religious beliefs collide. We have helped corporations establish a set of standards that monitor and control discriminatory behavior. Today, organizations make it clear that whatever your beliefs may be, religious or otherwise, when you come to work, you must behave according to the professional standards of the company or seek employment elsewhere.

Yet in our communities, locally and globally, we have been unable to have the same impact. Why? I believe we have outgrown our original vision. I think many of us are stuck in paradigms that limit us. We do not need to operate so narrowly as a profession. Our value is in how we see the world. We must push against these paradigms that force many of us to accept the idea that we can't impact individual and institutional behaviors that create great destruction to humanity.

Some might argue that diversity is out of its element when it comes to the world stage. I suggest that if we allow leaders and the populace to continue operating from a state of fear, it will lead to human rights violations that will erode our sense of freedom. Our history is filled with examples of these lessons: Japanese internment camps, Latino citizen deportations, Jim Crow and sterilization of African Americans, and the murder of Middle Easterners in Texas and Arizona during 9/11. If we ignore diversity tensions, civil society may erode.

As I write this chapter, I'm saddened by the recent assassination of Dr. Tiller and the attack on the Holocaust Museum. These events have occurred during the same time that Sonia Sotomayor, a Supreme Court nominee, was being accused of being a racist because she belongs to a Hispanic civil rights organization. Additionally, the diatribes directed at people who belong to different political parties or support gay and lesbian marriage, to name one issue, have reached new heights of conflict and turmoil.

I suggest that a framework is in place that supports introducing diversity to the world stage. The Universal Declaration of Human Rights (UDHR) was adopted in 1948 by the United Nations General Assembly during which there was a call for cooperation in "promoting and encouraging respect for human rights and fundamental freedoms." These freedoms encompass the human rights of all people, including political, religious, civil, economic, social, and cultural rights. The UDHR is a fundamental document that can frame agreements on how to live with respect, dignity, and freedom toward one another despite our vast individual and cultural differences. More importantly, it espouses a critical perspective from its preamble:

> Whereas the peoples of the United Nations have in the Charter reaffirmed their faith in fundamental human rights, in the dignity and worth of the human person and in the equal rights of men and women and have determined to promote social progress and better standards of life in larger freedom.

I entered Diversity to eliminate the "-isms." Specifically, I wanted to work on breaking down barriers within organizations that excluded people who were different by virtue of their race, ethnicity, gender, sexual orientation, and other diversity dimensions. It was important for

Latinos so they could enter into new areas of education and employment. Furthermore, it is good for everyone when organizations have values that supported treating all employees with respect and dignity.

I wonder if the Declaration of Human Rights and the thirty articles that were established in 1948 had influenced the social justice and civil rights movements. I ask this question because Article 1 states that all human beings are born free and equal in dignity and rights. Article 3 states that everyone has the right to life, liberty, and security of person.

When the Human Rights Declaration was established fifty years ago, it was driven by the horror of war and human atrocities. I question if society has become numb to the atrocities.

Clearly, there was a need for nations to come together and develop a set of principles that fundamentally value the dignity of human life. This perspective must not be viewed as a political issue solely. Countries that were socialist, communist, and capitalist all worked together to craft this remarkable document. Dr. Johannes Van Aggelen, who has been working with the United Nations since 1980, suggested that the Second World War was fought as a crusade for human rights. Unfortunately, there continues to be atrocities and violations of human rights. Fortunately, more groups are coming together to fight against these kinds of behaviors. I suspect the crusade for human rights is still going on, and with technology ever present, the speed in which the world community sees these violations will present challenges for countries.

## Diversity and Human Rights

The UDHR is an inspirational document. It is an example for us in the diversity field of what can happen when people and nations find a way to work past their self-interest for the greater good. Clearly, UDHR resonates with many of us in the diversity profession. Those of us who do diversity and organizational change understand how difficult it is to forge an agreement and get commitment between individuals. To think that a diverse group of nations signed this document to abide by a set of principles is astounding. I also think diversity practitioners intuitively recognize that this document represents the power of defining and agreeing on principles. The fact that nations from around the world successfully formed an organization that made it a centerpiece of their purpose is evolutionary.

UDHR can serve as an example of what can happen when a group of committed human beings strive to achieve freedom and justice for individuals who are at the mercy of their own government. As diversity practitioners, we help organizations evaluate the conditions of their work environment and its impact on individuals. We in diversity also look at freedom, equality, and justice.

UDHR and diversity are linked. Although the details are not always clear, we must explore the connections that exist. For example, a group of employees who fail to work as a team because of tension related to style and performance may not relate to HR principles in their situation. However, if the same group were losing their jobs because of their religious affiliations, I would imagine that they would relate to the UDHR document.

Originally, I thought UDHR represented the next level of diversity work as it evolved. So far, I have not been able to establish a solid business case to support this idea. When it comes to my work, I have only applied UDHR to one multinational corporation and a couple of nonprofit activist groups doing work in Russia, Latin America, and Asia. So I'm still working on how I can weave UDHR into my diversity work on a regular basis.

Nonetheless, I believe it is important for diversity professionals to study and embrace this profound document. We need to spend time with human rights experts to share and dialogue the similarities and differences of our work. This interchange has to include people from around the world.

Our world is in dire need of change. There are growing numbers of diversity practitioners, and we represent many different nations. We can learn from one another and create shared frameworks and a common language. In doing so, it will allow the profession to work collaboratively in support of change.

I moved into Diversity because I was not happy with the practices of our institutions. I have been involved in social action because I am not satisfied with our national set of values, beliefs, and practices. At this point, I am frustrated about the state of our world. I strongly believe that UDHR can make a difference, and Diversity can help.

As I mentioned, when I began to study and work on UDHR, I thought it represented the next step-up for diversity. Is it possible that diversity represents the next level for UDHR? Nations have adopted and agreed to follow and promote the UDHR principles. As I see it, implementing the principles is where the problem lies. Is it conceivable that diversity can be a tool or process for helping to implement the goals of UDHR? We need to explore how using a diversity approach can promote increased understanding and mutual problem solving to decrease injustice, stop global destruction, and address the underlining problems that engender terrorism and war.

## Next Steps

We have a road map in the UDHR. Although the details are not yet clear, we must begin to think about the connections that make sense. At this point, diversity professionals need to study and embrace this profound document.

As I have said throughout this article, we need a calling of the spirit to move us to the next level. The next level is the global stage. Our vision of diversity must operate at this level in that diversity is a global reality. Furthermore, the diversity issues that impact people in both corporate and government organizations are driven by tensions that are cultural, socioeconomic, religious, ethnic, and racial.

The beauty of D2K is the people who show up each year. They have a passion and spirit that drives many of them to be leaders and change agents. Of course, we don't all agree on a common diversity vision. Nonetheless, our ability to work through diversity tensions has improved with time.

Diversity professionals entered this field to address these issues. Many of us have heard that these kinds of issues would never be resolved. Many of us were also told we were just dreaming and that human beings would always treat one another unfairly and that organizations would always devalue its members.

The truth is that we in diversity have made a difference. So far, that difference has been primarily within corporate America. Again, I cite Vice President Al Gore's Best Practices in Achieving Workforce Diversity. The diversity profession is young, and what we have accomplished in twenty-five years is phenomenal. At the same time, the world is in dire need of change. There are growing numbers of diversity practitioners, and we represent many different nations. Our job is to come together under a common framework and a common language (principles) to work on these issues of our day.

If we move forward with vision and courage, we can change the world in which we live; our children deserve it, and the condition of humanity demands it. Diversity pioneers did this once before, and the only assurance we had was our faith. In our hearts, we believed in our calling. Now it is time to rise to the occasion on the world stage. As Gandhi said, "We must be the change we want to see in the world."

In the 1960s, we were not satisfied with our nation's values, beliefs, and practices. As a result, many people got involved to create change. It is time to do so again. Let us find that spirit that resides within us and allow it to move us into action. I end with this Hopi saying that I find critical for our times: "We are the leaders that we have been waiting for."

# LIVING MULTIPLE REALITIES
## AS A LATINA IN AMERICA

Santalynda Marrero, EdD

WHAT DOES IT mean to live multiple realities as a Latina in America, and why is this story so important to tell? For me, its importance lies in a personal midlife look at the good, the bad, and the ugly that shaped my identity and career choices as a Puerto Rican raised in New Jersey and later transplanted to California. On a broader plane, there are growing numbers of biracial and bicultural people in the United States who have new and evolving perspectives who also live multiple realities. The stories of immigrant and migrant women and first-generation children are largely untold, particularly those that come from the only Latino group to be considered naturalized citizens.[1] This is my story shared through my lens of survival that often takes place in the schism between two cultures. It is a story that I have chosen to share through defining moments that have impacted my life. These common touch points in the lives of multicultural individuals define the experience of living in multiple realities.

As I reflected on these experiences, I revisited places of great sadness, discomfort, and guilt. At times, the process felt raw and painful; and at times, it brought back memories of great joy. This path of discovery put me in touch with those whose lives and spirits are interwoven with mine. My earliest memory of living a multiple reality was based on my observation of the outside world around the age of four. Already, I was holding feelings of sheer frustration at not being able to control my home environment, which felt challenging even in the midst of so much love. Somehow, my association is that what I saw and experienced with the adults around me at home, how we all lived, and the stories they told and their experiences in our community left me feeling frustrated and angry. The way my elders were talked at, made fun of, were demeaned at work, and how they had to work to just get by with unfulfilling work that did not adequately compensate them financially was unfair. Even at such a young age, this was clear. I

---

[1]   The people of Puerto Rico, as a commonwealth, were made citizens of the United States by the passing of the Jones Act of 1917.

took note of the disparities. While I was to experience my own disparate treatment, in early childhood, it is through watching and hearing those around us, especially our parents, that we gain our earliest imprinting. At times, their defining moments become part of ours as did my father's in the stories he shared with me.

Staying conscious of the shifting in and out of cultural context has now become a purposeful part of my career, a calling to do the work of diversity awareness and inclusion training. The definition of this work has evolved and morphed over time. It began with race relations and focused on equal employment opportunity that was legally mandated and intended to ensure nondiscrimination. The next wave brought forth affirmative action to address historical underrepresentation across race, gender, and socioeconomic status. Within the last decade, the focus has been on self-awareness and strategic inclusion to leverage talents. Other relevant terms associated with the work are social justice, human rights, cultural competence, and talent management with a focus on engagement and addressing generational differences.

My training as a counseling psychologist and the lessons I've learned have helped me to frame the way I see my work in organizational, team, and individual development. Being bilingual, biliterate, and bicultural has afforded me the opportunity to work internationally. Diversity and inclusion and cross-cultural awareness are core to my work. The passion for my work lies simply in comforting the distressed and disturbing the comfortable to facilitate growth for individuals and their relationship to others. Not surprisingly, often the work of disturbing the comfortable is not solely reserved for others.

My background, as shared in story, includes the development and integration of two primary cultures creating dual ways of being in order to succeed in the United States as a Puerto Rican woman. This duality has created what I call living multiple realities as a first generation born in the United States to parents whom others would see as immigrants. As I examined my history and that of others, four common themes emerged that shaped this unique experience of living multiple realities. We all seem to share the following: (1)*defining moments—discrete points in time that shape identity;* (2) *a level of resiliency to overcome adversity;* (3) *an awareness that we must battle between acculturation versus assimilation;* and (4) *not forgetting where you came from by helping others.* Each of the stories to follow will illustrate how living multiple realities reflects these common themes. Our common touch points get shared in stories, vignettes, and dialogue that can augment training and development for those who are new to their diversity journey.

I believe our stories are worth telling because for many of us, it is through folklore that we manage the adversity and challenges of redefining ourselves while living multiple realities. Telling our stories has enabled us to survive and pave the way for others to have their voices heard. It is in the coming to terms with our past that we can honor it, learn to love ourselves enough to celebrate the present, and cocreate a future where we move beyond survival so we can thrive. Collectively, when we share our stories, we can learn from one another to better communicate and create communities of inclusion. By this I mean communities where we embrace and stimulate an appreciation for different cultures, languages, sexual orientation, class, and other attributes on the "wheel of diversity" beyond tolerance.

It is my sincere hope that by sharing a few of the defining moments that were most poignant for me, I will be able to provide an opening for those who want to relate to others living multiple realities and who may want to identify their own defining moments. It is also an invitation to the reader to reflect upon the question, Do we really live by the choices we make, or is it that the changes in life create the choices we make?

## Section 1: DEFINING MOMENTS

*The value of identity of course is that so often with it comes purpose.*
—Richard Grant

A *defining moment* is a unique experience that heightens the individual's awareness of "the other" or his or her own cultural reference outside of mainstream society. It can be haunting, provocative, and life changing. How we experience the incident shapes or filters our view of reality or multiple realities. What we internalize and project as a result of the experience becomes part of our identity. This experience oftentimes becomes a turning point wherein a conscious or unconscious decision is made in our interpretation, adding to our beliefs. These experiences generate the filters through which we interpret our world.

For those of us seeing life through a multicultural lens, whether we are immigrants or migrants, there are three kinds of common defining moments: defining ourselves as we discover the "other," experiencing discrimination for the first time, and wanting acceptance. Since identity is not experienced in a vacuum but rather in sociocultural and political contexts, these moments are key contributors to defining others and us. They serve to make sense of our world.

Defining moments are the prism through which our experiences color our identity. And sometimes it is our identity that colors our experiences. Either way, for some of us, a life's work, path, or calling emerges from these experiences. Ask yourself and others, How are these experiences similar or different to other Latinas or dual-identity cultures? What defines your reality around culture and identity?

## Shaping Identity: Learning about Self in Relation to Others

My upbringing as a Puerto Rican in New Jersey highlights the challenge of making sense of the disparities apparent in living within the context of mainstream United States culture as a first-generation Latina. I was born in 1952 with parents who were already forty years my senior, not very common in those days. My culture was handed down to me pretty much unfiltered as I was raised as if we were living in Puerto Rico. My parents instilled in my brothers and me a deep-rooted nationalistic sense of cultural identity. The cultural context set for me at home was different than the one I experienced at school as I mostly had non-Latino classmates. Learning life lessons, values, and ways of being that were taught to me by my parents, supported by extended family, and reinforced by a community were clear and uncompromising. My father would emphasize that there is a difference between my education and my schooling. For him, my schooling in the public schools was where I learned about non—Puerto Rican values, traditions, and beliefs. At home, he expected me to remain true to the education he and my mother provided for me to be a noble and good daughter. This difference in what I learned at school and how I behaved at school had sharp contrasts between the education my parents gave me every day at home. Early on, I learned to switch gears and decompress carefully so that I would not confuse what behaviors were appropriate in what setting.

This shifting between cultures began as early as I can recall. My behaviors, thinking, and processing happened in duality. Many would argue that this is a natural part of the socialization process. Be that as it may, during my tenure as a college counselor and academic advisor, my experience confirmed that when young people are faced with duality of cultures and class, they sometimes become torn, stretched, and isolated in the process. Some of us come to terms with the disparities, inequities, or commonalities without losing our self-esteem, our spirit, and ourselves. Others are not so fortunate, experiencing internalized oppression or disdain for their group of origin.

Basically, individuality is about the constant (conscious or unconscious) negotiation between self and others—a unique comfort with my mobility on the cultural identity continuum. While being raised ethnocentrically—meaning my reference point was focused on my ethnicity through interaction with peers at school—I became more ethnorelative. I could be an insider or an outsider in either culture depending on the circumstances. This is at the core of living multiple realities. Sometimes, the duality shows up as guilt for having at times disassociated with my ethnicity or in ludicrous myths and stereotypes placed on me by others. In talking with peers, I am affirmed and see myself in their stories as well. Other Latinas have captured their experiences in music, spoken word, drama, and literature. One of my favorites is Esmeralda Santiago, author of *When I Was Puerto Rican* and *Almost a Woman*. In the latter, the following quote captures the conflicted duality: "My world was dominated by adults, their rules written in stone, in Spanish, in Puerto Rico. In my world, no allowances were made for the fact that we were now in the United States, that our language was becoming English, that we were foreigners awash in American culture."[2] Perhaps the reader too can relate to these thoughts or is willing to explore another's story as a way to engage in an inclusive dialogue. Where are you on the scale of ethnocentricity and ethnorelativity wherein you have learned and become relative to other groups beyond your own?

A significant defining moment common among multicultural and non-White individuals is the experience that determines how much we might trust people who are different from us. I learned vicariously through my father's storytelling about discrimination. He shared a story about how Marie, an Irish American woman that would become my godmother, earned his respect. Papi rented a flat, and sometime later, Marie became the new building manager. The first week, she came to him to return five dollars she said he overpaid in his weekly rent bill. He attempted to set the record straight by letting her know she must be mistaken as his rent was

---

[2] Esmeralda Santiago, *Almost A Woman* (New York: Vintage Books, Random House, Inc.,1998).

twenty-five dollars per week, and that is the amount he had given to her. She responded, "Oh no, Mr. Santos, everyone pays the same twenty dollars a week." It was then that they understood the prior building manager had overcharged him.

Using her White privilege, Marie chose to confront the former building manager to ask him why he was charging Mr. Santos more than the others. His answer was simple: he is from another country, and he doesn't know any better, so you can charge him more. As she recalls the story, she asserted to him that the overcharging was unfair and discriminatory and that she would have no part in the scheme. She respected my parents as honest, hardworking people, and they respected her as an ethical and fair person. It is easy to understand why they chose her to be my godmother. At the end of the day, it left me with the understanding that some White people are good, and others can't be trusted. Imagine if the only experience one has with other ethnic groups solidifies a sense of distrust—this is at the root of prejudice, conflict, or racism. What did you learn about "other" in an experience relayed to you or that you experienced firsthand that led to trust or distrust? How might this experience feed stereotypes?

## Experiencing Discrimination

Discrimination takes many forms. Some of it is overt, for example, in name-calling. Early on, I learned that there is much power in a simple word. I learned it is more than being politically correct when choosing my words. For example, the word *spic* still brings a sting to my ear. I think it comes from "no spic English." Whatever its source, it came to be quite a derogatory reference to me and other Latinos.[3] On the other hand, institutional discrimination and racism is not as easily exposed and deeply entrenched. In this story, which helped further define and refine my filters, behind-the-scenes discrimination smacked me hard.

Upon graduation from Rutgers University, I was to become a teacher. Truly a dream come true. Or was it? It was 1974, the year I was student teaching English as a second language and Spanish at a middle school in New Jersey. I was lucky to be able to go back to my hometown to complete my assignment.

---

[3]   *Spic* is an ethnic slur used in English-speaking countries for a person of Hispanic descent. *Spic* can be used as a noun.

I recall asking Mrs. Lopez, the ESL chair, why she ate alone and not with the other teachers in the staff lunchroom. She smiled and encouraged me to join the others. She said we could talk about it afterward. After two shared lunches with other teachers in the staff lunchroom, I joined Mrs. Lopez in eating in our classroom, separate from the rest. It was obvious to me by their derogatory commentaries that they resented the changes in demographics in their school district.

About three-fourths of the teachers were White, and by the way, they were the same teachers who taught my brothers and me. The school administration also had remained the same for the past thirty years. What had changed was the student population. The students were no longer predominately White. The students were mostly Latinos from Puerto Rico, Cuba, the Dominican Republic, and other Spanish-speaking countries. Two days into my student teaching, my experience in the teacher's lunchroom made it clear that they were resentful of the change that "those people" (children, mind you) rendered upon them.

They made no excuses for their pejorative and negative comments about the students. I heard comments including "They're like animals" and "They don't want to learn." I remember meekly attempting to remind them that I came from their classes and from this very school. They were quick to patronize me by stating, "Yes, but you were one of the good ones." What I once interpreted as a flattering compliment now had new meaning. Joining Mrs. Lopez away from the teacher's lunchroom became my pleasure without question. The lesson learned was invaluable, opening my eyes with yet another etching for my identity and a defining moment in my career.

In working with the children, I found myself spending more and more time after school visiting their homes to help their parents navigate the social systems for food, health service, and all the basics needed for children to focus on their schooling. Teaching Spanish and English as a second language became secondary. Upon reflection, my behavior begs the question, were there other choices that could have been made from both parties? Today, what different choices do we consciously introduce in these open spaces other than retreating and avoiding?

Through these experiences, I came to better understand what Malcolm X meant when he cautioned that people of color face one struggle, but that the struggle has many fronts. Disparities in economic viability, health care, and access are still evident today. Some things change, and other changes are nothing more than pseudo changes for certain groups. What gave me hope was that I also learned that the more you are willing to learn about the struggle, the more you can do to make a difference. As a result, I made a conscious decision to enter graduate studies to become a psychologist.

## Wanting Acceptance

We all want to be accepted and included. The challenges abound for those living multiple realities as a result of a Latino ethnic experience within mainstream culture. From my earliest memories on through adulthood, defining moments would shake my core to remind me that wanting to be accepted and to fit in did not necessarily translate into being accepted.

As I moved on to higher education, ethnicity and race awareness took on even more complexity. In addition, the larger overarching issue of class also struck me.

I thought by the time I got to college, I had a clear understanding of who I was. This was based on the way I was raised, the awareness I had gained through experiences at school, and lessons I'd learned about exclusion as a Puerto Rican in America. Armed with solid core values, determinism, and—let's not forget—resiliency, I was centered. To my surprise, I quickly learned I was only partially grounded, and at times I was ill prepared for even more levels of ethnic and racial disparities. This realization presented a challenge to wanting to be accepted and being accepted. While the stage of young adulthood and attending college is jarring for most youth, for non-White youth, the experience carries more of a challenge. During my formative years, my encounter with other ethnic groups that included Jewish, Polish, Ukrainian, Hungarian, African American, and Chinese cultures enabled me to be more inclusive. With exposure and openness, similarities in family, values, and community became more evident over time.

Our challenge as Latinas was a two-edged sword. On the one hand, we did not all perceive one another in the same way. There were those for whom it was easier to assimilate. White skin, straight hair, language skills, lack of accent, and other factors made it easier for them to pass or at least opt to assimilate. They could be more easily accepted into the mainstream culture. On the other hand, those Latina sisters who had dark complexions or more African features at times found themselves between acceptance and rejection even within the Latino culture.

This dynamic of colorism in a culture that has many races and ethnicities is often a taboo discussion. Denial around the issue continues. The notion of good hair, bad hair, *bembes* (large lips), and refined European noses all have a host of negative and positive associations. Some antagonism and energy was rendered around who was more Puerto Rican or more Latino than whom. In the name of self-discovery, a privilege pecking order would again emerge. The late-night arguments of those who proclaimed mother Spain above mother Africa or above First Nations roots continue even today, no doubt. This is obviously an inheritance of colonialism, of colonial racism.

Our out-of-classroom learning came from dialogues around accepting one another as Latinas as well as being accepted and fitting in within the college community of women. One of the ways we were able to cope and find a place holder for ourselves was to live in a special-interest group dormitory.

La Casa Boricua was such a place. It was a way for Puerto Ricans to carve out a niche for ourselves in Douglass College at Rutgers University. Some would say that the existence of such a dormitory flies in the face of seeking acceptance while others would say it was a vehicle to promote acceptance. Noteworthy, there was always an inherent tension in our college experience around the theme of acceptance and our choosing to live separately. There was more to come in terms of what the non-Latinas, mostly white female students, living in adjacent dormitories thought of us. Their White privilege kept many of them from ever experiencing a non-White culture; most had never met a Latina. If they had, it was through a lens of class privilege. Their association was with a nanny, housekeeper, or gardener. I can recall a time when my parents came to visit and brought me food, aromatic rice and beans and *pernil* (roast pork). A few of the women who lived down the hall from me in the dorm exclaimed deliberately loud enough for me to hear them, "Ugh, what is that nasty smell!"

These experiences had an impact on me. They could easily have given me a sense of shame or pushed me to try and distance myself from my culture. This happens, this is a problem. From this experience, I learned that it is important to decide who you are and how you identify before someone else tells you who you should be. Americano culture did not, and generally does not, encourage immigrants and others to define themselves as anything but an assimilated American, and not to embrace first cultures. Defining one's self is a revolutionary act. While the internal struggle took root, the external struggle for presence and acceptance on campus juxtaposed. Social activism came by way of sit-ins and taking over campus buildings to protest the lack of admission and inclusion of Black and Puerto Rican and low-income students.

# Section 2: RESILIENCY

*A man carries success or failure with him . . . it does not depend on outside conditions.*

—Ralph Waldo Trine

The second common experience that shapes the worldview of multicultural individuals is a sense of resilience to survive both worlds. Charles Darwin is often quoted as saying, "It is about the survival of the fittest," but what he actually said is, "It is not the strongest of the species that survive, nor the most intelligent, but the one most responsive to change." Multicultural individuals are the benchmark for adaptability and resilience.

The ability to be flexible and pliable is at the core of resiliency. As a generalization, migrants' and immigrants' success depends on their ability to navigate through differences in language, cultural norms, and customs. Living multiple realities demands at least three kinds of common resolves that bicultural and multiethnic people have to our credit: to be strong in character, to be resourceful, and to filter out negative or challenging circumstances that get us through hardships.

As any child may experience moments of discouragement, my father consistently used his own life experiences to encourage and guide my sense of fortitude to overcome just about anything. One story worth telling serves a testament to the resiliency of migrants even when the choices are limited. It is one of many stories my father shared that demonstrated his character and made me take stock of what I needed to do when I thought things were too tough and I wanted to give up. Papi would tell us of leaving Puerto Rico as a mature man in his late thirties. In those early years, he worked at an industrial laundry facility. It was his first year on the East Coast when he experienced his first winter. Fortunately, working near the drying machines kept him warm enough, at least until the snow came. He did not have a winter coat.

He said he saw something soft falling from the sky and was so overtaken by the experience that he ran outside to touch and feel what was happening. You must understand this man had lived in the Caribbean his entire life in the early 1900s with no access to radio or television. In his small village in the mountains of Puerto Rico, he had no books and was schooled only to the second grade. Snow was a phenomenon for which he had no reference point. Soon he realized that he was wet and cold. He saw the snow accumulating quickly and piling up in a mound. With the curiosity of a child, he walked over to a mound of snow to investigate this white substance that had piled up. He noticed a piece of cloth sticking out from under the snow pile. As he tugged on it, he uncovered a sleeve. He continued to pull, revealing a sweater. This discarded sweater became his winter coat for that season.

This story left a lasting imprint of two key learnings: First, you can be proud of yourself regardless of how limited your resources may be. In fact, pride may be all you have to hold on to. Second, it helped me understand the fortitude of character that in essence says, "Do well with what you have." Later in my adolescence, I recall cruel incidents of misunderstandings about accents, frizzy hair, not-so-nice prom dresses, and similar trials of teenage life that were made less painful by thinking of that fortitude of character.

As I listened to others' experiences in the United States, I shared in the challenges of classism, poverty, sacrifice, and determinism that are so common in the lives of immigrants/migrants. To this day, the core value of resiliency sustains me in my life challenges and in the work of diversity and inclusion.

How might you get at understanding the impact of others' experiences when they do not have access to your world?

## Section 3: ASSIMILATION VERSUS ACCULTURATION

*He is free . . . who knows how to keep in his own hands the power to decide.*
—Salvador De Madariaga

Assimilation is the process in which one group takes on the culture and other traits of a larger group. It often assumes that the dominant culture absorbs the other. In the case of Latinos and most migrant and immigrant groups, it represents the decision to dilute or lose our culture and integrate into the dominant Euro-American culture. In this way, languages other than English are lost as are customs and traditions. From my perspective, it is a form of being overshadowed and marginalized by the other. Whereas the act of acculturating entails a conscious cultural integration of the other culture without losing language, customs, or traditions in the process. Both cultures are honored and not marginalized. The integration of a multitude of cultures today in the United States is more readily reflected in our mass media, sociopolitical influences, and communities than they were as when we were growing up.

Through the generations those of us who live multiple realities by being bicultural share the battle that exists between assimilating and acculturating. In this process, a few questions surface: First, how much of ourselves do we give up or give in to the other? Second, how do we negotiate walking in multiple realities without getting worn out? Third, how do we manage the stress?

The need to shift in and out of scripts between two cultures began early in life. Even in the "innocence" of cartoons young children see, early impressions can define the degree to which assimilation and acculturation can be in conflict. I recall seeing Pepé Le Pew, a silly skunk who was portrayed as sexy with his French accent while a Spanish accent was associated with the stereotype of not being as smart, less than, somehow inferior. There was a stereotypical hyper mouse who would say in a Spanish Mexican accent, "My name is Speedy Gonzales." Subliminal or overt, the messages abounded to associate with none other than the Euro-American culture.

One of my most painful defining moments imprinted in me the distinctions of assimilation and acculturation. The seeds for assimilation were introduced in elementary school down by the schoolyard. In 1960, when I was eight years old, our schoolyard was divided into sections. One section was for girls and another was for boys. Those lines were not to be crossed during recess. Actually, there was a third section. That was for the "retarded" children (in those days, this was the term that was used in our schools). They looked different than we did, they had what were described as funny-looking faces that did not seem to match the rest of their bodies, and some were physically challenged and had to use wheelchairs or crutches. They were different.

Over a period of time, I noticed that there were other children in the "retarded" group who looked like me and spoke Spanish like me. These were children that I knew because on the weekends, our families would come together to socialize around church, food, and fiestas. They sure didn't seem "retarded" to me. If there was a difference, it was that most of these children were older; I am guessing an average age of thirteen to fifteen. They also did not speak English, and both the girls and boys looked more physically developed than the rest of us. I remember either saying hello to them when no one was looking or diverting my eyes from theirs to avoid the hurt and humiliation that I expect was felt on both ends.

My struggle with my identity felt duplicitous. I was not like them at school. I was different in a good way—a way that was accepted and integrated in the Americano culture. I spoke English well—no foreign accent since I was born and raised in New Jersey. I dressed well, I knew what to do, and I was smart and well liked. These immigrant children I socialized with on the weekends, who lived near me, were like me but somehow different—less than. At school, they were labeled as defective.

There was no bilingual education then. So many of these adolescents dropped out of school and went to work as soon as they turned fifteen. I was tormented. It felt good at school to be accepted, so I had pride in being one of the "good ones," as my schoolmates and teacher would say. And then again, the humiliation and hurt I shared with and for my immigrant Latino peers were painful. I felt guilty for wanting to be included at their expense. To this day, those feelings of disempowerment, humiliation, and guilt bring me to tears.

## Shifting

While flexibility and making sense of multiple realities for bicultural and multicultural people are valuable in helping us succeed, the necessary moving in and out of self to fit in with others in mainstream culture is exhausting. Over time, this shifting is a process that stresses and gnaws at our sense of worth and self-esteem.

For many of us, the inequity and stigma in this duality of cultures, while helping to craft our identity, has come with a price. My interpretation led me to believe that I had to be smarter than all the rest and work harder and longer. I had to make sure that my dress was pressed, not a spot of café or grease on my homework, and when prompted, learn to say, "Yes, I am Spanish." I grew to hate the socks my shoes would eat, those that would slide down into my shoes when the elastic had stretched too far to be functional. God bless my mother, for she was as fastidious as me and as meticulous in her presentation as well. She colluded with the Americano culture.

We each find ways to navigate our multiple realities. My father on the other hand was more private and shunned some of the Americano ways. He cared less about the public image in terms of clothes, manners, and such. His focus was on being honest, hardworking, and even harder working. My parents advocated the American dream would come through hard work, not rocking the boat, and being honest. Staying faithfully within those parameters, I just knew I was on the right path. Wow, what a recipe for overachievement. I still can't break the cycle, which I find exhausting at times. These traits in my identity are a source of fun poked at me by those near and dear to me. I have learned to laugh at myself.

What I learned was that survival and, certainly, success is dependent on shifting between two worlds. In one world, you acculturate with your own, and in the other world, you assimilate in order to succeed. It seemed natural to share what I'd learned and to teach those like me how to speak the language of the other world and how to succeed. I even learned to distinguish for others and myself how to acculturate without assimilating and losing one's self totally. Coaching young professional Latinos to shift in healthy balance is key in my work. This is no easy task.

For myself, looking back now, I understand why as a child I acted out at home. I threw tantrums out of frustration from seeing similar inequities bestowed on good people, those I loved and who loved me. I became determined that I would always be able to take care of myself regardless of what others thought, said, or did. I'm not sure exactly when it occurred, but the emergence of this self-determination was a defining moment. There have been many defining moments that are clearly linked and have, without question, shaped how I chose to identify and led me to my career choices. The question I ponder is, Which really were conscious choices, and which were merely a dictate of societal norms charted by class, ethnicity, and gender? There are other parts of my identity like pieces of a jigsaw puzzle that still remain to be placed. At times, defining moments, like pieces of a puzzle, seem to have come out of another box (context) and mixed in where they don't have a proper place to fit. Maybe, since our cultural puzzles are often complex and multidimensional, I just haven't found where they fit yet. Maybe there is no proper place for some of the pieces. Any wonder why it takes a lifetime of introspection to make sense of it all?

## Section 4: NEVER FORGETTING WHERE YOU CAME FROM AND REACHING BACK TO HELP

*Be an opener of doors.*

—Ralph Waldo Emerson

## Reaching Back to Help

It is not uncommon for migrants and immigrants to pull together, sacrifice for one another, and share resources. In my parents' household, there was always one relative or friend living with us until they were able to get on their feet.

Members of the community who were more acculturated helped others get jobs, housing, and needed services. My parents instilled in us a core value of "never forgetting where you came from," which meant it was both a responsibility and privilege to reach back and help.

As my elder by ten years, my brother played the role of "cultural interpreter." He served in the army and explored in ways that would render him a worldly mentor to me. He was in touch with the Americano world in a way my parents trusted, even if they could not fully understand. He and I started our college experience as freshmen in the same year. His veteran benefits allowed him the opportunity, and somehow I am convinced that my father sent him on a deliberate mission to watch over his little sister. This is a practice I have seen repeated even today in other Latino families. I recall a time when my brother shared both his pride and concern for me. Pride in that I had successfully completed my doctorate. Concern in that my demeanor, being less than assertive and actually quite docile, would get in the way of my professional success. As a Puerto Rican girl, this demeanor was what was expected of me to show *respeto*. Fortunately, my brother helped me understand that the lack of eye contact, nonassertive handshake, and soft tone of voice would not inspire confidence in the clients seeking counseling.

With my brother Chuck's (the name Carlos Americanized) coaching and mentoring, I was able to learn how to shift and be flexible in my communication style, etiquette, and business acumen. Shifting again led to an understanding that *respeto* looked and felt different in each culture. If we had ever dared to look our elders directly in the eye, we would have demonstrated defiance, lacking respect and appropriate humbleness, which is so contrary to Euro-American cultural interpretation. Herein I learned one was to have direct eye contact so as not to be interpreted as having low self-esteem, lacking confidence, or being untruthful. And if I ever were to confuse the "look," Santos, my father, would remind me in no uncertain terms! I use his example in cross-cultural awareness training when addressing similar values and how they tend to show up differently, often creating miscommunication for the misperception and assumptions they generate.

The complexity of understanding others and ourselves as we live multiple realities includes the influence on our generational perspectives. I hold the perspective of a Latina from the boomer generation, which brings with it a filter different than other generations. I find these differences fascinating especially as I seek to understand how my son, James, who is bicultural, and other generations experience diversity. I witness how he and his inner circle of friends—which include a Christian Palestinian, a Muslim with roots from Libya, a first-generation Mexican American, a Japanese/ Pole, a German American, and three African Americans—all navigate their differences and similarities. I have shared in their development since they met in third grade and have watched them grow into young men. A few attend college locally, and a few are in different parts of the country. During their breaks, they all reunite and their bond grows stronger with time. Most seem to have clear identities, some shifting in and out of cocultures while others seem not to notice.

I am proud in how my son and I celebrate our identities, our realities, and our mosaic of cultures, experiences, views, and dreams. At the same time there are important voices that remind me that reaching back as we climb is a way to make a difference.

## Being Mentored

One person does make a difference in opening the doors once found shut. I have been fortunate to have had several mentors in my life who have made all the difference in my success. One such person who made a critical difference was my eighth grade homeroom teacher, Mrs. Seguine. She saw something in me that caused her to choose to make a difference. She went out of her way to be inclusive of me. This teacher was also the choir director and an educator who was innovative in her time by teaching eighth graders algebra when at the time it was reserved as a standard for high school only.

She ensured that I was included in her progressive classes and put me in the choir, not for my singing capability, of this I am certain. It is clear to me her intent was to help me gain confidence and see myself as having a place in the mainstream. It was at the end of this year that we were to complete our course selections for the ninth grade. So I chose the courses my social peer group of girls and I had discussed. Specifically, Typing 1, Steno 1, English 1, General Science, and Accounting Math. Like the few other Latinas around me, I was going to make something of myself, I was going to be successful, and I was going to be a secretary. My parents who had attended only the second grade thought this was marvelous.

As my teacher walked around to collect the curriculum forms, she reached down for mine and proceeded to crumple it up. I was horrified; I thought I had done something wrong! Much to my surprise, she replaced it with a form she completed in her best penmanship. The only thing I recognized was my name. She saw a different path for me. The courses she selected for me were English Composition, Algebra I, Biology 101, World History, and German. I swallowed hard and in a meek voice asked her if I could exchange Spanish for German. She smiled and nodded in the affirmative.

That one incident changed my scholastic tracking to college preparatory. Her mentoring, caring, and assertion was key in helping me become who I am today. I still get teary eyed at the thought of how she touched my life, and I feel compelled to do the same for others whenever I am able. There are many memories, both good and bad, that come to mind in terms of the individuals who opened doors and who closed doors for me. I sincerely believe every last one of them made me stronger, more resilient, and more determined.

## Mentoring Others

There are many ways to open doors for others. All too well I understood the social, economic, psychological, and academic challenges the students I've mentored have faced as they navigated through their education in a sometimes less-than-friendly environment. In academia, I served as the advisor facilitating workshops, overseeing student-run meetings, and directing developmental efforts in counseling with undergraduate students at my alma mater, Rutgers University.

In turn, there are many others I have mentored since then, including my son who of course represents the next generation of *mi familia*. To see ourselves in a new generation struggling to succeed in a new Americano way is part of the experience for many immigrants.

Of all those whom I have reached back for, the one that most touches my heart is Emilia, a young Chicana I met in the grocery store. She had attended more than five high schools as her parents moved throughout the state. When I met her, she was working to support herself and attended a local community college. It became evident that the road ahead of her was to be long as she made up for the basic learning she did not get in high school. So I would invite her over for food and friendship and slowly began mentoring her.

At times as we worked on her writing and math, she would fall asleep in my home. In sharing my story with all the trials and tribulations, we bonded as I saw myself in her, and she could see the possibilities reflected in me. Over the years, our relationship grew with a richness of *familia*. I am proud to say that I attended her graduation in 2005 when she received her master's in social work (MSW) from Columbia University. This for me has been mutual love made visible through her accomplishments. And what is most important for me is that she will take her knowledge forward to enhance the human rights of adolescents who are lost in the foster care system. I feel empowered through her success and contributions. She represents the ongoing promise of social justice work, expanding the playing field, and leveraging talent that I espouse in my work. Her generation is next in line to engage in the work of diversity. How will the upcoming generations Xers and Ys redefine this work? How will the next generations define success?

As I reflect back on my own success, I am reminded that it is said that success can be measured in terms of what you have given up in return for what you have received. That can be a chilling thought. The questions I ponder are the following: What parts of me did I give up along the road to success? Are there parts of my persona that have been forgotten or compromised for lack of self-expression? I think Bontemps (poet—Arna Bontemps, 1902-1973) says it best: "Is there something we have forgotten? Some precious thing we have lost; wandering in these strange lands?"

## We All Have Stories to Tell

Writing this chapter for the anthology has afforded me the time to reflect and tell pieces of my story brick by brick. I do not claim that my story is more worthy than anyone else's. What I do claim is my time to tell it. I encourage us all to look within and to relive and tell our stories. What better way to honor the spirits past whose shoulders served to let us see higher and farther? What better way to begin to understand one another than through sharing our stories?

Indeed, we all have stories to tell. Sometimes, we tell them to ourselves uncensored; and at other times, we filter them so that we can allow ourselves to be at peace. Honoring our past is paramount to self-acceptance. In so doing, it is important to honor the spirits of our ancestors and friends that have gone before us. With all the stories to tell—good, bad, and ugly—I know the ghosts will come out dancin' every chance they get. It is time to invite them to the party and make them welcome as the stories come flooding forth in memories.

Today, when I introduce myself as a speaker or facilitator, I often begin by saying, "I am bicultural, biliterate, bilingual, but not bipolar." All kidding aside, sometimes the shifting required to live in multiple realities has created real stress. Negotiating the schism continues to be a constant challenge. Many of us are resilient and channel our response to my stress in all the socially accepted and positive ways. For others, the same duality has played a role in suicide, mental illness, depression, and other tragic untold stories.

In listening to other's stories, it is clear that challenges of disconnect from the larger societal norm in America still exists today for immigrants and nonimmigrants, particularly those who are not White. It is clear to me that defining moments are as alive as the person living them. And what is to say they cannot be refined and redefined? Everyone deserves to live a purposeful and fulfilling life. To this end, I work with organizations, teams, and individuals to address challenges in interpersonal cross-cultural communication, and diversity awareness as core. For each of us, there is fertile ground to cover in addressing the disconnect around classism, gender bias, racism, and heterosexism—all the "-isms" that directly affect an individual's ability to be included and successfully engaged.

After twenty years as an internal consultant, I made the conscious decision to "hire myself" and launch my consulting practice. In living a purposeful life, a quote from Khalil Gibran's *The Prophet* comes to mind: "Work is love made visible." So with my academic preparation—the passport as I call it—and work experience, my career as a consultant has evolved. My clients include health care, institutions of higher education, fire service, and corporations throughout the country and intermittently a few international assignments.

## A Natural Evolution for Promoting Diversity and Inclusion

I came to diversity and inclusion consulting after several years of work as a human resources professional in corporate America. My work spans a broad range of experience, but the common theme has always been maximizing human potential. If I were to contemplate the path as I now see it in hindsight, the start was fueled by turmoil—visible collisions among races in this country. My history and experience of living multiple realities as a Latina in America helped me to see in others the struggle shared in (1) defining moments—discrete points in time that shape identity; (2) a level of resiliency to overcome adversity; (3) an awareness that we must battle between acculturation versus assimilation; and (4) not forgetting where you came from by helping others.

In my formative years, my role of change agent, advocate, and cross-cultural interpreter emerged. My consciousness was further fed by the civil rights movement and my access to higher education through affirmative action efforts. On the East Coast in the sixties, the Pan-African movement, the Black Panthers, and the Young Lords focused on economic disparity and the need for communities to come together for survival. The work focused on race relations with Black and White issues at the forefront. I can recall my first year as an undergraduate student at Rutgers University reading *Black Rage* written by Dr. Price Cobbs, whom I now am proud to say is in my circle of distinguished colleagues some thirty years later. Speakers such as Dick Gregory, Angela Davis, Nikki Giovanni, Eli Wiesel, and others influenced my thinking in those formative years. In tandem, the Mexican American movement was taking on a life of its own. Additionally, the feminist movement took hold with Gloria Steinem and others at the helm. Gender roles, careers, and barriers became a focal point. At times, race and gender issues were at odds; and in other circles, they were allies in the movement toward parity. It is a flashback to the spark of disparity I sought to make sense of as a child. Laws pushed us toward tolerance in a country that held fairness as its mantra. In some ways, we have made strides, and still in others we cope poorly with the disparity and dissention from the norm.

It makes sense to me that the diversity awareness and strategy toward inclusion is for me a calling by choice and by the chance of circumstance. Some of us believe that we are called to be change agents—socioarchitects for systems change. My experiences, my calling to work in diversity, and my academic preparation in psychology has brought me to a point where I live and work in a way that reflects what Galbraith once said, "In all life one should comfort the afflicted, but verily, also one should afflict the comfortable and especially when they are comfortably, contentedly, even happily wrong."

## A Call to Action to Be Part of a Diversity Exchange Community

Many of us live multiple realities with defining moments, and in these, I believe there is rich dialogue—a tool. When we come together and hear each other's stories, we can bridge the illusion of an abyss. It is the dialogue that we invite you to entertain. Whether we are pushing out of our comfort zones or getting real within them, we can expand ourselves, redefine ourselves, and support one another in development toward embracing diversity and being inclusive. Use the questions I offered and pose your inquiries in an appreciative and curious way. Hold truth and value your perspective in the asking as well.

This collaboration of the Diversity Community Exchange (DiCE) group represents to me a call to action to facilitate dialogue across diverse generations, classes, disabilities, sexual orientation, race, and ethnicity, circling the wheel of diversity. Within groups like DiCE, Diversity 2000, Diversity Women's Circle, Boards, and Black Brown Dialogue, I get to check in with myself, be willing to be challenged and be held accountable, and hold space for others to explore. It is within these circles that in telling our story and exposing defining moments that we connect, engage, and disengage in ways that are meaningful.

Research and literature most certainly have their place in the journey of diversity and inclusion. However, my experience confirms that it is in the ongoing process of dialogue that we break through assumptions, perceptions, and illusions that are key to intimate connection. A connection that renders authenticity and enables us to be allies to one another and have compassion as we embrace our vulnerabilities is challenging. It is said, there is a fine line between genius and insanity. Here too there is a fine line between others and me. For this reason, the many grassroots and professional groups I have participated in have been a mixed blessing. Accepting one another despite our style differences at times created conflict. Dialogue, while intended to invite us into "somewhere between right and wrong into a sacred space," too often would challenge us to listen with hearts open when we could not easily be neutral. Conversely, there are moments when we ponder each other's perspective, holding space without judgment. Certainly, growing personally and collectively as we face our demons and fears while exposing our thoughts and perspectives are well worth it. How else can we stay true to the work?

By nature, the inclusive process is in itself a contradiction of sorts. On the one hand, we strive not to marginalize our individuality and, on the other, commune in ways that support society. As social beings, we learn in context with one another. Whether in the role participant or facilitator, I recognize each time just how much like a rubiks cube we are in our challenge to align yet maintain our integrity and individuality. At the core of all organizational development, I have seen subcultures mixing, blending, and complementing where they were once at odds. Indeed, it is from our sameness that we come together and from our differences that we grow.

In the photograph on the back cover, you see the touchstone group that keeps me conscious and represents a living of diversity toward inclusion at its best. Throughout the ponderings, challenges, disequilibrium, frustrations, shared tears, and joy, we have created a community, offering both intellectual and spiritual connection. We have grieved the passing of two wonderful men, Marvin Smith and Sonny Massey. Our shared experiences and perspectives have reinforced for me as a practitioner that if we focus only on our sameness, we feed the illusion of replication and comfort. More importantly, we marginalize one another. When seeking to focus only on our differences, we are overwhelmed by the illusions that separate us.

My wish for you is to be moved to experience firsthand what we have in sharing and experiencing the full spectrum of one another in both similarities and differences held within our stories as we move beyond tolerance or even acceptance to a natural God-given appreciation. An appreciation that there are no degrees of separation!

# BRONX TO BERKELEY

Simma Lieberman

I GREW UP IN a working-class, Jewish family in the Bronx, New York. The Holocaust was a common topic among family and friends. I knew that six million Jews had been slaughtered by Nazis in the concentration camps. Neighbors and parents of my friends had numbers tattooed on their wrists, which let us know that they were among the Jewish survivors who had been rounded up and put in those camps. I would often hear stories from friends about their family members who had been murdered by the Germans. We knew how Jewish people had been gassed, shot, beaten, or starved to death. Although we were in the USA, the war was over, and everyone had been liberated, there was still a lot of fear that this could happen again if we didn't stick together. For many of us, being Jewish was scary, and there was a distrust of the other people who were not Jewish.

I shared this fear, but I believed that the key to our survival was to ally with people from different cultures. An early experience made me even more sure of what we needed to do.

We belonged to a small orthodox synagogue called a shul. I liked going with my father on the Jewish high holy days. One time when I was around eight years old on Yom Kippur, the holiest day of the Jewish calendar, I was sitting with my father in shul when all of a sudden, I heard yelling and things being thrown. A group of boys stood outside screaming anti-Semitic words and throwing things. I didn't know what was happening, but I saw their ugly grins and heard their laughter when the adults chased them away. They were older than me, and I would see them around the neighborhood. I couldn't understand how they could hate us and call us names when they didn't even know us. I thought that if people could know us and we could know them, then people wouldn't hate one another based on differences. I started looking for ways to interact with people who were different than me.

During that same time, I became friends with one of the few Black kids in school, a girl named Edith. She invited several kids from school to her birthday party. None of the other White kids were allowed to go to the party except for me and my friend Miki. One of the other parents said that she wouldn't let her daughter go because what if there were Black boys at the party and her daughter got involved with one of them. We were only nine years old, and this woman was so filled with fear for her daughter. My parents were by no means progressive, but even they were very surprised that the other parents would stop their kids from going. Miki and I had a great time, and the other kids missed it. Miki's parents were very involved in the civil rights movement. Her father had been a freedom rider.

One day after the party, Miki and I were walking past a Woolworths on 171st Street. I saw a long line of people walking up and down the street with signs. They were chanting, "1, 2, 3, 4, don't go in here anymore, 5, 6, 7, 8, Southern Woolworths, segregate." I found out that they were picketing in support of the sit-ins at the Woolworths in the south where Black people were not allowed to sit at the lunch counter. I thought of my friend Edith and the fact that she would not be able to sit at the lunch counters. I didn't know much about politics or race, but I knew injustice and joined the picket line.

At that time, I also became enamored by Harriet Tubman and read everything I could about her life. In the fourth or fifth grade, I created a puppet show using a diorama about Harriet Tubman, and of course, I played all the characters. It never occurred to me that someone might think it was strange that a ten-year-old white Jewish girl would act as Harriet Tubman.

I felt there was a connection between the civil rights movement and what had happened during the Holocaust. I started reading about Jewish people who had fought back during the Holocaust in the camps and the Warsaw Ghetto and slaves who had escaped and helped other people escape.

A few years later, I had the opportunity to attend the march on Washington in 1963, where I heard Martin Luther King for the first time. I had never seen so many people from so many different backgrounds in one place at the same time. I remember the electricity I felt when our bus entered the capitol. Both sides of the street were filled with people who were waving and cheering as each new bus drove in.

I also remember that after the march, as we were leaving Maryland, we decided to stop at a diner to get something to eat. They wouldn't serve the Black people who were in our group, and we had an impromptu sit-in. I was scared, but they ended up serving us all. It was a wonderful feeling to know that we took an action and won.

As I was leaving my immediate neighborhood, I also began meeting people from different economic backgrounds, many of whom were quite affluent. As conscious as I was about race and speaking out against racism or prejudice, I was embarrassed to be from a working-class family.

There wasn't a lot of money in my house, and financially, I couldn't keep up with some of the other people that I met. I was embarrassed because we lived in an old five-story walk-up building in the Bronx, and our furniture was old. Instead of the *NY Times* in our house, we had *Reader's Digest* and the *NY Daily News*. Both of my parents worked, and we didn't sit around discussing the theater and art like some of the new people I was meeting. When their parents would take me home after I had spent the day with them, I would have them drop me off on the Grand Concourse, which was a few blocks away and much fancier.

There were times I felt that parts of my life were disconnected. On one hand, I was socially aware and involved in the civil rights movement, angry at race discrimination; but on the other hand, I was embarrassed about my own background. I was very confused about who I was and where my life was going. I had a hard time thinking for myself, and without a sense of self came a serious case of low self-esteem. I was angry most of the time, and I didn't know why. I acted out in school by talking back and threatening teachers. Right before my junior high school graduation, my English teacher, Ms. Rinnel, noticed that I wasn't saluting the American flag and called me out on it. I told her that I couldn't salute the flag while there was still discrimination against Black people. The principal and the teacher told me I couldn't graduate unless I said I was sorry and promised to salute the flag. I did graduate and was even angrier and unhappy with myself.

From the time I started acting out the life of Harriet Tubman, I knew I wanted to be an actor. I tried out for the High School of Performing Arts in New York and got accepted. I was very excited about going to the school. Al Pacino had gone there, and there were students at the school who went on to become very successful. Unfortunately, I couldn't get past my self-esteem issues and walked around angry, self-conscious, and steeped in a big inferiority complex. So I didn't try hard at all to succeed. In fact, I felt that if I tried and didn't succeed, I'd look like a fool, but If I didn't try and acted like it didn't matter, I would still be cool. I ended up being asked to leave. Actually, they were going to give me a second chance, but I had already told myself I couldn't make it, so I declined the chance and left. I always said I was kicked out, but if I would have said I would make an effort to try, I could have stayed.

I ended up back at my neighborhood high school with five thousand kids. Throughout all this, I did maintain my involvement with civil rights, which was always important and gave me hope for the future.

On a civil rights march in New York, I met Robert, who taught me how to smoke pot. For the first time, I didn't feel angry. I didn't feel less than other people; I felt just right. I fell in love with drugs and eventually found my way to heroin. I was no longer afraid of anything. Life was manageable for a minute, although it wasn't. It never occurred to me that drugs were the reason I couldn't make it to school and had to drop out. It was the '60s, and the drug world was equal opportunity. I could sit around and nod out on heroin with the affluent people as well as people from different racial and ethnic backgrounds. We could talk about race and class injustice while we got high and didn't do anything about it. I thought I was happy.

Then reality hit. I was engaged to Jonathan, and we had just taken an apartment on East Seventy-Seventh Street in New York. I was spending the evening with my parents, and my mother was knitting sweaters for Jonathan and me. In the middle of our conversation, the phone rang. Jonathan's mother called to tell me that he had been shot to death. I couldn't believe it and couldn't handle it. I increased my use of heroin to mask the emotional pain, but at the same time, I started thinking about my life and what I was going to do. I was eighteen. I decided that I was going to stop using drugs. Between trying to stop and grieving, my anger returned and became an all-encompassing rage. I didn't know who to blame and directed my anger at society, the government, and nearly everyone else. I contacted some of my old friends and started getting back to the civil rights and antiwar movement. In my mind, people in the antiwar movement were those same "middle-class elitist White kids" with whom I was uncomfortable around. I couldn't understand what they were talking about, and I went back to feeling like I didn't belong.

One day I was walking down the street, and I saw a poster that said Capitalism + Dope = Death and then a picture of the Black Panthers. That, I could understand. I thought, *Yeah, capitalism is the problem, and if there was no capitalism, there wouldn't be drug addiction.* I wished that there was a group for working-class White people like the Black Panthers. I soon heard that there was a group that had formed in Chicago, called the Young Patriots, of poor White people mostly from the South that were allied with the Black Panthers. The Young Patriots were going to organize the White community. This group wanted to start a chapter in New York, and I was invited to join. I was very excited; at last there was a group for me, and I could be around other people like me. I joined and was a member for several years. I decided that a lot of my problems were from my economic background. Like a lot of other drug addicts, I didn't have a sense of control over my own life and felt that I had no power to change.

Instead of black leather like the Panthers, we wore dungaree jackets with our names on the back. We started free breakfast for schoolchildren programs in poor White neighborhoods like the Panthers were doing in the Black neighborhoods. We organized around poor housing conditions and brought poor White people together with Black people.

I loved the group at first, but the White people who were running the Young Patriots were from the south and had a very Southern culture. The radio was always tuned to Country music, or Country and Western as it was referred to at the time. As strange as it was, I wanted to fit. When I was alone, I listened to jazz and Motown; but when I was with the group, I listened to Country music. There were a few other Jewish people in the group that did the same thing. It felt weird not being the Jewish person I was, but these people were organizing in the White community, and I thought that if there was going to be change in the country, we needed to work with other White people, and the Panthers would work in their community. The Young Patriots and the Black Panthers were also allied with the Young Lords, a Puerto Rican organization, and we formed the Rainbow Coalition.

We talked with each other about race, culture, and how we could change the country. We envisioned a USA where people from all cultures would find commonality and live together, and there would be no rich or poor. It was good that we did get Puerto Rican, Black, and White people together.

At the same time, our group was really dogmatic. There was no room for disagreement with the leader. If you left, you were a traitor. Looking back, I wonder how we could have thought we were changing the country for the better. I would meet old friends who were glad to see me, but all I would do was spout slogans at them.

New chapters were starting in other states. I went with a couple of other people to Eugene, Oregon, to help start a new Young Patriots chapter and work with the newly formed Black Panther party. Having grown up in the Bronx, New York, Eugene, Oregon, was a major culture shock. By the second year in Eugene, the Patriots broke up, and people who had been in the Panther party and other organizations formed a new organization, the Eugene Coalition. It was a multicultural organization. We owned several houses, a farm, and a print shop. We were more dogmatic than ever. We only went to parties to hand out demonstration leaflets, did not acknowledge emotions, and had extreme rules. At the same time, we were a group of people from all over the world—China, Mexico, Nigeria, Ethiopia, Saudi Arabia, Iran, and different races and ethnicities from the United States. We lived together, broke bread, and supported one another through difficult times. Not everyone was a member of the Eugene Coalition, but we all worked on projects together. I was even part of a "guerilla theater group" that included Jews and Arabs.

While I was in the Patriot party, I was going along with everyone and with White Country and Western culture to the detriment of my own Jewish culture. One day after a rehearsal of our guerilla theater group, one of the Arabs, Khalil, said, "Arabs and Jews have so much in common. You're more like us than like the other White people in Eugene. You need to focus more on being Jewish." I took that to heart and realized that I had let go of my Jewish identity and needed to get it back. I really took his comments to heart. All that time in the Patriots, I wasn't happy because I felt like a part of me was missing. It had not been cool to talk about being Jewish in our organization because we were just supposed to be White. It was like a fog had lifted in my head. I wanted to leave but didn't know where to go. The Patriots eventually broke up, and I moved to Portland. I was away from dogmatism; people who had been in the Patriots weren't talking to one another, but I continued working with people from diverse backgrounds, and we continued our cross-cultural dialogues.

My experience with this group, ultimately, helped me to become more empathetic and want to understand people who didn't think like me because they were, from my perspective, so narrow-minded. I also realize now how much more conservative I've gotten in some ways. I've become one of those dreaded capitalists, but I believe in being a socially conscious capitalist and that everyone should have an opportunity to be successful and know that they have choices. To this day, I am not interested in collectivism or binary thinking.

I stayed in Portland for four more years. During that time, several of my friends founded a college that was named Colegio Cesar Chavez. It was formerly Mt. Angel, a Catholic college. Almost all the people associated with the school were Chicano, and many of the students were older farmworkers who had never had a chance to go to college. I had dropped out in my junior year several years before and hadn't thought about finishing. One of my friends at the Colegio approached me and told me that they needed some White people to attend and asked if I wanted to complete my degree. Since they told me I could get financial aid, I enrolled. I'm glad that I did. I might never have gotten a degree otherwise. I think I was one of two or three other White people at the school. It was a great opportunity.

After graduation, I knew it was time to try something new. I had dealt with some issues around physical health and had to change what I was eating and doing. I needed to exercise and manage my stress. I had help from a lot of different people. I was getting healthy and running between six to ten miles a day, so I decided that I wanted to move to San Francisco and study holistic health.

As I was getting ready to leave Portland and move to San Francisco, I realized that I was attracted to women. I wasn't sure what that meant in terms of my future. I had friends who were gay and I supported them, but I didn't think I was.

So in my midtwenties, I realized that I was too.

Several of my close friends came out around the same time, so I had a little group. It was like our own secret society. I was afraid to tell a lot of my other friends because I was worried about being rejected, and I had some serious internalized homophobia. When I did tell people, I was so grateful that they still liked me despite the fact that I was gay. That was a reflection of my own internalized homophobia and low self-esteem. Today, I can't believe I felt that way or cared what they thought. I would hear gay jokes and not say anything because I was worried about being accused of being gay. In fact, I started dressing more feminine and wearing even more makeup so no one would suspect. When people would ask me if I was gay, I'd say that I didn't believe in labels and I was just me and that I didn't want to be put in a box. I almost believed that, but looking back on it, I realized that it was a way of denying who I was. Denying who you are and pretending to be what you are not takes a major psychological toll. Changing pronouns and watching everything I said was exhausting.

I was living in Oakland, California, halfway out and halfway hiding who I was. I no longer blamed society for my problems. I wanted to make a good living, and I didn't think the end of capitalism would fix my life. I knew I wanted to be a corporate trainer and starting approaching organizations.

A national seminar company flew me to Kansas for an interview to join their team of trainers. I was really excited. I even went out and bought a new red suit to make a good impression. I thought it was going to be the beginning of a successful career. The four people who interviewed me were friendly and seemed to enjoy my presentation.

During the five-hour flight home, I thought about my experience in Kansas. Have you ever had someone smile in your face but you knew things weren't quite right? That's how I felt, and shortly after the interview, I received a letter that said, "We were looking for the perfect fit, and frankly you didn't fit in." I was devastated, so I called them up to find out why they rejected me and felt I didn't fit in. The answer I got was "We were looking for someone a little more all American." When I asked the person on the other end of the phone, she replied, "You would have to go to the South, and when we sent a Black trainer there, he got very low evaluations." When I told them that I had worked in the South and people loved me, all I got was silence. I suppose that Simma Lieberman from the Bronx was just not the image they wanted in the South. So many thoughts ran through my head: should I change my last name, should I get rid of my accent, or should I act differently? Like a lot of people who might be reading this chapter, I just wanted a chance to show what I could do. After wrestling with sadness and self-doubt, I got angry. I was already hiding my sexual orientation; I didn't want to have to feel bad about being Jewish. I decided I wanted to do the kind of work where I did not have to give up my culture and where I could be as Jewish as I wanted to be. That's when I began my journey to integrate my personal life with my professional life.

When I started working as a diversity professional, I thought I would be able to finally be my whole self. I never imagined that I was going to have to deal with the homophobia of fellow diversity colleagues. I didn't know that I would have to put up with gay jokes, hatred based on religion, and all-around ignorance about gay/lesbian issues.

## Early Homophobia among Diversity Professionals

I believed that the professional diversity community was a place where I could bring my whole self. I had been working on a community level before. I didn't realize that when consultants in diversity were talking about being authentic, being real, and everyone being included, there was a big part of me that was not welcome at the party. I quickly found that out when I began to hear disparaging remarks about gay people, and I saw other diversity professionals collude with clients and laugh at gay jokes. I was too busy trying to be accepted, liked, and invited to the informal networking events to let myself look at the hypocrisy of this selective inclusion.

As I got more into diversity issues on a systemic and environmental level, I started feeling like people were not really practicing the principles of diversity, but there were many times I didn't say anything. I'd talk about diversity and the importance of leveraging and accepting differences, but I was afraid to speak up about my own. It was very difficult to live a secret life, but I just accepted that this was what it is, and I'd work in the diversity field but go home and be my whole self. At the same time, I felt that I was being dishonest. Friends would tell me, "Don't worry, you're too paranoid." But to me, it was like a White person telling a person of color, "There is no racism" when how would they know? Because I didn't look like the stereotype of a gay person, straight people thought that I was one of them and could say anything they wanted about gay people.

I specifically remember attending a large diversity conference, and one of the main speakers made some homophobic joke. I was disappointed that almost everyone laughed. I was glad that several of us who did not laugh made eye contact and connected afterward.

## Being Closeted

I wondered what would happen if the other consultants knew that I was gay and in a long-term relationship with another woman, but I was too afraid to find out. This went on for a while but was causing problems in my relationship, and I was forgetting who knew and who didn't. I got psychically tired hiding who I was, leaving out pronouns, and letting people believe by omission that I was a single woman who had no life.

My partner worked in a primarily male profession, and we avoided any place where we thought we might run into anyone that either one of us knew from work. That meant we couldn't go to local blues clubs, attend community events together, or accompany each other to work-related celebrations. It got very lonely going to weddings, dinners, and group activities alone while most people brought their opposite-sex partner.

Other consultants thought I was such a good listener, but the truth was there was no way I was going to share anything about myself.

## Hiding the Evidence

Several times I had meetings at my house, and I would scramble the day before hiding any books, pictures, or knickknacks that anyone could construe as being gay related.

For many of us, we see coming out to straight colleagues as taking a risk that might mean losing a "friend" or, worse, being excluded from jobs. We have to deal with being excluded from informal networking activities because people whom we formerly spent time with are suddenly uncomfortable around us, or they assume that we wouldn't be interested. I would hear about straight couples getting together, and then people would hook up to work together.

## Coming Out

In the beginning, when I first came out to people, like other gay people in those days, I would be grateful that they still liked me even though I was gay. It was like we were happy for heterosexual crumbs of approval. Many of us felt we needed validation from heterosexuals, no matter how raggedy they were, to be OK. As I became more comfortable with myself, I came out more and more and was less concerned with what other people thought. Young LGBT people today are very different. Today, far more often, they are "We're here, we're queer, and we're not going anywhere."

Being truly comfortable with myself, not caring what other people thought, and just being out was a long journey, but I'm so grateful that I got there.

## Sexual Orientation versus Sexual Preference

It is sometimes frustrating to have to keep correcting people to use *sexual orientation* instead of *sexual preference*. Many people who are true diversity believers get it and are very open to the education. Others refuse to change and think that I am being nitpicky, but I am still going to tell it like it should be.

## Racism and Homophobia

When I was thirty-four, I met my partner, Sandra Brown. She was African American and originally from Berkeley. We were together for eighteen years. When we first got together, she worked for Country Road Construction. Sandy was the only woman on the crew, and they were very homophobic. I loved blues, but she was too afraid to go to any clubs for fear of running into people from work. We were both out in every other aspect of our life. It was feeling good not to have to hide except when we ran into workpeople.

Where I was extroverted and social, Sandy was introverted and shy. In many ways, we complemented each other. She liked to go out, but there were times when she liked to stay home. I always had a hard time sitting still, so she was like my brakes sometimes. I got to enjoy being home. She was passionate about film and loved all movies, from Bergman films to trashy horror. Sandy knew all about the history of Black cinema as well as gay cinema. Television was one of her pastimes. We must have seen every episode of *Law and Order* five times.

Our lives and relationship were a cross-cultural cacophony, and our house was clearly African American and Jewish. Our extended family circle also included Latin American, Asian American, and Middle Eastern people.

We were known for our multicultural seders on Passover and Rosh Hashanah dinners and Chanukah latke parties at our house. We went to her family for Christmas, Kwanzaa, and Easter. The food was always incredible, and we loved sharing our cultures with everyone.

I had always wanted to have children, and for a long time, I thought because I was gay it would never happen, until I started seeing a gay baby boom. Lesbians and gay men were becoming parents. After my parents died, I decided that it was time. I didn't want to live the rest of my life regretting not having children.

After Sandy and I were together for ten years, we had a son, Avi, who is now fifteen. We were like a lot of other "traditional" two-parent families. Right after our son was born, she stopped working for a while to stay home with him. We shared responsibility for housework and for taking care of our son. We had to deal with both racism and homophobia, but by the time we had Avi, we were very secure in who we were. Once people got to know us, they often changed their assumptions about lesbians.

We were very conscious of racism and anti-Semitism. Many times when I would be around White people, straight and gay, I would have to speak up for my family when the straight White people who thought I was just like them would think it was OK to joke or make remarks about gay people and Black people. There was and still is a moment of shock when I speak up. The gay White people would think it was fine to make comments about Black people and gay Black people. I would then let them know that my life partner was African American, and our family was interracial and interfaith.

Sandy and I had met through our mutual social scene because our social circles overlapped. Most of my friends at the time were people of color, predominantly Black. A couple of times, I'd meet other White people who had a hard time understanding that Sandy and I had the same friends. One woman even said to me, "How do you meet Black people?"

Although I was out for most of my life, I still had some issues with clients and colleagues who really had biases.

## Playing Down My Relationship

My partner, Sandra Brown, was always conscious of our physical safety being an interracial gay couple. I would think that it was hard enough being gay in the world, but to have to hide it from people who said they were committed to diversity was too hard. I had gotten into this work to integrate my personal life with my professional life, but this was not happening.

## Changing My Life Paradigm

It was life changing for me to become part of a larger diversity community where being gay was welcomed like anybody else, where I have a permanent seat at the table, where that seat has my name, and we are all family.

## Overcoming Internalized Oppression

I think some of those changes also occurred because I accepted and valued myself more. A part of me—like other lesbian, gay, bisexual, transgender people—had internalized the messages we heard from other people. I had to come to terms with my own internalized homophobia. Reflecting back on my actions, as a result, I realize how I had damaged myself and my relationship. Even though I had friends and a community who loved me, there was a part of me that still thought that I shouldn't be "too gay." Although I had been with my partner for eighteen years, there were times when I gave people the impression that we were not as serious or real as we were. I wasn't able to share with some of my diversity community how much love there was in my relationship. For some reason, my internalized oppression caused me to believe that if I talked about how deep our commitment was, people would think I was "too gay" and too different from them. It was easier to be seen as sort of single.

When I was able to let go of my fears and trust myself and others, I no longer was afraid of other peoples' judgments, not being hired or retained because of my sexual orientation, or losing economic security. When I was able to value and respect my whole person, I realized that I didn't care what other people thought and that no one had the power to define who I am.

When I had my son at forty-four, I knew that I didn't want him to have to keep secrets and that he would be proud of having two mothers. When I turned fifty, I decided that I was too old to worry anymore.

On January 26, 2003, my son and I returned home from being out all day. Tacked to our door was a note from the coroner telling me to call about Sandra Brown. I knew that something horrible had happened, and when I called, they told me that she was dead. She walked out the door one day, and then we never saw her again. Sandy died in the middle of her life. Avi and I were in shock. In one second, I was a widowed single mother. Avi was only eight years old. I don't know how we could have gotten through the last few years and come out OK if not for our diverse community. When Sandy died, my whole community showed up to support Avi and me and to honor my relationship and our loss.

It was amazing when I think about it. People came from my Palestinian/Jewish dialogue group, my whole diversity network, my synagogue, and my friends that I'd had for over twenty-five years.

Avi is proud of being raised in a multicultural family and of his two moms. He carries on the legacy of his other mother in his values and his life. He speaks up for his family and even has had to physically defend himself against kids who challenged his right to love two moms. And standing with him is his community of friends from all kinds of families and diverse ethnicities, gender, and backgrounds.

Sandy and I didn't understand the whole thing about gay marriage. Many of the gay and lesbian weddings we had been to seemed to be copies of heterosexual weddings. We didn't know about all the rights that came with marriage. I didn't think about them until she died. When she died, legally I wasn't considered next of kin. I had no legal rights to even view her body before she was cremated or make any of the decisions about her. Our son was not entitled to her social security, and legally, I couldn't even cash her last paycheck. It was a harsh realization that even though we lived in the San Francisco Bay area and the environment was one of tolerance, not everyone and every law shared that view. We had been together for eighteen years, more than a lot of straight married people. I was luckier than many other LGBT people because her family had always accepted us as family, so I didn't have some of the issues that others have had like not being allowed to attend a funeral or having a home taken away.

## Today

I am now sixty, I continue to live and work in diversity, and I have friends and colleagues of every age. I am out everywhere in my life, and most importantly, I am completely out to myself.

I started out facilitating dialogues among people who were different. Then I was asked to design and deliver diversity training. I realized that training alone did not create change, and I moved into process consulting and diversity leadership strategy. Today, I work with individuals and organizations. I am now a consultant, speaker, and author. I continue to meet new people, learn about cultures that are new to me, and hear new ideas. Creating the kind of world in which I want to live where diversity is celebrated, people are included, and our children can grow up in safety really is a journey, and I intend to be on that journey every step of the way.

For ten years, I've been a part of Diversity 2000 (D2K), a group of diversity practitioners that meet for four days every summer. Many of the people have become like family to me, and I love them. In 2002, Sonny Massey and Mike Vonada, two members of D2K, gathered a small group of people together to talk about diversity and discuss ways in which we could make change.

I was honored to be included in that gathering. As a result of our first meeting, some of us decided to continue. Our second meeting was held at the home of Marvin Smith in Oakland where we took the name DiCE—Diversity Community Exchange—and talked about our future as a group. In the last two years we lost our founder, Sonny Massey, and one of our founding members, Marvin Smith. I loved them both, and although we started the book before they passed away, we know that their chapters and this book are part of their legacy. I think that with the intellectual and diverse capital in DiCE and the memory of Sonny and Marvin, we have the ability to bring large numbers of people together and move toward creating the kind of communities, country, and world in which we want to live.

# IN THE AIR WE BREATHE
# AND THE WATER WE DRINK

Sidalia Reel, EdD

WHAT IS IT about diversity work that draws us in like a moth to a flame? Is it the nature of our society that privileges some people in ways that instantly keep others down? Is it so automatic and unconscious that acts of unjustified bias, prejudice, and discrimination occur naturally in our environment? It's as if it's in the air we breathe and the water we drink.

Diversity did not exist as a career field until I was well into my thirties and happily working in the corporate education and training world. In most organizations, equal employment opportunity and affirmative action departments dealt with issues of equity, discrimination, harassment, and how people were treated and/or allowed to compete for jobs, contracts, and compensatory rewards. About fifteen years ago, I was approached about leaving the education field in order to lead and expand my company's diversity program. At that time, diversity was just moving to the forefront of equity-related activity as a complementary endeavor associated with affirmative action and EEO. For me, my experience in managing customer service training and cross-cultural competency made me a logical candidate to move the company's diversity program from a focus on vendor-supplier diversity to a focus on workforce diversity.

The work of helping organizations and the people in them—to value, respect, and treat everyone fairly—forced me to realize that in my youth, I had experienced and witnessed a plethora of situations that exposed me to the conscious and unconscious bias toward differences and that I had learned lessons that could be shared with others. Racism was a constant source of the ways I have been mistreated, and it has opened my eyes to all the other ways people are discounted, devalued, and put down.

Now that I've made a career out of helping people to value the differences in others, I know that this is some of the most challenging, undervalued, and thankless work to undertake in organizations. As a professional African American woman working in high tech and academia, I have both experienced and witnessed bias and discrimination on the basis of race, color, gender, age, sexual orientation, disability, religion, and even native language. Differences across cultures, differences between the races, genders, sexual orientation, thinking styles, and differences across all other dimensions of diversity are often deemed acceptable only if the perceiver of the difference still feels the difference lifts him or her up while putting the other person down. By and large, the messages in our world tell us that being different is not OK. Bias and prejudice come so naturally to people. Again, it's as if it's in the air we breathe and the water we drink.

In this chapter, I'll share some of my experiences from early childhood through today that demonstrate over and over again how much work we still have to do if we are going to overcome the prejudice, bias, hate, and discrimination in our world. Each of my stories is connected to one of the many lessons I have learned from my parents and family, from people who have inspired me, from school, from my work, and from my life experiences.

## My Inspiration

I am inspired by my sons and other young people in my life to help them see past the false sense of privilege and entitlement they enjoy. I want them to realize that insidious forces out of their control conspire to keep them down, if only in their own minds. My studies on unconscious bias and stereotyping have confirmed for me that bias in the form of racism, sexism, ethnocentrism, and heterosexism is so pervasive in US culture that it is as difficult to unlearn as forgetting how to walk. Our propensity to treat people differently if they are not like us is an unconscious act, and being different continues to be viewed as a liability rather than an asset. Again it seems as if bias is in the air we breathe and the water we drink. The drive to overcome bias, the pollutant in our human relations, keeps me pushing forward despite the difficulty of the journey.

While the young people in my life inspired me to write, my professional work also compelled me to write. My doctoral dissertation addressed the topic of automated stereotyping (i.e., the unconscious biases about other people that we all learn and internalize as very young children). My findings indicated that it's difficult but not impossible to find ways to inhibit stereotypes. Writing this chapter was a cathartic experience that freed me to remember and record the stories of my own experiences of being the target and sometimes the perpetrator of bias. I hope my lessons and stories will inspire others to join me in the journey toward a world free of bias.

# Respect Your Past

On many levels, the experiences and lessons from childhood shape who you are as an adult. I was born and raised in Berkeley, California, in the 1950s-1970s. The Berkeley of my childhood was the very definition of diversity and multiculturalism. As a college town founded in the late 1800s, from its inception, the diversity of Berkeley existed on a social, class, racial, and ethnic level. Portuguese fisherman along the bay; a turn-of-the century Finnish community; working-class families of all races in the flatlands; predominantly Black neighborhoods in south and west Berkeley; a constant stream of foreigners from all over the world who were teaching at or attending UC Berkeley; and a steady influx of immigrants from Mexico, Latin America, the Philippines, Japan, China, the Pacific Islands, Southeast Asia, and Europe all combined to make the Berkeley community a tapestry of cultures. The Berkeley Hills, however, remained a White enclave of affluent families whose neighborhoods were protected by redlining, covenants, and the like until well into the 1960s.

In the 1940s, my parents came to Richmond, California, from Northeast Texas to work in the World War II Kaiser Steel shipyards. My older brother was a prepubescent only child being cared for by my grandmother and the Kaiser day care facility. In the early 1950s, the family moved to Berkeley, and I was born shortly thereafter. I'm sure that home ownership on our quiet, family-oriented street was the American dream in the minds of many families during the postwar Eisenhower era. The stability no doubt allowed them to expand the family, and once I was born, my parents had four more children in five years, ending with a set of twins. For a few years, my family lived the TV-land lifestyle of the 1950s. My father went off to work in San Francisco, and my mother was a stay-at-home mom who kept busy cooking, cleaning, sewing, painting, and caring for her litter of children. That changed when the twins entered kindergarten, and my mother went to work outside of the home.

My best friend in my early elementary school years was a Japanese American girl whose parents endured the internment camps during World War II and then settled in Berkeley. My immediate neighborhood included a preponderance of mainstream Americans (i.e., Anglo-Saxon European Americans) and also Japanese, Portuguese, Norwegian, Chinese, Italian, Irish, Dutch, Filipino, and Black families. The Black families who settled in Berkeley brought a variety of differences, defying the monolithic stereotype of the Black family portrayed by the politicians and social scientists of the day. There were other Black families from Texas, as well as Black families from Louisiana, Arkansas, Oklahoma, Alabama, Mississippi, and Georgia, who ate different foods, had different pastimes, and even had values that were different from my own family. As an adult, I look back on my upbringing with the respect it deserves in making me who I am. Now I see that it is within this backdrop of a multicultural community that I learned my first lessons about diversity and the harsh realities of being different. Things are not always as they seem, and in all situations, it pays to go beneath the surface to find what lies deep in the hearts of others before you bestow trust and faith in them.

## Don't Judge a Book by Its Cover

UC Berkeley enjoyed a very liberal reputation worldwide, and as the home of the free speech movement, exposure to people of all sorts and types was to be expected. And yet, outside of the campus and on the streets of my Berkeley neighborhood, racism reared its ugly head. I was just a seven-year-old innocently skipping down the street on my way to a piano lesson when two White men blocked my way and yelled at me, "Nigger, walk on the other side of the street. I don't want you walking in front of my house!" Just three blocks from my home, the irrational hate of the color of my skin imprinted an internal message that I wasn't good enough to walk on a particular sidewalk and that White strangers did not want Black people in their midst.

As I mentioned earlier, I am the second of six children, but my older brother is twelve years my senior. He graduated high school and left for the US Army when I was going into kindergarten, so I grew up as the de facto eldest child. We were loved and cared for by our parents, my loving maternal grandmother lived about a mile away, we saw our other relatives frequently, we had enough of everything, and we were happy. However, we were quite sheltered by our parents' strict rules about staying away from strangers and about playing only with one another in our own backyard, a rule that remained in effect until our teenage years. Playdates and sleepovers were definitely out of the question in those days. As a result, my parents' strict rules about staying away from strangers were validated by my encounter with the two racist White men in my own neighborhood. The liberal book cover that Berkeley touts and even exploits hides the realities of the intolerance that resides in the neighborhoods of this "liberal" city. Even in Berkeley, a town renowned for its liberalism and multiculturalism, hatred and bigotry toward an innocent child happened. If it happened here, it could happen anywhere. It gives me pause to admit that the feelings that lie just below the surface that are fueled by experiences of being discriminated against stay with me and, to this day, manifest as feelings of inferiority when I least expect it.

## Learn to Control the Self-Hate that May Take Root in Childhood

Looking back, I see that the seeds of self-hate are sown early. For me, another of the earliest experiences I recall happened when I was nine. I discovered that the self-hatred that I harbored inside me about being different was influenced, in part, by a television news story promoting the adoption of foreign children. The reporter interviewed a White couple who adopted two Chinese children and had them growing up in an all-White city where they lost all their Chinese identity.

I, along with my sister who was eleven months younger than I was, watched the program with a feeling of shock and horror. What we saw in this story was that your parents, or whoever claimed to be your parents, could make you grow up to be whoever they wanted you to be, and you could have a completely different identity than the one you are born with. We decided that we were adopted because we weren't the same color as either of our parents. My mother's nearly white skin, blue eyes, and red hair starkly contrasted with my father's dark skin, brown eyes, and black hair. Our looks fall somewhere in between our parents' features, so we believed we didn't belong to either one of them.

We packed up a few dolls and clothes for our journey to who knows where to find our "real" parents. Just as we were slipping out of the side yard gate to run away, my mother yelled out from the front porch and stopped us in our tracks. Mom interrogated us about where we thought we were going and why. We proclaimed, through our tears, that we knew that we were adopted because we didn't look like her or Dad, so we wanted to find our real parents. With her hugs and kisses, my mother helped us calm down, and she described everything about each one of us that came from her or my father—my father's nose, my mother's lips, my father's cheekbones, my mother's hands. As an adult, I now know that my sense of humor and my joy in telling personal stories come from my mother's wonderful gift of storytelling. From my father, I inherited confidence and a sense of personal integrity. Who would have ever thought that my father, the perfectly groomed and stylishly dressed businessman who rode the commuter bus to San Francisco every day, was carrying his barber tools and a .38 pistol in his briefcase as he made his way to his barbershop?

When Mom got to the root of the problem (i.e., that we watched something on television that we didn't understand and that we transferred what we saw in the adoption of Chinese children to our own family), she probed us intensely until she discovered that what we were really upset about is the fact that people were always asking us if Mom was our real mother because she looked white. Mom told us not to let other people tell us who we are. Her own African, Scottish, and Apache roots made her indefinable from a race perspective. Many years later, when I talked to her about the diversity work I was doing, she reminded me of my runaway attempt to find my real parents, and she shared with me about how painful it was to be mistaken for White and how she was called mixed, mulatto, or half-breed or multiracial at a time when interracial marriages were socially unacceptable. She went on to tell me how she had often had her race "corrected" on job applications and other documents where she wrote Negro, only to have it crossed out and replaced with Other. She warned us that people would hate us just because the color of our skin was not the same as theirs. She defiantly instructed us never to let anyone get away with thinking that they are better than we are. She wondered out loud if the day would ever come when race didn't matter.

The internalized oppression that causes many people of color and other groups who are marginalized because they don't fit the mold of what an "American" looks like carry with them this feeling, often unconsciously, that they are not as good as or not as valued as people in the dominant White culture. As the people of the United States become increasingly bicultural and multicultural, people are becoming more accepting of people of different races and cultures. I have to catch myself when I start to feel devalued because I'm being ignored or when my opinions are challenged or when my work is discounted. I fight hard to overcome what social psychologist Claude Steele calls stereotype threat, meaning the stereotypes about groups, in my case African Americans, that challenge our self-image and may negatively influence intellectual performance or other abilities. I remind myself that it's about me; it's not about them. I'm the one who controls my image of myself, not anyone else. Overcome the feelings of self-hate and self-doubt by continually reminding yourself that you are in control of who you are.

# Treat People with Dignity and Respect

One of the dangers of feeling oppressed is the possibility that you will become the oppressor. It is a law of nature—the survival of the fittest, the law of the jungle, or whatever saying people use—to justify mistreating those who are weaker, smaller, or anything perceived as less than they are. My parents worried about me being too nice and too trusting of people. I see now as an adult that I understood, even as a child, that it's not OK to treat other people badly because they are different. In fifth grade, I befriended a boy who was mentally challenged, what my mother called a Thursday's child as in the nursery rhyme line "Thursday's child has a long way to go." Stanley was in my class, but he was years older than the rest of us. He was twice our size and larger in stature than most adults. He had pale white skin, thick red hair, freckles, and a wide buck-toothed grin. I was never sure if he just suffered from what was then called mental retardation or if he was also deaf or just unable to speak well, but he could not engage in conversation. Probably in today's educational system of special education for special-needs children, Stanley would not have been mainstreamed with other children. I suspect that because his aunt was one of the most tenured and respected teachers at the school, she was able to ensure that her nephew attended regular school with whatever supports could be provided to him.

When Stanley tried to run and play with other kids, they were either afraid of him or did mean things to him, like throwing rocks or spitting on him. I felt sorry for him, and despite the fact that I was a little afraid of him, I talked to him. From time to time, I helped him with his lunch, and I told other kids to leave him alone when they were bothering him. I was teased about being nice to him, but I continued being a friend to him. Once, during recess, a girl who was one of the schools best-known bullies was trying to take money from Stanley by running up behind him and reaching into his pockets. I snatched her away from him and was ready to fight her, but she backed down from me and ran away. I'm sure that it didn't hurt that I was one of the tallest girls in the entire school, which made me seem more powerful. I imagine that the diversity tenet of treating people with dignity and respect started in me with how I treated Stanley back in the fifth grade. It's not on the same level of the real dangers children face today, but standing up for Stanley was one of the bravest things I did as a child.

My demeanor is contrary to what you'd expect, given the experiences I've had with bigots and strangers. On occasion, I've been criticized, as a child and as an adult, for being too freehearted, too positive, and too welcoming. However, when I see people being mistreated, it does cause me to react. One of the activist statements that truly resonates with me and the work I do is "If it's going to be, it's up to me" (author unknown). This was a small example of standing up for someone else. I hope that you will also find the courage to stand up for others when they are being mistreated. We should all develop the ability to treat people with dignity and respect, especially those who are different from us.

## Someone like Me to Believe in Me

I grew up as a bookworm who loved to read, jump rope, and play piano and violin. My elementary school had one of the most diverse school populations in Berkeley, and at that time, our school was an exception to the more segregated populations at other schools. I took for granted the array of teachers I had—teachers that came from many ethnic backgrounds (including Irish, English, Italian, Mexican, Chinese, and Hawaiian.) My teachers' ages ranged from twenty-something new college graduates to those with one foot into retirement and everything in between. Integration of the Berkeley public schools occurred in the mid-1960s as I entered junior high school. It was the end of what felt like a diverse and welcoming school experience in elementary school where I was a top-performing student. Virtually overnight, my school experience switched to one in which I was tracked into predominantly White classes where I always felt that I didn't belong.

I was already shy and not very vocal in elementary school. I became even more withdrawn in junior high, partly because I was experiencing a feeling that my teachers didn't think I was good enough to be in the top track and, I'm sure, partly because I was experiencing the changes of puberty. One of my junior high school teachers told me that integration was an experiment and that I was "special" because I was a smart Black girl in the top track, and I would have the best teachers. I certainly didn't feel special. I was too young to understand what was going on around me and too naive to question what teachers and authority figures were telling me.

My junior high school guidance counselor, Mrs. Wilkerson, was my savior. She was a strong Black woman who talked to me regularly about expanding my horizons and using my gifts. She told me I was bright but that

I was too shy and timid for others to know it, so she encouraged me to take drama and act in plays in order to develop public speaking skills. She told me to pursue sports because I was athletic and that I could benefit from being a team player, so I ran track. She encouraged me in ways I never realized at the time and that I now appreciate as an adult. I was a record-setting track-and-field athlete in junior high and high school, and I ended up in the training profession where good public speaking skills are essential.

To have someone in your corner who is outside of the family is incredibly motivating. Following Mrs. Wilkerson's example, even though I am not a guidance counselor, I have challenged and encouraged many young people over the years. I hope that everyone will make time to encourage the young people you encounter. Moreover, in the work world, mentoring has been popularized as a key ingredient in career development. Whether formal or informal, mentoring relationships support and encourage others, particularly those who are perceived as different. Difference is an asset, not a liability if you believe in yourself.

## Make Your Out-Group the In-Group

Because I studied hard, I did well academically in junior high and high school. Although I was not overtly discriminated against, I always felt different. My parents, especially my mother, taught me to hold my head up high and not to be bashful and timid about asking the teachers questions or talking to them when I didn't understand what was going on or when I didn't like the way I was being treated. Mom worked in some capacity at every school I attended (from noon schoolyard monitor to cafeteria worker to girls' gym matron) and kept a watchful eye over everything going on. Despite the fact that she wasn't a PTA mom (i.e., she was only interested in taking care of her own children, not anyone else's), the school administrators came to know my mother quite well because she confronted and challenged them on a regular basis. She even coached other parents on how to make school administrators respond to them.

By the time I entered Berkeley High School, I grew accustomed to being in the minority in all my classes except physical education. Berkeley used an academic tracking system that grouped students according to academic performance. As one of a handful of Black students in my class to be placed in the top (college-bound) track, I was almost always the only Black student in my academic classes. Athletically, I enjoyed success on our unintentionally all-Black track team.

I also had the privilege of being a founding member of an all-Black social club, the Soul Syndicate. I wanted to be a part of it because it was a more positive alternative to the pseudo-Greek letter clubs my affluent White classmates participated in. I was invited to be a part of this exclusive White in crowd, which was essentially the high school version of college sororities and fraternities. My handful of experiences as an invited guest for these Greek-letter style parties made me feel that I did not fit in. The parties included drugs, drinking, orgies, and other unsupervised, unchaperoned activities in the homes of the rich kids living in the hills who partied unabashedly while their parents were out of town.

Conversely, in the flatlands on the poor side of town, the members of the Soul Syndicate rarely had house parties but instead raised money through parties hosted by the YWCA and held car washes and other fund-raisers to sponsor bus trips to Santa Cruz Beach and Boardwalk and the state fair in Sacramento. For all intents and purposes, the Soul Syndicate was providing a service to the community, which was getting Black teenagers off the streets with fun, safe, and legal activities. Except for the occasional fight or drug-laced punch bowl, our parties were pretty harmless. Given that this was happening in the late 1960s during the time of the rise of the Black Panther party, the civil rights movement, the Martin Luther King assassination, the Vietnam War, and all the social upheaval of the that era, I felt lucky to have an outlet for having fun and hanging out with other kids like me.

I realize that the sense of belonging and acceptance I felt in the Soul Syndicate not only gave me a wealth of experience in planning and completing projects, but it most certainly helped me to overcome my pubescent low sense of self-worth in ways that I had not recognized until years later. I'm grateful for experiencing inclusion as part of the Soul Syndicate—arguably the ultimate out-group in 1960s Berkeley.

## Work Twice as Hard

In contrast to my supportive and encouraging junior high school counselor, my high school counselor did not take any interest in me. He was a bitter older man who had probably worked at Berkeley High School when it was built. He was a condescending White man whose only guidance was to advise me to take typing classes and go to secretarial school. I don't think he ever looked at my transcript to see that I had good grades and that I was tracked as a college-bound student, not a vocational education student. The way he treated me was positive proof that no matter how hard you work, some people will still stereotype you because of the color of your skin and put you down. As you can imagine, my ever-present mother berated and harassed that counselor incessantly for his prejudice and narrow-mindedness, and I'm sure her deeds influenced his decision to retire.

Although it wasn't cool to be a bookworm, I totally own the fact that I loved school and liked learning new things, so I worked hard in high school. In addition to the Soul Syndicate and running track, I had an after-school job working as an office assistant at the US Department of Forestry. When it was time to apply to college, several of my teachers who saw promise in me advised me to apply to a number of colleges and wrote letters of recommendation for me. I was accepted by all the colleges to which I applied. When I finally settled on a women's college, I attended on a full academic scholarship. It was both exhilarating and frightening to go hundreds of miles from home with my modest belongings and live on campus in a dormitory.

The affluent student body was composed of girls from very wealthy families from all over the world. Many of my White classmates had cars, expense accounts, new wardrobes every season, and spent their summers in places like the French Riviera or Rome, winter break skiing in the Alps, and spring break on shopping sprees in Hong Kong. Some of the girls were living lavishly on what was essentially the interest income on their personal bank accounts. It's hard to conceive that academically I was among equals when such a disparity in wealth existed between us. My parents did not have the means to pay for college, so the only way I could attend was to obtain a scholarship and pay my own way. After six years of working and saving for college throughout junior high and high school, my money paid for books and incidentals, and it was all gone by the end of my freshman year.

My first days as a freshman further showed me that no matter what you're made of, some people will still put you down because you're different. As summer preparation for entering the freshman class, I received a booklist of classic books that I should have read in high school, including the *Odyssey, Great Expectations, Moby Dick*, works of Shakespeare, etc. These books would be the basis of the English placement exam that all freshmen were required to take. I had barely read half of what was on the list and hopelessly tried to jam in some summer reading time in between my summer jobs. Once I arrived on campus, to my surprise, when I entered the blue book examination room to take the English placement exam, I found only questions about books I had read, and I effortlessly wrote pages and pages of essays. I passed the exam with flying colors, and I was exempted from having to take any English classes to fulfill my college graduation requirements.

The only hurdle I had to cross was to discuss my exam with an academic advisor. When I arrived at the advisor's office, he had a confused look on his face and asked me who I was. I told him my name, and as he looked at the name on the front of my blue books, I pointed to my name and told him, "Yes, this is me." He asked me to write my name on a piece of paper and compared the two signatures. Naively, I assumed this was part of the process, so I complied with his request and waited patiently. When he saw that the signatures matched, he then took out a list of names and asked me if I was an EOP student (the Equal Opportunity Program for disadvantaged students). When I said no, he asked me about my GPA, my SAT scores, my admissions letter, and other questions to validate who I was and that I was academically worthy of being a regular academic scholarship recipient as opposed to an EOP student. He even asked me additional questions about the books I wrote about in the exam. He signed and stamped the English Exemption form, and he brushed his hand in the air in front of me to dismiss me. He told me to take the form to the registrar's office without saying another word or giving me eye contact, much less acknowledging in any way my accomplishment of passing the placement test. It was then that I realized he thought someone else wrote my exam, perhaps a White student.

Thankfully, this experience with prejudice was not repeated in my classes, but I felt scarred by being questioned about the authenticity of my work and my name. I knew then that I would have to be self-reliant and self-motivating to make it through college when I encountered other situations like this one. Words my father told me rang in my ears and kept me going: "All you've got is your good name, so work hard and do your best to live up to it." It was definitely instilled in me that my name and my reputation was not only my own, but it was also my family name, so I always worked to make my parents proud of me. I hated the fact that my intelligence and integrity were being questioned because of the color of my skin.

At seventeen, I couldn't imagine what I could do about being treated this way except to work really hard and prove that I was competent. The fact that African Americans have to work harder to overcome the negative preconceived notions about us is something I live with every day. It's an automatic manifestation of the internalized oppression that lives within African Americans. I think back to the years of innocence growing up in Berkeley, and I know that the seeds of self-hate were planted even then with the various subtle and random acts of bias against me, my family, my non-White friends, and my neighbors.

While there is also the possibility that class plays a role in the discrimination I experienced, class differences can be overcome or, at the very least, masked superficially with a new wardrobe or speech lessons or other image enhancements. But it's not likely that changing the color of my skin is possible. A litany of sociocultural phenomenon reinforces stereotypes and fuels prejudice. Things that contribute to stereotypes include everything from the negative messages about Black people in the media to the spate of social welfare programs that are set up to fail and, most disappointingly, the professional training and brainwashing that feed stereotypes by attempting to force every square peg into the round hole of the dominant Judeo-Christian, European American culture. These institutionalized mechanisms are enablers that fuel law enforcement and other people in positions of power and authority to respond to Black people out of race-based fear. I expected that racism would rear its ugly head to cause people to fear, distrust, and disrespect me, but I wasn't prepared for the rejection I experienced from students of my own race.

## Read Between the Lines

One of the greatest changes for me in leaving home to enter college was the loss of a sense of belonging that comes from being part of a large close-knit family. The experience of being the only Black student in class was not new as I had experienced this in junior high and high school. No matter what I experienced at school or out in the world, I enjoyed the ever-present love, safety, and security of my family when I got home. But when I entered my dorm and discovered that there was only one other Black student there, I shuddered to think that I wouldn't be surrounded by people like me when I went "home" to my dorm room. My dorm roommate was a Latina whose family hailed from El Salvador, and she grew up in San Francisco, so I was fortunate in being paired with another Northern Californian whose family, like mine, was not wealthy. She introduced me to one of her Black friends from high school who attended one of the other colleges within the cluster of colleges in my college town, and we became lifelong friends.

As I became acclimated to the campus, I met other Black students, and I assumed that I would be accepted by other people like me. I quickly came to the realization that having black skin in common did not guarantee acceptance. Social class distinctions, being from up North versus coming from Southern California (particularly Los Angeles), attending college on an academic scholarship, coming from a large family, having parents from the South, not being a student government leader in high school, having a part-time job while going to college, and any number of other factors suddenly became the criteria to separate me from the other Black students. Whether it was in my own mind or from actions and messages from the others, I felt inferior to them.

To complicate matters, I was dealing with the sexual tension and temptations all around me. While I knew that my relationship with my boyfriend back home would probably not survive the separation (and it didn't), I was not prepared for the onslaught of potential beaus in my midst. I quickly learned that some of the attention from the opposite sex was not so much about me but about the fact that coming from Berkeley and with my ever-present allergy-red eyes, it was assumed that I had the hookup for good drugs from Berkeley.

I felt that I was being rejected and accepted at the same time for all the wrong reasons. Was I supposed to deny who I am and pretend to be someone else? Should I feel ashamed of my family, should I try to act cool because my red eyes made people think that I was always high on something, and should I stop being studious? Of course, the answer to all these questions was no. As I was looking for guidance on what to do, I received some valuable coaching from one of the advisors from the Black Studies Center: Watch, listen, and learn before you act. Approach every new unfamiliar situation as if you are a visitor from another planet trying to learn the culture, and read between the lines. Then look for the commonalities as a way to build relationships so that you don't have to change who you are. I was able to put this advice to work in befriending some of the other Black students with whom I was unable to connect with previously. To this day, some of the people I met in undergraduate school are among my closest and dearest friends, and we have lifelong bonds that exist, no matter how bookwormish or sappy or naive they think I am. I learned the hard way that you cannot make assumptions about how other people perceive you. What you do need to do, however, is speak up for yourself.

# Tell, Don't Ask

I earned my undergraduate degree and went directly into graduate school. Shortly after earning my masters from an Ivy League university, I worked hard and felt that my scholarly success would make me undeniable in securing a great job in the world of work. My first job out of graduate school was with the state department of education in Massachusetts, and although I was happy to be hired early with the job waiting for me until I graduated, I was dismayed that I was one of four Black women from the same masters program who were all hired into the same entry-level job category. We formed what appeared to be a ghetto of highly educated Black women working in low-level jobs among a sea of other employees who held higher-level positions and did not possess graduate degrees or work experience that warranted their elevated status. I was appalled when I discovered that one particularly voluptuous, provocatively dressed blond White woman who flirted unabashedly with the men in authority positions was promoted into a job for which she had none of the requisite qualifications. While I had hoped that my qualifications would help to level the playing field, this was not the case. I thought racism was the only barrier I had to overcome, but now I knew that I could not and would not compete on the basis of sex appeal. I left shortly thereafter.

For my next major position, I moved to Washington, DC area, and I accepted a position with a Black-owned engineering consulting firm as a training specialist. A colleague, who was also an African American woman, attended a railroad engineers' conference with me. We were attending the conference to acquire knowledge and make professional connections for a new consulting contract. When we arrived at the conference, we found ourselves adrift in a sea of several hundred middle-aged male White engineers. There was one other Black face in the room besides ours and a handful of other women. My colleague and I intentionally split up to work the room and expand the possibility of finding prospective resources for our future work.

As we waded into the room and attempted to make conversation during the cocktail networking hour, I noticed how uncomfortable I made the men I approached to start conversation, and not one of them initiated conversation with me. As I introduced myself and held out my hand for a handshake greeting, I did not always get a handshake. When I made conversation by asking questions, I received abrupt yes/no responses without any elaboration on the topic, and I saw body language that told me to keep my distance. I even got pushed off on someone else when one gentleman responded to one of my questions by saying, "I don't know, but I'll bet Jake knows, so why don't you go over there and ask him?"

Before the networking hour ended, my colleague and I gave each other knowing glances across the room, made our way to one another to go into dinner together, and attended the rest of the conference together, taking a few notes during the lecture presentations. Once we refrained from initiating conversations, we had no further interaction with any of the other attendees because they were certainly not reaching out to us. In contrast, our manager—an alcoholic White ex-military man—schmoozed and boozed his way around the conference, and he connected with a few people who gave him some resources that were useful for our project. He certainly knew the rules of the game in terms of networking, reading the crowd and the individuals in it, and knowing when and how to close the deal. And more importantly, because this was a White male—dominated gathering (I'm guessing that 98 percent of the participants where White men), the White men at the conference were more comfortable with him simply because he was more like them.

This large professional conference experience, where I felt excluded and like an outcast, has been repeated many times in my career. The way people responded to me wasn't entirely due to racism and sexism, but that's how it felt. To counteract this feeling, a coping mechanism I have developed is to kill them with competence by becoming one of the conference presenters or content advisors. This made me among the people being sought after rather than having to navigate the conference as someone vying for the attention of others. This meant that I had to make a switch in my thinking about how to attend professional meetings. In these settings, I have shifted the way I approach others by starting the conversation with what I am about and what I have to offer them as opposed to seeking people out for what they can do for me. The positive act of giving information about yourself and relating your own experiences to the other person counteracts the negative act of taking information from and interrogating others. Networking is not just about collecting business cards, but it's about establishing relationships and exchanging information.

I've also embraced some advice from one of my mentors who told me to "act like you know what you're doing until you figure out what to do," and people will be less likely to question what you're doing. I find this advice to be useful in diversity work because we are so often forging new territory and new ways of doing things. More often than not, diversity practitioners in organizations do not possess the position, power, and authority to make decisions or lead large teams, so we have to use our influence to persuade the key authority figures to follow our recommendations in making decisions, whether it's implementing new policies or endorsing people or events or funding initiatives. The "tell, don't ask" lesson is about taking initiative, and it is probably just an extension of the "work twice as hard" lesson, but ultimately the ability to exhibit confidence, competence, and credibility results in a successful record of accomplishment.

## Suspend Judgment

The field of diversity presents challenges that defy the very nature of humankind. In the new age of the knowledge worker, we are constantly bombarded and barraged with overwhelming amounts of new information to process, a dizzying array of choice points and numerous requests to make decisions about everything—from which e-mail messages to read or delete, to selecting Facebook friends, to what cable channel to watch, and more. This means that sometimes, we have to be discriminating and go with what we know just to limit the volume of decisions we have to make and to get through our day.

To make living in the information age practical and efficient, we have to discriminate in order to narrow down our choices and make decisions based on familiarity, prior knowledge, past experience, and intuition. Discrimination creates a comfort zone of similarity and familiarity. To be honest, the process of gravitating to differences in people is counter to our instinct to gravitate toward similarities and requires learning new patterns of behavior that ask us to pause and think rather than assume and act on what is comfortable and familiar. I realized that my own assumptions and stereotypes get in the way when I least expect it.

Not long ago, I was driving through the affluent city of Palo Alto, the home of Stanford University. I stopped at a traffic light, and I noticed a plainly dressed thirty-something White man walking alongside my car. He had a backpack, and he was conservatively dressed in a plaid shirt, crew-neck sweater, slacks, and loafers. He had an unshaven face, but his neatly combed hair made me think he was just going with the ruggedly handsome movie-star look of a George Clooney or Matthew McConaughey. I also assumed he was a student or somehow connected to Stanford University.

As the young White man reached the corner, he knelt down and reached for a discarded pizza box on the sidewalk. He grabbed a slice of pizza out of the box, brushed it off, and began eating it. I thought, *There but by the grace of God go I.* In the age of abundance and overindulgence, America's obsession with wealth bothers me. But the ravages of White poverty and homelessness are the societal ills that I have never wanted to pay attention to. I know that it's a media-manufactured lie that most poor people have black and brown faces. I suppose that's one of the reasons why I don't buy into White people, especially White men being poverty-stricken. The television news story about the shabby old White man panhandling on the streets of San Francisco by begging for food in the summer and then spending the winter in his condo in Florida seemed to support my thinking. So did my attempt to give food to a downtrodden and dirty White man sitting outside of the post office carrying a Will Work for Food sign. When I offered him my apple, he said angrily, "Can you give me a couple of dollars instead?"

So when I saw this seemingly ordinary young White man eating the discarded pizza off the ground, it tugged at my heartstrings. Yes, hunger, poverty, and homelessness strike all people (although at disparate rates). Recent catastrophic natural and man-made disasters show us that we're all just a calamity away from having our worlds torn apart. And while it may feel like it's easy to clean yourself up, go out and get a job, and work hard at any job you can get, life is just not so simple for some of us.

In that moment, I realized that the very thing I feel victimized by—that people make assumptions about me and react to me based on that assumption, not reality—I had just done to this young man whom I assumed was a Stanford man because he was a regular White guy walking just blocks from the campus. It just goes to show that you never know what another person's reality is. The hardest thing to do and the answer to how to overcome stereotypes is to suspend judgment. Pause to think before you act, or listen before you speak.

## Going Deeper through Dialogue Circles

Once I made the transition from corporate education to corporate diversity work, I decided to gain exposure and increase my expertise in the diversity field by attending Diversity 2000 (D2K), a conference of diversity practitioners. At D2K, the freedom and openness made possible through the use of Harrison Owen's open space technology allows you to set your own agenda for learning, sharing, and engaging in the kind of dialogue that rarely occurs in work settings. An interesting dialogue session that was convened nearly twenty years ago was on the topic of what White women and women of color need from each other. The result of that very rich dialogue was a commitment to convene a woman's circle that still thrives today. The true lesson of being in circle with others is that you do learn to trust, appreciate, challenge, support, mentor, and learn from one another. Once a container of safety and support is created, no subject is off-limits, and the opportunity to discuss the undiscussable continues to be the stuff of great dialogue.

One of the most challenging themes the circle has tackled is whether gender issues are subordinate to racial issues. Our circle of White, African American, Latina, and Asian women, straight and lesbian, US and Canadian, and Christian and Jewish women weighed in on this topic years ago. I realized then and now that the many life experiences I have had that made a personal and professional impact on me revolved around issues of my race more than about my gender. After much debate and discussion, we concluded that race issues have more impact than gender issues. A very difficult part of the dialogue that led to this conclusion was the many deep and complicated discussions about White privilege and the fact that as White women, there is not the same continual bombardment of race issues that women of color endure. By and large, the dominance of White culture is assumed and taken for granted by White women unless whiteness is raised by women of color. Even after many years as a women's circle, we still find that the subject of White privilege has to be revisited periodically. Dialogue circles are hard work that requires members to be committed to the circle and to be clear about what you're willing to give and receive from the circle.

The longevity of this women's circle is unique because with many circles, a much shorter period of engagement is established up front, and perhaps there is a less compelling reason to exist. I don't recall ever having a discussion about how long we would exist as a circle. It seems to me that the question of what White women and women of color need from each other is a conversation that could continue for a lifetime. More importantly, the sisters of this circle have formed a bond with one another. During the early years, we met quite frequently—five to six times a year despite the great distances some members traveled. In recent years, there are fewer dialogues and less time to connect because life has presented itself and interrupted our flow with the inevitable losses and gains of life, including spousal and parental losses, illnesses, empty nests, marriages, divorces, relocations, job losses, retirements, grandchildren, and the gift of aging.

Since this first circle experience, I have joined other circles, and I know that this type of interaction inspires my work and enriches my experience as a diversity practitioner. However, I have not seen the special bond that the D2K women's circle created occur in other circles. I've come up with the following questions to ask if one is interested in convening a lasting circle. Can convening a circle be too contrived? What are the lessons to be learned from one another in the circle? Are you willing to be egalitarian in your sharing as well as your listening? Are you willing to be changed by the dialogue? Will you know when it's over? The women's circle reminds me again and again that we are all on a lifelong journey of learning to value one another as human beings with similarities and differences and that the differences are sometimes subjected to close scrutiny from others and by holding up the mirror to inspect ourselves.

## Diversity and Organizational Change

I consider the diversity work I do today to be the most significant way in which I can make a difference in the lives of people in the workplace. Above all else, diversity work helps individuals make changes in their behavior toward people who are different from them. At the organization level, this work entails three areas of focus: recruitment, development, and inclusion. A brief description of each focus area follows.

The objective of diversity recruitment is to intentionally seek the best talent from all segments to bring into the organization. The smart companies go beyond attempting to meet diversity representation goals and instead search as broadly as possible to find the best talent everywhere. The goal is to cast a broader net to seek candidates in new places and use new methods. Implementing practices for attracting and hiring diverse talent include participating in nontraditional and diversity-focused conferences, searching for talent on diversity-focused job boards and websites, and advocating for diverse candidates by promoting these candidates with recruiters and hiring managers. While certain diverse populations get more attention than others due to US Affirmative Action (i.e., women and people of color), there is a growing emphasis on equal employment and equitable treatment worldwide for people with disabilities and for the LGBT community.

The development of diverse populations focuses on how high-performing employees gain visibility and receive opportunities for advancement and promotion. In particular, when women and people of color join an organization, they experience a different career development path from their White male counterparts. I have seen the career trajectories of women and people of color take many years longer than their White male counterparts who possess the same credentials and experience. (Cross-industry research on the career advancement gap is documented in *Breaking Through: The Making of Minority Executives in Corporate America*, David A. Thomas and John J. Gabarro, Boston, MA: Harvard Business School Press, 1999.) My work involves identifying, tracking, and then advocating for diverse candidates during talent and performance rating discussions so that subjective criteria such as personality traits and "style" differences are not used to evaluate the results and performance of women and people of color. This work also includes participating in talent discussions, designing diversity considerations into talent selection processes, and providing coaching and mentoring for the individuals and their managers so that diverse individuals receive the feedback and development opportunities they need to successfully progress in their careers.

Inclusion, the third focus area, encompasses the ways in which the work environment makes employees feel welcomed, supported, and able to thrive. For many years, I have worked with others on formulating the policies and practices that make the work environment harassment-free, equitable, and fair. This work includes implementing a diversity training curriculum; events and communications to raise awareness about cultural differences; developing work-life programs and resources such as flexible work schedule arrangements, part-time/job sharing, telecommuting, and providing resources to help manage work/personal life needs such as finding child care and elder care; and managing and supporting employee resource groups (also called employee networks or affinity groups).

Ultimately, the overarching goal in corporate diversity is to hold the leadership team accountable for creating a diversity-friendly work environment where everyone can do his or her best work. The positive and significant actions in support of diversity from the company's leadership team provide an important signal to the rest of the company about the importance of diversity in the company's success with shareholders, customers, marketplaces, and the communities where the company does business.

Diversity as a field of endeavor is evolving, and in many corporations, diversity organizations are being combined with other human resources organizations such as employee engagement, organizational effectiveness, staffing, and talent management.

The shifts occurring in the corporate landscape, coupled with completing my doctor of education degree, compelled me to think about making a change in my work environment. As a result, I recently moved from a corporate work environment to academia for the opportunity to work in a newly established diversity and inclusion organization and to launch an initiative that focuses on equity and inclusion for university staff. The same need to focus on the areas of recruitment, development, and inclusion of employees exists in the academic environment. No matter what environment you're working in, the work of diversity is still the same—helping people to become self-aware of their own biases and how they impact other people, finding ways to enable everyone in the organization to fully contribute to achieving the common goals of the organization, and striving for behavioral changes that will bring equity in how people are treated.

I am struck by the parallels between the corporate and academic work worlds in terms of who we serve, what we offer, and how we impact the world outside of our work environment. I realized that in moving from a corporate to an academic environment, I have traded a corporate focus on customers, selling products and services, and philanthropic endeavors that benefit the community for an academic focus on excellence in serving students as the customer and changing lives through groundbreaking research and public service. Implementing diversity efforts take years to accomplish, and in most environments, results are not achievable or sustainable without collaboration and commitment of other departments and the active involvement of leaders who champion the work.

Progress happens, and while some organizations hype diversity progress in highly visible ways, other organizations seamlessly absorb diversity progress into changes in policies and practices related to work culture without bringing attention to the diversity organization. My hope is that my professional journey in the diversity field is motivating to others and that they will examine their own life experiences, determine what role they can play, and decide to join me in this work.

## DiCE

I am indebted to the group of diversity professionals in the Diversity Community Exchange (DiCE) because I feel nurtured, supported, and validated by each of them for what they help me to be, see, and do in my work. What comes to mind for me in being a part of DiCE is Kahlil

Gibran's quote: "Work is love made visible." DiCE was conceived as a group of diversity professionals of varying backgrounds who came together to provide the kind of intimate learning community and support group that is not possible in larger groups. When Sonny Massey convened the original DiCE group in partnership with Mike Vonada, the original intent was to include people whose lifework is not in the diversity field, including medical practitioners, entertainers, environmentalists, and others. It soon became apparent that it is difficult for people who are not significantly involved in diversity work to be capable of making the same contribution to a group such as DiCE as would individuals whose career focus is in diversity work.

Drawing from the Diversity 2000 Conference, a diversity learning community that meets annually in Northern California, a group of diversity practitioners were invited to become a part of DiCE. Diversity work is challenging, and what our DiCE members have in common is our passion to have our work make a difference in people's lives. It just so happens that over time, those of us doing the work are not simply called diversity practitioners. We have many different titles ascribed to us, including educators, consultants, change agents, and other titles. The combination of corporate, academic, government, nonprofit, and consulting environments in which we work gives us the opportunity to expand our knowledge through sharing what we are learning and helping each of us to see what we cannot see for ourselves. The thought-provoking, activist, philosophical, practical, whimsical, tearful, and joyful connections we have with one another have sustained me through many difficult challenges, both personal and professional.

During the writing of this book, we have lost two of our members, Marvin Smith and Sonny Massey. I believe that each of us are holding the space for Marvin and Sonny in our hearts and minds and that with this book, we offer to everyone who is thinking about a career in diversity work a wide assortment of motivations and reasons for doing the work now and forever.

## Change the World One Person at a Time

I always assumed that those of us who serve as change agents in our organizations—whether under the auspices of diversity, culture change, organizational effectiveness, social justice, or whatever other label is bestowed upon us—would be able to make an impact on our organizations and the effects of bias. I have learned through training, one-on-one relationship building, and continued exposure and awareness building about our differences that there are many ways to chip away at the bonds of prejudice. The key to successfully overcoming the bias in the air we breathe and the water we drink is to be self-aware and do the deep personal work that will enable you to stay strong and keep your personal integrity intact as you tackle the challenges and opportunities of the work.

I've shared ten of my personal lessons with you that have made me strong in doing diversity work: (1) respect your past; (2) don't judge a book by its cover; (3) control the self-hate that may take root during childhood; (4) treat people with dignity and respect; (5) be a role model for others; (6) your out-group can be the in-group; (7) expect to work twice as hard; (8) read between the lines; (9) tell, don't ask; and (10) suspend judgment.

One final lesson comes from Mahatma Gandhi who told us to "be the change you want to see in the world." What I now know is that to affect behavioral change, you have to make an impact on people one individual at a time, and when enough people are impacted, the organization will change. Through dialogue and personal stories, I have learned how I can have a personal impact on people. Diversity work will always be a part of me and how I operate no matter when and where I call upon my life experiences to inform my work.

In the spirit of helping one another do well in this challenging work, I'd like to close by sharing a story that has inspired me. The "Star Thrower" story tells us that no act is too small to make a difference.

## The Star Thrower

Written by Loren Eiseley and adapted
by Joel Arthur Barker in the film *The Power of Vision*

An old man was taking a sunrise walk along the beach. In the distance, he caught sight of a young man who seemed to be dancing along the waves. As he got closer, he saw that the young man was picking up starfish from the sand and tossing them gently back into the ocean. "What are you doing?" The old man asked.
"The sun is coming up and the tide is going out; if I don't throw them in they'll die."
"But young man, there are miles and miles of beach with starfish all along it—you can't possibly make a difference."

The young man bent down, picked up another starfish, and threw it lovingly back into the ocean, past the breaking waves.

"I made a difference for that one," he replied.

That young man's actions represent something special in each of us. We are all gifted with the ability to make a difference.

# NOT EXACTLY

Nadia Younes

I AM NADIA YOUNES, and I was quite literally unable to escape the field currently known as diversity and inclusion. I was born in Canada in the middle of a blizzard to an upper-class Egyptian Muslim father and a working-class American Christian mother. Immigration laws in the '60s combined with the luck of a large Canadian research grant and the rigors of cancer research my father was doing at the time were the reasons behind the Canadian addition of my three potential citizenships. My father was so worried about the collision of these three countries causing a mess for them at my birth that I was nearly born in the back of a taxi that was being raced toward the US border in the hopes of the delivery of a healthy and little *unquestionably* middle-class US citizen.

Perhaps he was unconsciously onto something big. He was trying to design a life for him and his family that had less cultural conflict than his did. This would not pan out as possible in his lifetime, and our cultural, religious, and class differences would create the biggest divides and cause much tension throughout my family's history and my own path in the world. But what if we could consciously "design" families, communities, organizations, etc., that work across all the inevitable differences that exist? What if we changed our behaviors to look for and build understanding, respect, and connections rather than assumptions, mistrust, and divisions? How could we do this with all our differences? In discovering and sharing my own story with a small group of people widely different from me (and my coauthors in this book), I found that it is precisely the power of our stories and experiences, when openly shared and listened to, that can transform us as individuals into something greater than any one of us could have developed into without the others. We have become—by design and perhaps a bit of divine intervention and grace—a very functional, multicultural family. So I'll share my story and hope that you find some connections, but more importantly, I'll urge you to discover and share your own and seek out the stories of others in your family or community so that you are inspired to consciously create and design multicultural communities that work.

Chancellor Merkel in Germany declared the failure of multiculturalism too soon. We do not have the option to let multiculturalism fail if we want to live well in the world that exists or the world currently being created for future generations. Multiculturalism is not an experiment, it's a reality. Each of us likely belongs to a family that has relations from different cultural backgrounds, educational and socioeconomic levels, beliefs, and other differences. And we all likely live and work in communities that are becoming more multicultural with each passing day. Each of us has an opportunity through the listening to and the sharing of our stories to be a part of designing a world, one family and group at a time, which holds the hope of working better for everyone.

So my story may be unique to me, but in its telling, I hope to incite you to tell your own and to crave hearing the stories of people widely different from you in order that you may also start to create a shared set of hopes and positive relations that expand and enrich your life and the lives you have the opportunity to impact along the way.

## My Story

From my first memories as a child, I remember being the odd one out or, in *Sesame Street* terms, the *one of these things is not like the other.* Initially, this realization came from the questions people often asked me. Was I Christian? Not exactly. Was I White? Not exactly. Was I or my family from one place in particular? Not exactly. Was I bilingual like many in my family? Not exactly. And more recently, during a post-9/11 revival of a kind of "nationalism" filled with hate, fear, and a renewed sense of us versus them, was I proud to be an American? An Egyptian? Not exactly (since my personal mix of cultures was something many on both sides of the world immediately distrusted and held grossly uninformed and negative stereotypes of). As an adult, these questions are still put to me. The difference is that now I am more consciously aware that my answer of "not exactly" comes from my own multicultural identity born out of sheer raw ingredients, a lifetime of being a part of an extremely quirky and reality TV—worthy multicultural family living in a variety of places and often humorous life experiences. The raw ingredients you already know about, so what about my family?

My mother is Christian (Episcopalian), and like many of any faith, she practiced and was active in her church to varying degrees throughout the stages of her life. She grew up in a working-class family that lived near Detroit, Michigan, and reminded me of the 1970s TV family, the Bunkers. My grandfather could have been Archie Bunker filled with his prejudices and biases and limited exposure to cultural differences. My grandmother was definitely a kindred spirit of Edith Bunker—generally believing all people were good and kind but never wanting to disagree or upset her husband. Being 100 percent agreeable to everyone at all times was the sign of being a good wife—always pleasant and unchallenging. This background would shape how my mother would try and be a good wife. It didn't prepare her to know how to be a good wife from my father's cultural lens, but she had a much better fit the second time around when she remarried a man from a similar cultural, religious and class background as the one she was raised in.

My father, now in his eighties, is a Muslim who grew up in an upper-class family in Egypt. He was remarried to an Egyptian Muslim wife from an even wealthier family than he was raised in. The combination of his age and Muslim second wife have led him to practice his faith with more of the regularity that was likely a part of his youth but that was in the shadows during much of his adult life while working in the States and being married to a practicing Christian. He grew up as the son of a highly educated and prominent politician in southern Egypt. He grew up with servants—a cadre of cooks, drivers, nannies, and house cleaners that are still a part of his class and family today in Egypt.

My maternal grandmother was Jewish, and this was the unspoken not-so-secret in our home. My paternal great-grandmother was English—something of pride to my father and his generation since the English ruled in the colonial era of his youth. Ironic, of course, since our English relations, whoever they may be, have certainly never claimed us or kept ties with their North African family. I am doubtful they were so proud to have "gone native" during the time of colonial rule, and it is likely that my great-grandmother risked losing her family over what has been told to me in our family's oral tradition of an epic and gracious love story between my Egyptian great-grandfather and his English love. I'll come back to the concepts of love and grace because they have become central to who I am, who I believe we are all capable of being, and how I believe this work of inclusion and diversity will have any chance at helping us reach our own human potential.

I have one older sister. She is an engineer by trade and a wonderful mother of two beautiful children by life. She is a kind and good woman who has chosen to not be Muslim after very thoughtfully considering it along with other options. She has done this knowing that it would cause a severe division between her and many of her relatives. This choice has cost her and her children any relationship with our father, and he too is in much pain over this division.

Our father has built an impenetrable wall that his practicing of both cultural tradition and religion has forged between them, and my niece and nephew have no idea what they have done to alienate a grandfather who chooses not to know them. If having Jewish relatives was an unspoken not-so-secret, openly admitting to our father that she didn't feel Islam was a fit for her was an even bigger taboo and one that brought—albeit unintentionally—much shame to our father. He didn't actively practice his faith growing up so we were only partially exposed to it when we were visiting family abroad. We did Ramadan and other traditions when we were there but these practices didn't consistently make their way into our home life in the States. Even though our dad must understand why she would have not connected to his childhood faith, he couldn't separate the cultural and social pressure that all of his children should be Muslim.

The faith, as I understand it, would say that Allah knows what is in your heart so you should follow this faith only if it is in your heart and not out of social pressure. Many never actively question whether the faith they were born into and raised with is one that works for them or one they choose to have guide them. It takes courage to choose a faith you weren't born into I think. The one of your family feels betrayed when you leave and the one you join may never really accept you at all or accept you as a sort of second-class "convert" and question your practice and faith with twice the scrutiny of those born into it.

Subtle and not so subtle messages were sent to us growing up about religions that were not in the Judeo-Christian—and even within this tradition, Judaism, received many comments that made conversations around the Canasta table with our Jewish great grandmother uncomfortable for me.

Grandma Bea, as we called her, was a great card player. She wore a green banker's visor with a light attached and was a keen competitor. Over 80 years exposure to the game and an excellent dozen moves ahead thinking ability just may have made her the better player but the number of comments about her shrewdness, cautiousness with money and the meager bets that were made in the game all circled around her being Jewish. When she responded tersely even the nature of her response was credited negatively to her religion. She couldn't win at the prejudice game but she sure could clean everyone's clocks when it was about the cards and I was always glad when she won. I hated the way digs were taken at her for her religion and I also didn't like when they treated her like a child because of her advanced age. If I ever live to be in my eighties I know I will not take kindly to being talked to like a child with little to no life experiences. Just one "So how was your day sweetie?" said with the syrupy intonation used to address toddlers might just set me off—or—maybe I'll let it roll off me by then. I don't know but it is a pet peeve now.

Another time I recall was when I was first introduced to the deliciousness of real bagels from a Jewish friend that lived in my neighborhood who had given me some homemade ones to bring home. I was told we didn't eat or buy bagels because, "no offence to my friend and her family, but we were not going to support Israel". That put the sour in the sourdough for me and I remember being furious at what I thought was complete absurdity. I had what must have been my first political argument at the time and it was over all over a bagel! I understand intellectually that I was raised predominantly in the part of the world that mostly believes in the separation of church and state and that there are other parts of the world where the two are closely intertwined or inseparable but the connection to bagels (or other such bizarre connections) is still lost on me.

Growing up the confusion about our family's religion came out during the holidays especially when mom was active in church without her family. I had friends' parents quiz me and tell me they'd pray for my soul. At Christmas, it took some time to pass before friends understood that I would be no worse for the wear if I did the tree, stockings and giving to charities pieces of Christmas without the core focus of rejoicing the birth of baby Jesus. We acknowledged that this was the reason for the holiday and my mother did truly rejoice in her faith but for myself it was a holiday about giving, love and charity (and as a really young kid—honestly, it was about amassing as many of the new toys that my parents and the wonderful Santa would think I was worthy of—much like the Christian and Catholic kids I grew up with.)

As for me, I jokingly tell people that I am the religious equivalent of Switzerland and want to be known for my neutrality in this area. My faith in God and how I live my life on any given day is more important to me than the religious label others seem to need to categorize me. In my experience, organized religion is often used to divide people and put them at odds with one another, and I believe any spiritual or religious path should actually accomplish the opposite. That seems counterintuitive to me and not at all what I believe God intended for us. When pushed with the question "What religion are you anyway?" I often reply that by birth, I am a Muslim, but I don't always get that right when it comes to the rituals and traditions since I wasn't raised with them with any regularity around me. I am, however, trying to consciously develop myself into the kind of woman God would want me to be and one that I myself would admire. I'm not quite there yet, but living a good and honorable life seems to be about continuous improvement and giving of oneself.

So if I love candlelight Christmas services that focus on love for humanity, Ramadan with the emphasis on being grateful and giving thanks to God and helping those poorer than you, and the overall concept of doing good deeds or doing mitzvahs, then I think I am all the better for being exposed to all these. I have read all the main books of these religions at one time or another, but I enjoy more in observing the daily behaviors that guide really good people. These truly good and honorable people I find come from so many religions that I never felt the need to claim just one to guide me as it seems to me that if there is any judgment day, then HOW you have lived day to day is what I believe will get judged in the end, not which religious team you signed up for or were born into.

I find it ironic that in Jewish tradition, you ARE Jewish if it is on your mother's side; and in the Muslim tradition, you ARE Muslim if it is on your father's side. So does that make me both?! Not exactly.

Before I realized that I didn't have to pick one, I sort of visited various organized religions while growing up due to my family's interfaith nature. I found religion fascinating especially since I was taught in any of the religions I was exposed to that there was one god and that we were all his creatures (although it seemed that each one telling me these tenets also believed that their people somehow had it slightly more figured out and were slightly more favored than those other folks of "the Book").

I had the privilege of knowing and loving my Egyptian and American grandmothers and my Jewish great-grandmother. I have fond memories of all these wonderful women, and when I think of the great divisions, heartaches, and crimes against humanity their inherited backgrounds have endured in generations before and after them, it is only a reminder of just how important the work of inclusion and intercultural connection is. There is still so much division to overcome, and often, the reasons behind these divisions become clear very early in life.

Growing up in Pennsylvania—in a small German and largely Protestant community—I quickly learned that Islam was suspicious at best, Judaism was intolerable, and Episcopalianism was too close to Catholicism to be fully accepted as Christian but was the lesser of the other non-Protestant evils. Not everyone held this view of course, and the locals are incredibly nice people by and large, but the messages I received growing up in the '60s-'80s were clear. "You are not one of us". The few other minority or immigrant families that lived in there when I did were the families where I felt most accepted. There was an unspoken bond between myself and the Indian, Vietnamese, and Black children who went to my school. The five or so of us often laughed about our differences with the community at large but only in private and with one another. The rest of the time we spent like most youth, trying to fit in a culture that we just were never going to be fully included in. Some of us sort of stopped trying, and a few resorted to more of a conversion approach.

Our Vietnamese friend for example changed his given name to a more American and Christian-sounding name. I remember thinking in my teenage youth that his going from a Vietnamese name, whom few bothered to learn to pronounce let alone spell, to some soap opera—sounding name like Todd or Thad was a bit extreme. In the end, people in the town laughed at his new name almost as much as his old one—never really understanding that it wasn't about what he wanted to be called but about trying to create an identity that felt more real to him and in sync with the two cultures he was blending as he grew up. In any event, many in the town simply missed out on knowing this warmhearted and funny young man whose life experiences would likely have made for some very interesting story sharing. This could have offered both parties insights they would never have been able to get anywhere else in the area.

There wasn't much acceptance of any diversity at that time and place. Active Klan chapters existed just miles from my doorstep, and the one Black family and my other more visibly minority friends stood out more than I did. I often found myself intervening when people said rude and ignorant things about them when they weren't there. I was welcomed into this outsider group more often than the majority group, what with my father and his accent and unpronounceable name (known as Mike by the locals) and my mocha skin and lion's mane of thick dark curls. Race, still a confused and avoided topic in America, was something that I wasn't sure about. My dad wasn't White, and he wasn't Black either, so people really didn't know what I was. If a guess had to be made though, I was lumped into the non-White category in the small town I grew up in.

Many a school yard taunts had bias and prejudice as their cause. My older sister often defended me when I was being called a nigger or a sand nigger as I was later referred when one of the more brilliant bullies put together that I was half Egyptian and Egypt had a desert. I had no idea what these terms meant or why they were being spit at me at the time I first heard them I just knew that the meaning was intended as an insult.

When my childhood best friend and I got into a little-girl squabble and she went crying to her parents to help us resolve it, I remember her father saying to her loudly that if we weren't getting along, then she "should just stop playing with that nigger girl." I had no idea what he meant, but I understood that it wasn't considered good and that her dad would be just fine if I weren't in her circle.

When I came home in tears and my father heard what was said, I was forbidden to play with my friend or go to their home. She was my best friend, and to any little girl, this was pretty tragic. We played in secret for a while but eventually drifted apart. Perhaps we would have drifted anyway over time, but the circumstances made this instance stand out, and it wouldn't be the first time that being different would distance me from a level of intimacy or belonging I craved. I was likely only about seven years old, and even then, when taunted with words I didn't understand, my reply was always an exasperated "Oh yeah! So what if I AM what you said?!" So what if I am—out of the mouths of babes, and still this phrase goes through my head when someone infers or says negative things about a group I am a part of (or someone else is, for that matter). My sister tells me that was the phrase she used to defend me with and that for her it wasn't about denying the name they were calling me rather it was about denying them the RIGHT to label me. I am thankful I internalized the phrase because it has guided a more conscious look at what I am and how I view other cultural differences.

The cultural differences were evident and went beyond race perceptions. You couldn't enter our home without immediately knowing you "weren't in Kansas anymore." From the smells from our kitchen to the volume of our discourse and foreign decorations all over the house, you knew we just lived differently.

I still have a picture of my best friend and me in elementary school in our matching red, white, and blue tennis dresses. Hers was a cute miniskirt and had a halter top. Mine was way below the knees, and despite the one hundred degrees and 100 percent humidity, I was wearing long dark socks and sleeves. My sister was older than I, and the cultural outsider picture that comes to my mind from her school years was far more embarrassing to her.

For her Spring dance, she was not allowed to purchase a normal cocktail dress. These were too sexy and adult looking, according to my father. Instead, my father gave her the most beautiful bright turquoise formal *galabeya* I had ever seen, a sort of African frock or muumuu with fancy gold stitching. She looked like a princess to me and at five years her junior I would have loved to play dress up in the same dress. Her peers at the dance however must have thought she was dressed for Halloween. I don't remember her attending any dances after that until she left home and went to college.

It wasn't just my best friend and her father's racial barbs that attempted to categorize me—even from my minority friends, the curiosity and questions still came. It wasn't until I was older that I realized that we were all just trying to understand where we belonged, where we might be accepted, and what our intercultural identities really meant to ourselves and others in the world around us.

My whole life, these categorical kinds of questions kept coming from all directions, and I grew to understand that I would need to come up with some sort of answers although none of them seemed to clarify my cultural identity to those who asked about it . . . and everyone did. I experimented with a wide variety of answers when I was younger, trying on different pieces of my identity as one would try on a piece of clothing and looking for the right fit and style. All of them fit, but none of them matched each other, so I had to learn to wear my polka dots, stripes, paisleys, and solids all together and not worry that it wasn't really the fashion at the time.

When Obama was elected and held up as "the first Black president," I wondered if he felt a bit at odds with himself in accepting that title. Does being the first BLACK president ignore the fact that he is half White? He's been very open about his biracial background, yet both Whites and Blacks, for different reasons I suppose, ignore his White half. And in this, how much can a person choose their identity versus what is chosen for them?

My sister identifies with being an "Apple-Pie American" and I identify as being Egyptian American. Culturally, I was raised in a household that was certainly not like most other American middle to upper middle-class families nor was I raised in the traditional Egyptian ways. My darker skin and features also made me look more ethnic than my sister, and people often assumed I was Latina or at least mixed with something. Some tell me I look very Egyptian, and others say I don't. There are many looks to Egyptians, and half the time, the people who tell me that I do not look Egyptian don't actually know any. Just as a point of clarity on the matter, Elizabeth Taylor really didn't look Egyptian when she portrayed Cleopatra. I'm just saying. In the end, I just say "thank you" for the compliment whenever someone asks if I am Brazilian, biracial, Middle Eastern, Italian, Mexican, or Greek.

The third culture that was inevitably created was something that had pieces of both countries, elements of both classes, and the basic values contained in many religions. As I got older, I would consciously choose the pieces that felt authentic to me and matched how I wanted to live.

This notion of authenticity is very important to me and serves as my magnetic north, but finding what feels authentic in my mix has taken some time. When my father's wife, for example, reproached me for not bothering to learn the suras from the Koran in classical Arabic or praying with the prescribed motions of the five prayers a day, I tried to explain this notion of authenticity to her. I am privately a very spiritual person, and I talk, privately, to God very often—giving thanks, asking for guidance, and praying for the well-being of loved ones and the world around me in general. If I were to replace these prayers with the rote memorization of phrases in a language I do not speak, this would feel inauthentic to me. I think I would be doing this more so that people like herself would judge me as a better Muslim. It is far more important to me that God knows what is in my heart and sees that I am trying to be a good person, and I just personally don't think he is so concerned about these specific rituals in any religion. He's just got to have bigger concerns than these!

Being authentic and learning how to define myself and my own cultural and ethnic identity was an important part of my journey into this work of diversity and inclusion. I began to understand the psychology behind my squirming and wanting to be able to clearly say yes or no to questions that would firmly establish me as fully included and accepted in the groups behind the questions. The world of diversity and cross-cultural work that would later call to me and guide my life in more ways of being than simply my professional life began in these early questions. Wanting to fit in and be a part of the group, whatever the group may be at the moment, can be a powerful force in one's life at any age. Adults fool themselves when they say they don't care if they *ever* fit in. At times this can be true, but if you find you are *rarely*—if ever—a part of the socially preferred, understood, and/or majority culture, this constant tension influences who eventually becomes your in-group. It can also make you a bit of a philosophical wanderer that has others labeling you as too intense because you actually spend a fair amount of time consciously considering yourself and your culture—or cultures as the case may be—in relation to those around you. I spend a lot less time trying to frame or craft an answer to the WAYA question "What are you anyway?" now than I used to, but I've learned to listen to the subcontext because it varies.

## Diversity Practitioner Disparity

Even among diversity and inclusion practitioners, there can be silly power and "-ism" dynamics that play out that as a field, we really need to just stop. I do not believe that experiencing these "-isms" is in any way unique to me, and as these things go, I've had it easy, and I know it. This, however, only strengthens my commitment to the work of diversity. I know the "Yeah, if you think YOU had it bad" one-upmanship that can happen among diversity practitioners across races and classes, and people in general will not help us as a people to move forward to a more inclusive, forgiving, and loving world. When a blind colleague told me about the power dynamics within the disabled community around which disability has more privileges and the same dynamics were echoed across the GLBTQ (gay, lesbian, bisexual, transgendered, and queer) communities, it makes you realize just how much work we have ahead of us. Earlier in my career when I was hired as a diversity manager, I distinctly recall the outrage of some of the Black employees who felt that the diversity position should only be filled by a Black leader, and I was expected to sort of prove I was diverse enough. They held me at a distance, and it took a lot of trust building for them to understand that I was committed to being a strong ally and advocate for equality and inclusion for their group as well as all others.

Sometimes, the questions about how diverse I am or what my diversity makeup is seem to be an attempt to classify me and find common ground. When a neighbor or colleague ventures into conversations that mention the holidays, weddings, baptisms, etc., this WAYA question inevitably comes up, and usually, my answer baffles them because I wasn't raised in a single-faith home. I found I was also on guard a bit when I answered their questions because it wasn't unusual for me to be held at a distance once they realized that I either wasn't familiar with or didn't share their specific traditions.

As a young girl, I remember being scolded as insolent when I politely and quite ignorantly whispered in an elderly woman's ear on Ash Wednesday that she had a smudge on her forehead. I remember being so embarrassed and hurt at the woman's accusation that I was an intentionally rude and ill-mannered immigrant girl. Years later, I realized that my mother took part in this and in many other traditions at her church but rid herself of any trace or mention of these before entering our home so as to keep peace in the household. This need to practice her faith without exposing it to her children was very hard on her and, ultimately, on the marriage between her and my father.

My father had more of an uphill battle because in Islamic tradition, the children in an interfaith marriage are to be raised Muslim especially if the father is Muslim. Although this was their agreement upon marrying, my father's faith was one we visited when we went to see the family on our summer vacations to Egypt rather than one we were steeped with at home. Given the area I grew up in, my father's very long and erratic work hours, and the fact that the nearest Muslim community was over an hour away, I don't fault him for not being able to fully raise his two girls as Muslims in the traditions he would have loved for us to have adopted as our own. My mother certainly couldn't have filled these shoes either, so we were left to experience religions the way a tourist experiences a new and exciting destination. We knew just enough about Christianity, Islam, and Judaism to get by but not enough about any to fit in, so both my sister and I set out on our own to find our spiritual paths. And in doing so, neither of us feel particularly lost today in spite of the sympathy or pity we sometimes receive from people wishing we could have really experienced their religious upbringing.

Both of my parents abridged their birth cultures so much that they created something of a hybrid, and this didn't work for either of them. After their divorce, they both happily, and with varying degrees of success, immersed themselves in their birth cultures by remarrying spouses with similar cultural and class backgrounds and living more in accordance to the cultural traditions they grew up with. My dad still struggles with this concept of home culture though and currently is sort of a man without a country.

I'm told by my family that my father's strictness is more old-school Egyptian than is true for most Egyptians today. His immigrating to the United States when he was thirty had him using Egypt in the '50s as his reference point to what was appropriate for his children being raised in the United States largely in the '70s and '80s. This disconnect from his home and culture has never really been mended.

Upon retirement from his practice in the United States, he anxiously moved back to Egypt to split his retirement time and immediately began noticing how disappointingly different Egypt was not like the United States. Six months later, he'd find himself fed up with the States and rail against how it was lacking in comparison to Egypt. This pattern has lessened over the years of his traveling back and forth between the two, but he still seems a bit trapped between cultures, and there is an unsettling dissonance for him that I can relate to (and perhaps have inherited). I tell people now that my home is wherever I am currently living since my family now lives in the United States, Egypt, Europe, India, and South America.

For my sister and I, going back to our "home" culture to find a sense of acceptance and inclusion was far more problematic, and for my sister, the feeling of home within a religious community was harder to create given the background I've shared. As an example, when my sister married a non-practicing Methodist, she realized that if she wanted to raise her children with an organized religion, it would be her that would lead this effort. She began, with the support of her husband, to research options she was exposed to while growing up in an interfaith family. She had already decided that Islam wasn't a fit for her and not the religion she would raise her children in but in this choosing, she unintentionally became estranged from most of her Egyptian family.

I, on the other hand, have pieced together a tapestry of the beliefs as I understand them and as they resonate with me. For example, in Islam, no one is closer to God than anyone else, and your relationship with God is really only between you and him. There are religious scholars and imams, but they have the same relationship with God as anyone else. There are no intermediaries. I like this. It feels more authentic for me. In Christianity, concepts of love, grace, and forgiveness are so woven into being a good person and Christian, and I really like this. In Judaism, ideals of critical thinking, environmentalism, and consciously practicing acts of goodness regularly are woven into the practice, and I like these traditions. When an Egyptian cousin married an Indian man and I learned about the concept of continuing on a path toward nirvana through multiple reincarnations, I decided that a more practical approach for me was to try to evolve to the best of my ability in this incarnation since I am unsure of what might be after. But the process of creating what works for me only really happened as a result of the mix I was born into. Most people never choose a religion; they seem to be born into the traditions of one, don't question it, and continue in the same path as their families did before them. Later, they may choose another religion, but this seems to happen very rarely. When people do choose to leave or enter a religion not theirs from birth, it seems to cause ripples in many all directions.

I understand that this cafeteria-style religion/spirituality and identity is very hard to fathom for some and downright offensive to others, but it is simply inherent in who I am and how I organize my world. I am what sociologist Ruth Hill Useem coined as a third-culture kid (or TCK), and it wasn't until graduate school in pursuit of my MA in intercultural communication that I stumbled upon the book of the same name (*Third Culture Kids: The Experience of Growing Up Among Worlds*, by David C. Pollock and Ruth E. Van Reken, 2001, Intercultural Press). My own personal world was falling into place. I had never in my life been so excited and connected to a book. To learn that my struggles and experiences while growing up among worlds was something that actually had patterns of behavior and commonalities with others was so affirming.

A third-culture kid (TCK / 3CK) or transculture kid is "someone who, as a child, has spent a significant period of time in one or more culture(s) other than his or her own, thus integrating elements of those cultures and their own birth culture, into a third culture."[1] TCKs tend to have more in common with one another, regardless of nationality, than they do with non-TCKs from their own country.

Having more in common with the Indian, Vietnamese, Black, and Jewish families in the small town where I grew up made sense in this context, and to date, some of my closest friends and easiest connections are also TCKs.

I grew up exposed to so much variety. My parents' backgrounds and upbringings not only differed around ethnic, geographic, and religious background but also in socioeconomic and educational backgrounds as well. My family sort of hybridized all these things, and it was only after my parents remarried partners who almost identically mirrored them on these dimensions that they were able to be resettled into their own previous identities. As a TCK, my experiences repeatedly reinforced that I was somehow different and that my home culture was a bit of a moving target.

Early experiences growing up were often of not really fitting in or of exerting an awful lot of inauthentic energy in order to be perceived as fitting in. Full inclusion, even within my family, was unobtainable due to language, geographic, and religious barriers to name a few, but I tried multiple approaches before I was able to fully embrace the notion of being a third-culture kid. Later in life, I too would find a partner in someone who had a cultural mix and background more like my own in many ways. The evolution of this relationship and living and working outside of the United States are two experiences that have brought me closer to feeling at home than ever before.

If I fast-forward to my adult life, going from single to married to divorced to remarried was all about finding a better cultural fit. The same may be said of finding any partnership that works, but for me, because of my mix, finding a relationship with a partner that works has had additional layers that had to be sorted through.

I grew up not being allowed to date. As a young teen, I remember the first time a cute, wholesome, and truly sweet boy walked me home from school carrying my books and flirting innocently with me. My fantasies at the time involved me holding his hand. It was that innocent. My father was home when we walked up, and he immediately came out of the house with his hair on fire. This boy—who was my first love, the kind whose name you wrote on the bottom of your sneakers or on your notebook and in hearts inscribed TLA (true love always for those not in tune with the old-school puppy love terminology)—was so shocked. That was the first and last time I was walked home from school. For the rest of my adolescent life, any relations I had with boys—no matter how innocent—were in total secrecy from my father.

My first puppy love married his high school sweetheart, and hopefully, they are still living happily ever after somewhere. For me, finding intimacy meant finding someone with whom being myself was easy and at least somewhat understood, but with my hybrid orientation, this proved to be a bit more difficult.

I fell head over heels with my first mature love at age seventeen or eighteen. He was a mixture with a Spanish surname but hailed from Louisiana and had a smile and heart the size of the bayou itself—still does, I imagine. We dated innocently enough for years, and then on a bold move on his part, he moved to Boston where I was going to college to be with me. It didn't last, and later I would realize that he was my only real adult practice with dating before I married. I think not being allowed to date seriously impacted my ability to learn how to choose a partner that would be a good fit for me.

The second serious relationship I ever had turned into my first husband. He was more of an all-American boy from a working-class family from a small town outside of Pittsburgh's steel country. He found me exotic, and I found him stable and mature, and neither of us was. I loved his family, especially his father who was a gentle and loving man. He didn't rule his family as my father did. Instead, he wore his heart on his sleeve and readily gave affection to children and his wife. He was macho in that you would almost never see him cry, but he had a gentle and strong spirit I really loved and admired. When his son and I parted ways, I missed him far more than anyone and often found myself wondering if I would have been able to stay married had the son been more like the dad.

Our families were very different though. When I first saw the movie *My Big Fat Greek Wedding*, it so reminded me of our two different cultures that I found it laugh-out-loud funny. His family was certainly the far more quiet and reserved one. At their family dinner table, the sound of silverware and plates passing dominated while in my family, overlapping conversations at increasing volumes and with lots of hand gestures ruled. You couldn't have heard a plate shatter let alone the clanking of silverware. And yet we both enjoyed and felt at home at our family dinners . . . just not at each other's.

My family would find my first husband boring, and his family would find me excitable or full of life. In the end, we grew apart, each wanting very different things in life and feeling most comfortable in very different types of communities. I also learned to be cautious when men described me as exotic and different because in the end, these are traits most wanted to sample but did not want for a lifetime. Had I had more supported dating experience, I might have learned this earlier in life. I watch my sister guide my niece and nephew, and I think that they will get very important practice in learning how to decipher the good and not-so-good fit when it comes to choosing relationships with any future partners. I know the success rates these days are not so high, but their earlier guided exposure should hopefully increase the odds of success. I certainly hope so for their sake!

When I would go to Egypt to visit my family in my college and post-college years, there would always turn up some random man. My aunts would happily proclaim, "Look who has come to join us for dinner! Ahmed . . . such a good boy from such a good family!" No doubt they all did, but this matching really seemed inauthentic, and I think I might have been super doomed had I been matched with someone who was looking for the perfect Egyptian and Muslim wife. My father would later realize this to be true and would soften to my Peruvian and Catholic-raised future husband, but we would have some hurdles to overcome in order for me to stay connected to my father.

I warned my partner Victor that my family would be the difficult one. His was simply glad he was happy and, when they met me and saw how I behaved with him and their family, immediately welcomed me with open arms. My mother and sister did the same with Victor, but my father and his wife were a different story. They had a whole battery of criteria that they wanted to judge Victor on, and they all revolved around culture, class, and religion—my big three growing up where I was mixed and they weren't.

Oddly enough though, their own values around culture, class and religion in these three often collided. Once after graduate school and well into my thirties, I was mentioning to them that I had dated a man that I had met at the gym. He was a pilot, Harvard educated, dabbled in real estate where he owned several properties, and was very fit and active. He made me laugh and had a very literary and intelligent sense of humor. My dad's wife was adding all this up and thought he sounded just perfect until I revealed that he was Black. She just couldn't wrap her mind around that and, in the end, said something like, "What a pity" and said I should think about any future children we might have before I took it further. Her question asking how dark-skinned he was spoke volumes about her own biases. My reasons for being lukewarm about this gentleman had nothing to do with his race, but she would never understand that.

Somehow, I knew that the only man my father and his wife would immediately accept was the one I would likely never meet or fall in love with, and that realization took the pressure off. Finding the religious, cultural, and class perfect match for them was less important to me. Class seemed to be where they ended up getting the most hung up, and certainly their own upbringing and distinct divisions across class made this tough for them. Classism is what I struggle with most in Egypt and other countries that have strict delineations.

Being raised in America where there is at least the stated belief in equality, acting like you are from a superior class just because you have more money or education is typically frowned upon. It happens of course, but people like this are generally considered snobs, and it isn't unusual for Americans to define classy behaviors as very different from wealthy ones. Having the luxury of having staff to do your shopping, cleaning, tending to children, caring for elders, and keeping homes in working order may still seem like a dream to many Americans however. To pay for all these services in the United States is beyond all but the richest of people. In Egypt, servant families have grown up parallel to the families who rely on them, and although there are also unwritten rules that the upper-class families should abide by regarding how to treat their servants well, these rules fall far from anything we might consider egalitarian in the United States.

Knowing the cultural component behind the class divide doesn't change the fact that I think having a servant class that is treated as "less than" is wrong. I know this is my American egalitarian upbringing, and I also know that there is a wide variety of treatment among the domestic help that runs households, raises children, and feeds families in Egypt and throughout much of the world. I still carry a bit of shame when I recall several instances that are considered socially appropriate in Egypt at the time and that I cringed at when they were happening.

On one occasion, we were at the beach and Salah, my father's cook and house helper, had come inside and was attempting to wait on me. I was just getting a glass of iced tea after spending hours on the veranda lazily reading my book. He had been working like a dog all morning in the humidity and heat—cleaning, moving furniture, doing things in the yard, etc. These were all part of his job, and he was of course being paid, however small a pittance the working wages were for him. When he saw I wanted tea, he stopped what he was doing and came running to do it for me. It's a funny thing. I don't mind being waited on in other contexts, but this class context drives me crazy. I told him not to worry and that I was fine and proceeded to pour him a glass as well as myself, and I motioned for him to sit and have some tea and rest for a minute as he was clearly exhausted. He was uncomfortable immediately, and I knew I had committed a major faux pas. I knew he wasn't worried about any gender or flirting assumptions because this was never even a hinted at in our relationship. He was a bit younger than I, and I had known him for some time, sent clothes with him for his wife and kids, and tried in my best broken Arabic to communicate with him—he was always giving me vocabulary help when I needed it. We were simply friendly with each other.

I should have paid attention to his discomfort and not forced my American ways on him because when my father came in and saw him casually sitting on the chair in his dirty work clothes, he erupted. Salah's immediate reaction was to slink to the floor, eyes lowered. He was literally sitting at the foot of the chair looking like a puppy that had been scolded for being on the furniture. I had brought this on Salah and felt angry at myself, angrier at my father, and ashamed overall that a simple act of kindness could cause the cultural clash that it did. How any culture can justify this treatment of another human being is still beyond my personal comprehension, no matter how much I learn about different cultures—sometimes the values collide. I know that my family in Egypt is from an educated and privileged class and that my father comes from an older generation and that his age also plays into how he sees class differences. There is an emerging middle class in Egypt, but it will take a long time for this to change cultural patterns.

The social rules vary a bit of course, and my younger cousins and many of my aunts share meals and have a more friendly employer-employee-like relationship with their servants, but their place as second-class citizens and servants is still considered their appropriate place, and people behave accordingly. I have to be very careful when I am in Egypt as these values collisions can arise for me, and they aren't always in my home.

On another occasion, I found myself crying in a police station in Cairo, desperately trying to get Salah's papers, which he must carry at all times, back to him. We had gone to the bazaar together, and I had bought many gifts to bring back to friends, so I had many bags, several of which were bulky, yet Salah would not let me carry any of them. My walking around bag-free while he struggled to carry all my purchases made no sense to me, and I was embarrassed to have him carry all my bags. To me, this seemed ridiculous, so I playfully argued with him, and as we were smiling and clearly bantering with each other about who was going to carry the bags, a policeman from the tourist police branch came and harshly interrogated him. He was yelled at and literally dragged to the station. I followed and, with increasing temper, demanded to know what was going on.

The sergeant had seen us and immediately knew that we were not of the same class because of our appearances. He also assumed that Salah was out of line with me and perhaps was even trying to rob me. I explained to the officer in my halting Arabic that he was my "friend"—not knowing or even wanting to use the exact word for servant. The use of the word *friend* immediately triggered the officer to think I was a Western tourist covering for a local thief I took pity on. Hours later, after calmly explaining that he worked for our family and then finally resorting to tears, we were released, but Salah was given a harsh reprimand by the authorities and told to come the next day to retrieve his papers. I made some excuse to my father that I needed Salah the next day to help me with some more shopping, and we went together to retrieve his papers as he needed his "employer" to vouch for him in order to get them back. Given the reality of classism in Egypt—especially among my father's generation—I knew that at least at first, Victor's background would be questioned.

"What does his father do?" "Where did he go to school?" "What is his degree?" These were some of the first questions that my father asked when he learned I had more than a passing interest in Victor. I knew that his father had a similar background to my Egyptian grandfather. Both were politicians at a fairly high level in their respective countries, were well respected in their communities, and provided well for their families. Victor however had not finished college but had a great job in an oil company in Peru, so he had left school for work before he graduated. Later, when he was told in the company that in order to progress any further he had to become fluent in English, he moved to the States and in six months had perfected English enough to learn a new trade and find a job in computers, allowing him to live independently and reroute himself away from a career in the oil business to something he also now really enjoyed.

I found that pretty amazing and couldn't imagine that most people could accomplish the same in six months in a foreign country and culture. To me, I saw how intelligent and resourceful Victor was. To my father, our educational gap caused him concern, and he wanted to make sure Victor wasn't after what he perceived as a free ride.

When I met Victor, we matched each other on so many dimensions—in our religious and spiritual views, both opting for the day-to-day good living versus the organized practice. His kind and easygoing nature, how he cared for his family and friends, and how much he enjoyed socializing with people all seemed to feel more of a fit. He was also raised and had lived in different cultures spanning different socioeconomic levels and countries.

When Victor said that he would become Muslim to marry me, this eventually won over my father who, I know, realizes that neither Victor nor I will ever win the world's best Muslim prize but that we would be good and honorable people together all the same. Of course, his becoming a Muslim isn't something we will advertise to his Catholic family, but this is part of living across cultures and learning to just live and let live. His parents and family are very tolerant and open, and they do know the religious mix in my family and so were more concerned about whether or not I lived honorably and could be loving to their son.

My father fretted over this until he met Victor and saw that he was internally motivated to always be learning and that he was very intelligent and independent. Perhaps between my father's and my own advancing years, he put up less resistance than he would have had I been a younger bride-to-be, but now that he knows Victor and sees how we live, he is always asking about him and giving me advice on how I will need to act in order to be a good wife to him. Victor and I laugh at this, but I know it means that he's been fully accepted into the family.

Our first test as a couple would be when I was offered a job in Switzerland. We sold our cars and left sunny Southern California where we were living in separate places to begin a life together in a foreign country. Living in a foreign country was new to me although I had been exposed while growing up to many cultures and had travelled a lot. Victor, on the other hand, had lived in Peru, Venezuela, and the United States and already spoke several languages. He hadn't travelled as much as I had, but his international living experiences had prepared him for the culture shock that was ahead of us.

Switzerland is a beautiful country, and it has taken us awhile to get used to the ways of the people here. The first time I was scolded by an older woman for not waiting for the walk light at a crosswalk, I was mystified. There were no cars in sight and it was late at night, yet she stood there waiting for the green walk light. At the time, I didn't speak German at all, so I had no idea why she was scolding me. Later, both Swiss and German friends told me that I was likely being reprimanded because had a child been present, I would have been setting a bad example for them and teaching them behaviors that would put them in danger.

This rule-following culture can be exasperating as can the unfathomably high costs of things here, but Switzerland works. People here do not seem as obsessed with consuming as much as they can as prices make this unthinkable with the exception of only the filthy rich. They know they have a beautiful country, and they have planned to keep it that way with recycling and an environmental concern for their surroundings that is admirable.

The other nice thing about their practice of self-policing is that it has built a certain safety and security here that is not found in too many other places in the world. Public transport is an example of how deep the honor system is here. To ride a tram or bus, you must have a ticket or a pass, but rarely do you have to present this to anyone as it is largely on the honor system. Plain clothed enforcement agents do occasionally ask to see your ticket, but in the last three years, I think I have been asked five times to present a ticket, and out of carloads of people, I have only ever once seen someone without a ticket. I could relay countless stories of lost valuables being returned by strangers or correct change when someone has overpaid being quickly returned.

We bicycle a lot on the many wonderful trails throughout the country, and there are fields of flowers that are also on the honor system. The first time I encountered one of these, I thought I had landed in Oz. Rows of gladiolas, sunflowers, dahlias, etc., were in a large field. No one was there—just a cardboard sign with the prices by stem of each flower, some pruning shears and string, and a small metal box with a coin slot. You pick what you want and deposit your money, and that's it! I couldn't help but think how that system would play out in Southern California where I had come from.

There is a flip side to any culture, so the three riot-gear clad police who showed up at 11:30 p.m. at the mellow dinner party we were having on our roof deck one Saturday night came as a surprise. We had gotten a noise complaint because there is a rule that after 10:00 p.m., you must be quiet. I had to give my passport and permit numbers as well as my boss's name and phone number. When I went in to work the following day, I wondered if Ella Fitzgerald on our iPod player was going to get us deported! My boss laughed and just said, "Welcome to Switzerland."

Similar rules around flushing toilets at night and when you can do basic home things like gardening, laundry, washing your car, and hanging up pictures are all far stricter than anyplace else I have lived. We laugh at these anomalies now and just try to follow the rules. There are a lot of them, and the Swiss seem overly fond of them, but they do have an orderly and peaceful society. When it seems too sterile, we hop on a plane or train and easily visit plenty of places with more color, but we have truly grown to appreciate how this society functions and are trying very hard to be respectful guests here. We don't know where we will call home yet, but for now, it is in Switzerland where we are yet again experiencing "which one of these things are not like the others." It helps in living internationally to be used to not fitting in, and since there are many people from other countries here, it has been easy to meet people from all over the world. We've enjoyed it so much we have even sought out ways to do more of it through home exchanging and couch surfing.

These communities are not for everyone as you have to generally trust that people are good and verify them through a series of e-mails and references. In the end, you open your home or stay in a home of complete strangers.

My experience with these communities has been really good. Home exchanging, where you swap homes for weekends or longer, seem to be set up to swap like for like, and so you typically end up staying in a home comparable to your own (or you at least try to). Couch surfing takes intercultural relations even further, and for the connections it fosters, it really is fantastic. The name had me thinking that it must only be for hostelers and partying college kids until I was asked by a good friend in her fifties who hosts regularly if I wouldn't mind meeting up with a couple she was hosting but had a schedule conflict with.

They were a terrific couple from Israel, and our walking tour of the city and stops for snacks and a coffee had us connecting across our cultures in ways that likely would not have naturally presented itself. I found myself wondering how this simple personal connection might have positively impacted some of my Egyptian relatives, and I was glad I had the opportunity to share personal time and stories with this wonderful couple.

The whole idea of couch surfing really fits into the field of diversity and inclusion, so for me, it has been a really nice way to build an extended community and get exposed to local cultures and places. I have been hosted and/or connected with a local contact in Norway, Brazil, New Jersey, Germany, the UK, and the Czech Republic. I have hosted people from France, the United States, Columbia, Germany, Israel, and Italy and will keep on doing this as there is nothing like seeing a place and experiencing the culture with people from there and being able to share your own.

This community polices itself as well, and I have not had a bad experience. Low-, middle-, and upper-class homes have all opened their doors to me, and the commonality is the love of making these cross-cultural connections and understanding different cultures through firsthand encounters. I have heard more personal stories and shared my own all over the world through this community, and it has been a really nice way to make real connections. A simple social media platform does the initial connecting and ongoing organizing, but it is the people participating, nearly 2.5 million people in over 245 countries, which are reaching across many dimensions of diversity to understand one another and build a connected global community.

So it is with couch surfing that I close my still-unfolding story. My quest for meaningful, inspiring, magnetic, and growth experiences across cultures will continue (beyond couch surfing) as I am a bit addicted to the cause of bringing diverse people and communities together. I hope to continuously get better at helping others do this also—be they in my family, my circle of friends, or the corporations and communities I work with.

Once I started hearing the stories of my coauthors, I knew that we would stay connected, and I am ever thankful for the grace, love, and inspiration each of them feed me with. My life is so much better for reaching out across cultures to create an extended family, and although for me, this was born out of necessity—what with my family so spread out and disconnected—I'd have it no other way. The world's a small place, and the power of your story is just waiting to connect you to someone. We can all take part in designing a multicultural world that works—one family member, one colleague, and one story at a time.

# ONE LIFE TO LIVE:
# A CRISIS OF CONVERGENCE
# AT THE CROSSROADS

Tommy Smith

THERE WAS NO doubt about it; the time had come. The delays, the further ruminations, the introspection, and the soul searching had furnished all the relevant data for consideration that they could provide. Unfortunately, the outcome of this exercise was precisely what I had feared—and expected; I had to make a choice. I suppose on the one hand this should have been flattering. In three separate and distinct (some would even say opposing) professional directions, I had been requested to play a significant leading role. Each was an area that I am passionate about, each was an area that I had the good fortune of demonstrating a greater-than-average degree of proficiency in, and most importantly, each was an area that could ultimately improve the status of my people. The questions I could no longer avoid answering were the following:

1. Should I pursue my plans to open up a consulting engineering firm?
2. Should I accept the pastorate at one of the largest African American Baptist Churches in Hayward, California?
3. Should I accept the department head position leading affirmative action and diversity at one of the premier research and development laboratories in the nation?

In the pages that follow, I look forward to sharing with you the decision that I ultimately made and how I went about making it. Before doing so, I think an equally interesting story is how I came to have those three options in the first place.

My interest in telling my story stems from the fact that beyond the aspects of it that concern me, I believe it is in many respects characteristic of a multitalented, gifted, yet abused people who had to find this out for themselves the hard way. America's socialization process for African Americans not only seeks to withhold our fundamental identity, but it also seeks to obscure any and all notions of the gifts we hold within this identity. The biggest tragedy in this process is that many of us believe this nation to be credible, and thus when told that we have no worth, we sadly, and with reservation, go on to believe it. For those who, through enlightened upbringing, sheer contrariness, or simply the grace of God, refuse to believe it, it is not uncommon to not only discover the lie but to also realize that you may have more talents than life to use them in! No wonder they try to keep it a secret!

## An Engineer by Any Other Name

Of all the elements that make me who I am, my technical nature, the engineer in me, is perhaps the most prominent. I say this because it flavors how I view and perceive the world, how I approach problems, and how I determine expectations. My belief is that even though something this fundamental is probably born and not taught, how basic tendencies such as these are nurtured and enabled greatly impact how well they are ultimately developed. For this reason, I would like to start my story with when and how the engineer in me was first recognized.

"Tell me why." Those three words do more than simply sum up my primary mode of interacting with my parents as an inquisitive youth growing up in Oakland, California. They actually form the title of the first book I remember receiving as a gift. As I recall, the book was huge and full of intricate and colorful pictures and illustrations about how all kinds of things worked; cars, bicycles, magnets, rain, and electricity were among its many subjects. Losing myself in its pages both satisfied and further stimulated my thirst to know how things worked. Why I wondered about such things, I couldn't tell you. Nor could I say what I intended to do with the information. I had no grand designs to seek a career in science. I hadn't an inkling of what an engineer was, and no one in my family was in any way connected to science or technology. It was just plain curiosity. I just wondered how things worked. I suppose that, if we are born into this planet predisposed toward certain talents or abilities (or "hardwired" as a physicist friend of mine would call it), this simply was mine.

## A Mother's Insight

My mother appears to be the first to identify this tendency within me. She was fond of telling the story of watching me press the cushion down on her living room couch, intently and studiously pondering the cushion's almost "magical" ability to spring back to its original shape after being pressed down. As an engineering student, I would eventually come to realize that this property is called the material's modulus of elasticity. However, since preschoolers know nothing of such things, I came up with another method to solve this mystery. My mother goes on to say that I disappeared into the kitchen and soon returned with a pair of scissors and proceeded to cut the cushion open to observe its springiness firsthand! Being the remarkable and innately intelligent woman that she was, my mother did not wish to completely drive my inquisitiveness out of me (perhaps knowing that one day it would yield dividends to me as a researcher). However, she did wish to spare her furniture (not to mention radios, sewing machines, and kitchen utensils) from my further experimental investigations! And so, even though I did get disciplined for cutting up her furniture, my parents did buy me that tell-me-why book to help nurture this aspect of my personality. This was followed by several other items of the same genre—building sets, microscopes, and related toys designed to nurture an interest in science and learning.

Buying books and educational toys were not the only ways my parents expressed their commitment to learning and education. Although neither of them was college educated, they clearly valued education. Their work schedules and their own academic limitations kept them from being as personally involved in our learning as many parents are today. Even so, in their own way, they made it clear to us that education was very important. For example, I can recall my mother asking almost daily, "Did you get your lesson out?" even though I cannot recall her ever actually helping me with my homework.

The emphasis on education in my household was much greater than in the community at large and especially within the subculture of hardheaded boys that I ran with. This led to the establishment of what would eventually become a consistent recurring theme in my life: the dichotomy of reconciling positions that, while frequently in opposition with each other, somehow managed to come together in me. Holding traditionally divergent views did not bother me, but handling the divided loyalties that they frequently engender has often been challenging. Valuing education in the midst of friends who had little regard for it was an early introduction to these struggles, but it wasn't my first. That unfortunate circumstance grew out of an incident that, though it occurred almost a half-century ago, continues to be a painful and disquieting memory.

THE DiCE GROUP

# Cindy

This story involves a little girl in my kindergarten class named Cindy. She was short, very dark-skinned, and looked exactly like the pictures I'd seen of little slave children down South. I had no notion of romantic love at that time, but Cindy was my favorite person to be with in the whole world. We would run and play together at recess, and I genuinely enjoyed being with her. Even now when I think of her, I can see her face totally taken over by her sweet and innocent smile. But what I didn't know was the Eurocentric aesthetic standards of this society had defined Cindy as ugly. I wasn't supposed to like Cindy. According to my older siblings, who were Black girls themselves and had already begun to buy into this deception, she was undesirable. They began to tease me about liking and playing with little *Black* Cindy. And so, consistent with what I have come to recognize as a personal character flaw of epic proportions, I abandoned Cindy.

I never believed the hype about Cindy. I knew she wasn't a bad person. I knew she wasn't unkind or mean. I knew I still liked her. But I abandoned her just the same because my sisters said she was ugly. I abandoned her because of her dark skin and archetypical African features. I abandoned her because she was *Black*. Ultimately, I abandoned her because I was too weak to take the stand that I knew I should take. I abandoned my principles and someone I loved for the fear of losing the love of others. I wish I could say that this was the one and only time I abandoned someone I loved (and who had good reason to assume that they could count on my love), but sadly, it isn't. On two other occasions, each successively more treacherous, I repeated this spiritually colluding, soul-eroding behavior.

Getting back to education (and, unfortunately, more contradictions), I did have to find a way to reconcile the fact that I personally valued education a lot more that my homies did. Fortunately, this situation was favorably resolved primarily due to two factors. The first is that I never did run with the true delinquents. I actually never had much interaction with those who were intractably bad and clearly on the fast track to reform school and prison. Since the disdain of education was directly proportional to the degree of social pathology, the friends I did have were not as educationally resistant as the most extreme guys. The other factor that worked in my favor is that just as I approached the age when this issue would have assumed more prominence in my life, our family moved to a better neighborhood. As a result, in the middle of the sixth grade (my last year of elementary school), I transferred to a more academically focused school. This was also my first school where Blacks were a minority, a condition that would remain true for the rest of my formal education.

In my previous school, I was a good student, but socially, I was rather unremarkable and average. However, I had the presence of mind to realize that being the new kid would allow me to reinvent myself. A few days into the new school, I remember asking a fellow Black sixth grader who the king of the school was. In my former school, this was the title given to the person who was the best fighter in the school. However, my new friend was unfamiliar with the terminology and asked if the king of the school meant the smartest person (which it logically should have meant in an academic environment). Feeling smugly superior, I told him what I meant. What I didn't tell him was how secretly relieving it was to know that I was now in a place where academic achievement was at least as valued as fisticuffs.

In retrospect, I don't know how I would have fared had my family not moved from Brookfield. My Cindy incident clearly shows how important the esteem of others was to me. Would I have been strong enough to be a good student in the light of the antiacademic ghetto mentality around me? I honestly don't know. But I am grateful to have been spared the struggle. I was still a young Black male, and I still wanted to be cool. But now I could at least accommodate within that persona a healthy component of academic achievement. Thanks to my parents' unrelenting drive to improve their lot (and no doubt a bit of serendipitous divine timing), our family's move in early 1966 helped to put me on a course of being someone who could always be down with the brothers while simultaneously embracing the value of intellectual development. Even today, when I have occasion to visit the hood, I am still able to fit right in.

## The Middle Passage—Formative Events in Adolescence

I went on to be a very good student in junior high and high school, typically being thought of as one of the smartest people in the class. My social development also progressed well. I played sports, went to dances, and generally participated in most school functions. Another part of my character and identity also began to develop during this time. My junior high and high school years coincided with a great deal of racial turmoil in the nation and in the Bay Area in particular. It seems as though my personal experiences paralleled Black America's struggles with the identity formation issues of the post-civil rights period in the 1960s. The anger expressed in the riots, the confusion after Dr. King's death, and the immense sense of pride that accompanied the introduction of "natural" hairstyles and James Brown's "Say It Loud—I'm Black and I'm Proud" all seemed to apply to me in the same proportion as to the country at large.

The new feelings of pride I began to experience as a result of self-identity and self-affirmation and also beginning to emerge in the Black community began the process of helping the world to make a little more sense to me. Studying slavery in school and seeing the differences between my community and those I saw on television made it very clear to me that a fundamental injustice had been done and was continuing to occur to my people. As a young man, the militancy of the Black power and Black pride movement—particularly the Black Panthers—was a response that I could relate to much better than the passive acquiescence that I assumed had been our response up until then. I strongly resonated with the idea of Black men standing up to the wrongs we had endured and, if necessary, using force to protect our rights as free citizens. However, this period of identity formation was not without its challenges.

## Fernando

When my family moved from Brookfield in 1966, one of my new best friends was a boy named Fernando Martinez. As you might have guessed, Fernando was Latino. We played sports and were in Boy Scouts together and spent a fair amount of time at each other's homes. Fernando and I were such good friends that I still find it hard to believe that the events that I now refer to as treacherous act number 2 ever could have occurred. But they did. They occurred on a date that for other reasons was already assured to live on in infamy. Unfortunately for me, I managed to make April 4, 1968, an even worse date than it already was.

I was in the eighth grade; we had just finished showering after gym class and were on our way home when we got word that Dr. Martin Luther King Jr. had been killed. I don't remember any of the names or faces involved, but I and the six or seven young brothers I was with that afternoon were angry, indignant, and looking for revenge. We were neither social critics nor politically astute, but we knew that Dr. King was a good man who advocated nonviolence, and he had been violently slain. And if that's how White folks wanted to play it, then we were ready to bring it on!

So there we were, looking for a White boy to beat up and take out our collective rage on, and who should show up but Fernando. As Fernando approached, what we all knew but didn't vocalize was that he really wasn't what we were looking for. He wasn't "White." But on the other hand, he wasn't Black either, so the group-think of the moment was, *He'll do!* I knew their thoughts, and I knew that I wasn't comfortable with this. It wasn't right, and I knew I should have spoken up and said it wasn't right, but I was somehow frozen. As he got closer and one of the guys shoved him and another grabbed him, I could feel my pulse quicken, and these awful feelings of embarrassment, shame, cowardice, and most of all, confusion began to overwhelm my thinking. I needed more time! It was coming too fast, I couldn't sort it out fast enough—things I heard in church, things I knew about loyalty, but loyalty to who? My friend Fernando or my people?

The confusion, the hesitation, and the fear seemed to swirl around in my mind. I knew what I *should* do; common decency demanded that I step up in front of Fernando and between the brothers and say, "No, man, he's cool, he's my friend—we've got to find someone else!" But that's not the way it happened. I did not step up. I did not interfere. I did not rescue Fernando. I did not come to his defense. I at least had the decency to refrain from the assault and from actually hitting him, but that was too little too late. Worst of all, I did not (could not) look at him. Dr. King's was not the only death that day. A friendship died. And along with it, another little piece of my soul.

I managed to keep living, growing, and developing after that incident. I suppose like most shortcomings, I simply rationalized it away enough for me to continue on. But even though I'm sure I tried to banish the incident from memory, my subconscious mind stubbornly refused to comply. I don't recall all the self-talk I engaged in attempting to reconcile that incident, but what I can recall is becoming more and more militant. As I completed junior high and went on to high school, the movement grew and my Afrocentric consciousness along with it.

My identity was also influenced by a number of written works. These to me all seemed to collectively express the consciousness of a Black culture no longer willing to passively wait for White society to give us equality (e.g., *A Glorious Age in Africa, Africa's Gift to America, Manchild in the Promised Land, The Spook Who Sat by the Door,* and *Message to the Black Man,* among others). These books all taught me something factual about my heritage and gave me something to be proud of, but by far the most impactful of all was *The Autobiography of Malcolm X.* Of all the voices giving expression to the Black experience in America, Malcolm's spoke most directly and eloquently to my soul. His passionate devotion, sharp intellect, and verbal fluency all deeply impressed and inspired me. But what I admired most

THE DiCE GROUP

of all about Malcolm, and the reason that to this very day he remains my most revered African American hero, was his uncompromising courage. I admired Malcolm's courage as demonstrated in his willingness to stand against enemies. Not only did I aspire to emulate this courage in the face of enemies, I suspect that on a more subconscious plane, I longed to also be able to direct it at friends when necessary.

After the incident with Fernando, I had no other non-Black friends until going away to college. I'm not sure if this choice was conscious or unconscious, but I am sure that it was the result of me being so immersed in the movement that no one non-Black ever had a real chance of getting close to me. However, even though my friends were all Black, I continued to have difficulties in the area of friendships. A good example of this is what happened when my friends began to experiment with marijuana.

Rather than join in because it was the cool thing to do, I resisted the peer pressure and instead read a massive volume on the subject called *The Marijuana Papers*. I did this partly because I wanted to wade through the hype provided by both sides to find out the truth about marijuana, but I also had a subtler (and less healthy) reason for doing so. For whatever reason, it was important for me to outperform my friends. I didn't think I was better from the standpoint of being from a better family, being better off financially, or being better in a religious or moralistic sense. I just needed to know that I could do something that they couldn't. In this case, I decided to be the one that didn't smoke weed. I would be the one who was able to stand firm even if everyone else in the crowd bowed to the pressure to indulge. I didn't take this stand because I thought marijuana was so wrong. I took it because deep inside, I felt it demonstrated that I had a superior level of mental discipline than my buddies did.

I did not recognize this at the time, and it is difficult to admit now, but I have come to realize the reason for this behavior. In our world, guys were cool if they looked especially nice, dressed well, had a nice car, were star athletes, or were major thugs. I was none of these things, but I had an iron will and just enough self-confidence to not have to rely solely on peer approval for self-esteem. Therefore, even though I had no trouble partaking of wine or beer at parties, when it came to weed or cigarettes or stealing, I was completely impervious to peer pressure. This was my way of standing out. I suppose this could have been viewed as a positive trait, but deep down inside, it troubled me. It bothered me to know that inside I was competing with my friends—guys who had no clue that inside I was betraying their trust by secretly trying to best them.

Although at the time I was able to ignore my discomfort with this willingness to misrepresent my inner truth, eventually it became too difficult to do without sacrificing my integrity. Fortunately (and quite painfully), I was never able to force my conscience into submission on this behavior, which ultimately led me to embark on a course to confront my duplicitous tendencies head-on. Like most major character-impacting decisions, this was not a simple matter of glibly making a choice one day. Instead, it marked the opening foray in a protracted struggle for authenticity. While I am happy to report many victories in this war, I cannot say that it is over. Indeed, some vestiges of it continue to this day. But while I can't claim complete victory in this war of what I have now come to describe as collusion, I can say with confidence that I am committed to authenticity, and this in and of itself is a victory.

My high school experiences, the Black power movement, and collective literary voices, with brother Malcolm's leading the way, helped to mold me into the archetypical angry young Black man. By high school graduation, I was defiant, confident, self-motivated, and self-defined as could be, but beneath the surface, telltale indications of inner conflict were there—albeit hidden by the tough, threatening Black militant exterior.

## The Cal Poly Experience

In the fall of 1972, I arrived at California Polytechnic State University at San Luis Obispo as a fiercely independent, intelligent, angry young Black man. This university of over 15,000 students had a Black student enrollment of only 250. Although my junior high and high schools were integrated, I had never experienced anything like this degree of whiteness. Needless to say, the person who emerged from this institution two and a half years later was not the same one who went in! In a scant thirty months, my views on life, personal identity, and especially race relations were radically altered. Recalling all the circumstances that contributed to these changes would require a book in itself. However, one incident in particular captures the essence of the greatest changes I experienced—those in my views concerning race.

## Getting Unstuck

In high school, I had developed the habit of spending time alone in reflective, contemplative thought. My preferred locations for this therapeutic activity were initially the hills of East Oakland. However, Cal Poly's proximity to some of California's most beautiful beaches offered many more locations for me to carry out this thought therapy. One day, I had driven my car out to Pismo Beach to indulge in this favorite activity of mine. When I got ready to leave, I discovered that while the parking spot that I had chosen offered excellent vistas of the ocean, it offered almost no traction for tires. In other words, my car was stuck in the sand. After trying to no avail to rock myself out of this predicament, I realized that I was only making the situation worse and digging the hole even deeper. At this point, I remember trying to calm myself down by thinking logically about the predicament; but no matter how I approached it, the answer was still the same. I was helplessly and hopelessly stuck in the sand, and getting out was completely beyond my ability.

At this point, as I began to realize my complete helplessness in this situation, two individuals came upon the scene. These were not just any two individuals. They couldn't have been. I am convinced that they were the two people in the state who best contradicted the thoughts of a nineteen-year-old budding militant who had just reached the conclusion that the sole interest of White Americans in life was to exploit and marginalize all people of African descent. These two shaggy-haired white hippie types came up to me and said with a totally unsuspecting and cheerful friendliness, "What's going on, man?" After I explained my predicament, they offered to give it a try. As I watched in complete amazement (accompanied by a combination of dread and denial), these two guys did what I couldn't. After a few syncopated rocks back and forth, they freed my 1963 Ford Fairlane from what I was sure would be its seaside grave. With a closing "Far out, dude," they continued on their path and soon disappeared into the dunes. Despite my most Herculean mental gyrations, I knew there was but one explanation for their actions—complete altruism—which in turn left only one description of my earlier conclusions about race relations—complete bull!

## Enter God

Those two young White men at Pismo Beach forced me to look in the mirror and make a choice: to go on living a lie or incorporate what I learned and continue seeking for truth. Needless to say, I admitted the error of my ways. Convinced of my myopic perspectives, my searching continued and eventually brought me to God.

My relationship with God actually began much earlier than college. Although my family wasn't particularly religious, like many African Americans of that generation, we attended church on a regular basis. The theological understanding that this produced wasn't particularly profound; I would describe it roughly as knowing that God was real, and we human beings owed him some amount of homage—even if it was only perfunctory. As I grew older, my theological views evolved somewhat, but they were still fairly basic. By the time I left for college, I essentially felt that God is real. He expects humanity to behave a certain way. If we do, all will be well, but for those who don't, there will be a day of reckoning.

My Cal Poly years altered these views somewhat. It's not so much that they were replaced, but they were certainly expanded. As I met people from different religious persuasions, I gradually began to question the exclusivity of my protestant theology. In particular, Eastern religious traditions not only appealed to my contemplative side, but they also complemented the learning I was receiving in science classes about how the universe operated. An example of this that I still quite vividly recall is while sitting in a physics course learning about ballistic motion, as the instructor explained that a ball in flight would follow a curved path completely determined by the angle and magnitude of its initial velocity vector, I distinctly remember thinking, *How does the ball know to obey these rules? What if it wants to take a different flight path?* These early musings of mine eventually culminated in a fairly comprehensive systematic theology (which will be the subject of a future writing project). More germane to this story, such thoughts marked the beginning of a religious/spiritual influence that would eventually come to dominate the landscape of my consciousness.

Developing my religious stance was a process that was just as animated and dynamic as my political journey. The strong influence of Malcolm X already had me a little curious about Islam. Meeting people from the Middle East and Africa at Cal Poly caused me to look even deeper into this faith. Eastern religions were the next stop along the way. These had a special appeal to me in the way that they easily accommodated the metaphysical blending of spiritual and physical things. While my exposure to these faiths could only be called rudimentary at best (I did some reading of the Koran, Bhagavad Gita, and the Nine-Fold Path), I did appreciate the new perspectives and insights they brought. And although their influence was never strong enough to replace Christianity as my chosen faith, they did allow me to do just that—to *choose* a faith, as opposed to blindly accepting that of my parent's by default.

Although my religious persuasion remained Christian, I felt no hesitation about modifying it to accommodate elements of the other belief systems that I found compelling in my search for truth. I felt no hesitation, but perhaps I should have. After all, with no formal training or guidance, I was brazenly critiquing and resynthesizing religious philosophies that had been under development in some cases for millennia. What if I made a mistake? However, there is no need to treat this idea hypothetically because the fact of the matter is I did make a mistake—a huge mistake. I meant well, but the fact is my homegrown theology contained some pretty serious flaws. The most significant of which, without a doubt, was my feeling that spiritual insight could be enhanced by certain chemical/biological substances. I found out the hard way that this is not true (at least, it wasn't true for me). In fact, this belief led me to one of the most severe crisis points I have ever encountered in life. The story is too involved to go into here, but the short version is that in 1977 (after dropping out of college and living as a jazz/funk/rock band musician for two years), I experienced an event that made it unequivocally clear to me that my homegrown theology was also bull (to go along with my earlier views on race). Suffice it to say that mythical Icarus was not the only person to have flown too high!

My hippie-musician phase ended in a chemically induced crash landing in March of 1977. In its aftermath, I left the band, joined a *real* church, traded in my homegrown theology for orthodoxy, and entered the next phase of my life—adulthood.

## Starting Over

In April 1977, I started over. I do not mean to imply that after this point, my life became problem-free. My turning point did not eliminate problems, but I think it may have done something even better. After my spiritual conversion experience, I entered an approximately three-year period of almost constant church attendance, Bible study, and prayer. What happened to me during that period resulted in my having a continual awareness of God's active participation in my life. That is, I now knew that my life mattered to God.

Since this idea is taught in countless Sunday schools across the nation and the world, it may sound a little melodramatic for me to tout it as this remarkable, life-changing epiphany. Be that as it may, I finally got it. I realized that God was interested in my spiritual development and that he was continually present in all my thoughts and activities. His presence was not as a traffic cop waiting to write me a ticket for every infraction. Nor was he an overprotective governess preventing every potentially hurtful collision or misstep. He was a mentor. A wise observer who would caution against some things, encourage others, but always allow free will to be exercised and learning to occur. He valued instruction, experience, and reflection—all predicated upon good faith. This I learned was his way. This I learned was his way with me. I left that experience convinced of his love. I left it convinced that God had my best interest at heart. I left it knowing that my best interest was at the heart of his design for my life. And I left it committed to living my life in a way that is consistent with this design.

Thus I embarked on the journey of my new life with God as a constant companion. I have no doubt done many things that have disappointed God since this time, many of which have been equally disappointing to me and caused deep regret. This includes the most difficult experience of my life—a traumatic marriage followed by the protracted, agonizing, and ultimately futile struggle to save it. But with each flawed decision and with each error in judgment, I have rediscovered and been affirmed and comforted by God's unconditional love, timeless wisdom, and inexhaustible mercy.

Since my life-altering experience happened in conjunction with ending my band days, a very practical next move was reentering the workforce. This I gladly did and with entirely new results due to my new mind-set. I suddenly saw the world as an interconnected system of labor in which our quality of life was dependent on each member of society doing their part by making their contributions to the common good. Prior to this point, I had not done much in the way of contributing to the common good, but I now desperately wanted to. I began working with a total commitment to quality and excellence and soon landed at one of the nation's premiere research and development facilities, the Lawrence Livermore National Laboratory. While at the lab, I reenrolled in university and eventually became the first (and only) African American to win the laboratory's undergraduate Technical Scholarship.

In parallel with my technical education, I was deeply involved in studying the scriptures. While this did not include formal university training or seminary, I had managed to develop some fairly effective study skills. Aided by the insightful guidance of my pastor and a voracious appetite for reading the scriptures, I immersed myself in rigorous and comprehensive Bible study. Although I am somewhat at a loss to explain how, I thankfully acknowledge God's blessings to me in this area. In time, I became known as a thorough Bible scholar and teacher and an effective speaker. Eventually, I accepted the call to the ministry. The denomination and church that I worshipped in at that time did not put a great deal of emphasis on seminary training, so I continued with my technical education during this time. In fact, my newfound spiritual insights were complementing my technical studies and vice versa. This union of science and theology has contributed to a fresh perspective in many aspects of my ministry and spiritual understanding.

After completing my engineering degree, I went on to work on a number of challenging assignments that in my wildest dreams I never would have thought that I would be able to contribute to. But contribute I did, including leading the design of (and being awarded US patent no. 5,017,779) an electron energy spectrometer system I co-invented as a part of the nation's Strategic Missile Defense Initiative (SDI).

Although I enjoyed the work I was doing tremendously, by the end of the '80s, I was beginning to feel an urge to move on to something new. This was due to a combination of factors, including the recent breakup of my marriage, having experienced a few race-related incidents in the workplace, and receiving an unsolicited offer to enter a consulting business. I had also recently passed the professional engineers licensing examination—a necessary prerequisite for conducting a consulting business of the type I was asked to consider. Although none of the above factors alone would have sufficed to cause me to make a major move, the combination of them all was persuasive. After much thought and pondering, I decided that I would leave the lab and begin a consulting business. The one caveat was that since most of my actual engineering experience was in esoteric research and development areas and the consulting market was in the area of engineering for conventional buildings and facilities, I decided to transfer to the department of the lab that did this type of work for a couple of years to gain a bit more experience before leaving.

So that was that. The plan was made. I still wanted to live my life God's way, and I still didn't have a crystal ball, but I thought I was making better, higher-quality educated guesses. The plan wasn't perfect, but I felt it gave me enough latitude, opportunities to rely on proven strengths, and potential for excitement to make it worth pursuing. It also left the door open for me to engage more fully in Christian work and ministry—something that I was being more and more encouraged to pursue by people in my faith community. This last point would become increasingly important over the next few years.

I had recently joined a new church, and even though I tried to keep my ministerial credentials incognito, that all changed when I was asked to deliver the keynote address for the Black history program one year. Over the next few years, my reputation as a speaker and teacher continued to grow, but I wouldn't find out until later just how much it grew and to whom. Getting back to the laboratory, I had made my decision to leave and had taken the initial steps to execute the plan when a completely unanticipated suggestion came my way.

## Enter Diversity

The suggestion had to do with a new idea beginning to emerge on the lab's corporate scene—workforce diversity. Unbeknownst to me at the time, the laboratory had fared poorly in an affirmative action audit conducted by the US Department of Labor (i.e., the Office of Federal Contract Compliance Programs [OFCCP]) and was under some pressure to complete a number of good faith actions intended to affirm its support for workplace equity and affirmative action. One such action that eventually came to my awareness was the creation of a position entitled Minority Issues Program Leader. This position, along with its women's issues program leader counterpart, was formally advertised as a 30 percent time position in which the selected candidate would continue to work on their current job for 70 percent of their time and spend the remaining 30 percent working with the newly created Employee Equity and Compliance Center on programs and activities designed to increase career advancement opportunities for minorities and women at the laboratory. I decided to apply for this position for two primary reasons: The first is that since my high school days of being the Black Student Union president, I had maintained an active and energetic social activist interest. The second is that since I was planning on leaving the laboratory within the next couple of years, I felt helping to make the lab a more hospitable place for people like me would be a nice parting gift.

My candidacy was successful, and I was appointed to the job in 1991. The next two years were truly fascinating. I experienced a crash course on the "people" side of the laboratory, which proved to be an entirely different world from the technical environs that I was used to. Then to complicate matters further, the lab experienced its first ever large-scale diversity-based workforce complaint. As I worked through these situations and challenges, I began to notice first that the prospect of helping people to feel better about their chances of experiencing fair treatment at work was really gratifying, and second is that it was really difficult. I continued to keep in mind my plans for a consulting business. I even did a few projects during off-hours as an introduction to the field, but I also found myself increasingly drawn to diversity work. So far, my diversity involvement was exciting and refreshing, but it had not yet reached a stage of presenting me with any dilemmas. However, in very short order, it would.

During the two years that I held the part-time diversity position, I continued to work in the laboratory's facilities engineering department where I learned the ins and outs of performing the kind of engineering that would be helpful in future consulting endeavors. In parallel with this, as my two-year tenure in the diversity position drew to a close, the laboratory was facing a major budget and workforce restructuring challenge. Its response to that challenge included offering an early retirement program for employees in certain administrative areas. One of the areas involved was the (newly renamed) Affirmative Action and Diversity Program (AADP). It turned out that the seven senior-most leaders of this twenty-one-person program were retiring, including its director. My name surfaced at the top of the list of possible replacements. And thus we return to the place where I began this story.

## The Choice

I was faced with three choices involving three excellent opportunities in three areas that were near and dear to my heart. The first was the decision I had made two years prior to prepare for starting an engineering consulting business. I had made the transfer to facilities engineering and had completed enough side jobs and logistical preparations to officially launch the effort. With the city of Oakland having minority-owned business participation goals of 46 percent, the time to go into business would probably never be better. The second opportunity was diversity. Not only was my name at the top of the replacement department head list but I was also offered the position. The third choice involved ministry. Only a few months before receiving the AADP offer, I was asked to be the interim pastor in my new church after the pastor announced his retirement. Three great opportunities. All in areas I loved, all in areas I had demonstrated success in, and all capable of fulfilling what I sensed as a life calling.

I needed to make a choice. I chose diversity work. One of the biggest influences on the outcome of this choice was an individual who began this DiCE journey with us: Marvin R. Smith. Marvin was at that time a manager at the laboratory and, several years back, had the very job I was contemplating accepting. Marvin's counsel to me at that time was meaningful and timely. This had much to do with his wisdom and wealth of experience but most to do with the man himself. Marvin was a fearless, bold, powerful personality. Although he had a large frame and imposing presence, he had mastered the art of deemphasizing his power but not negating it. He was kind, friendly, always ready to unleash his powerful and comforting laugh, but equally capable of being completely resolute when the situation called for it. Of the many things I learned from Marvin, one of my most treasured is how important it is for underrepresented people to have an advocate in the workplace who is in every way the equal of those in power.

Marvin has since moved on and is now flying with the angels, but his encouragement helped open the door for me to make my decision. What helped me through it was the sense of purpose that I began to discern around my involvement in diversity work. It wasn't clear enough for me to articulate at the time, but retrospectively, I now see what made this work and choice so compelling. Looking back on the key pivotal events of the story I have shared, a pattern begins to emerge that I now feel made my choice of diversity inevitable.

## Cindy

The struggle to affirm Cindy's friendship in the face of my siblings' ridicule was my initial exposure to the politics of exclusion. Although it was perpetrated by the people closest to me in life, it was born out of the vile, dehumanizing racism America invented to justify the wholesale inhumane treatment of Africans (and other non-Europeans). My reluctant and shame-producing complicity in ostracizing Cindy made me uncomfortable enough, even as a kindergartner, to know that something was wrong with my world. A world so distorted by hegemonic racism that it forcibly stole her obvious beauty away from her through the blind complicity of those who should have most valiantly endorsed and protected it.

## I'm Black and I'm Proud!

The Black power/Black affirmation movement of the late sixties gave me a foundation upon which to frame my interface with society. My inner struggle to deny racism's claims of inferiority and assert our validity and complete equality as a people began as a silent one. As the movement developed, so did I; and eventually, the silence was finally broken when James Brown gave it musical expression, the Panthers gave it action, and brother Malcolm gave it purpose! Stepin Fetchit (the shuffling image of Black inferiority personified by actor Lincoln Perry) was dead. This is who I was. This is who America would have to deal with!

## Fernando

But what about Fernando? What about my friend? What if, while you try to take the time to sort it out, it ends up being too late? As painful as that incident was, I did not leave it with complete clarity on how to deal with divided loyalties. However, I did leave with this: my personal integrity is more important than group approval.

## Pismo Beach—Getting Unstuck in Mind and Manner

I thought the rules were clear. I thought the battle lines were drawn. I thought I knew how to deal with White folks. I thought they were the enemy. A stuck car in the sand convinced me otherwise. Integrity demanded it. The White calculus professor who told me I couldn't do math was real enough. But so were my rescuers. All were individuals, and I had the obligation to treat them all as such. Melanin content offered no insights into human character. I had no justifiable reason to systematically deny to any segment of humanity the respect and consideration that I myself would want.

## Salvation

And then there was God. The one who silently sat back and observed all these traumatic experiences I lived through. The one who did not intervene and physically prevent me from carrying out utterly inane actions. The one who allowed me to get married and divorced. The one who allowed these lessons to shape my soul. And throughout it all, the one who managed to unequivocally convey to me his complete love and acceptance to me *despite my shortcomings*. Of all the things I felt compelled to address, none was clearer than this: I had to let others (not just church members) know that despite it all, whoever we are, whatever we do, however we struggle, however we fail, whatever our weaknesses, across the entire human spectrum, we each matter to God.

The five lessons mentioned above were more than casual observations; they were powerful and profound episodes that had the effect of forming fundamental pieces and aspects of my character. They helped me to become who I am and continue to remain a part of me. For this reason, although I chose to perform diversity work, I did not choose to leave these elements out of my life. Rather, I chose diversity work because I felt it offered me the greatest opportunity to integrate and address this combination of interests. Just as my Christianity has been broadened by respecting other perspectives and my engineering effectiveness increased by viewing it as an acknowledgment of God's handiwork, my approach to diversity is not precisely canonical. In performing diversity work, I seek to remember and help others understand that

- we all lose when we allow peer pressure to obscure "Cindy's" beauty,
- all people need to and have a right to feel proud of their heritage,
- standing up for the rights of others is a prerequisite for personal integrity,
- sooner or later, each of us will be forced to choose between denying truth or our prejudices, and
- God has a passionate love for each one of us (including those outside of our range of acceptability).

## Convergence

I made the choice to do diversity work, but I was not and am not convinced that the choice must be mutually exclusive. Just as I have woven the five themes above into my approach to diversity, I believe that scientific and spiritual ideas can be added to diversity to create a holistic approach to uniting our species. That is, I believe that what began as a crisis of mutual exclusivity at a crossroads of careers can ultimately help point the way toward synergistic spiritual convergence.

I believe that the challenge of diversity is the fundamental problem of human existence. Biologists and geneticists consistently conclude that there is no biological basis for the concept of race. While it is true that our ancestors did *develop* on different continents and geographical regions, we are a single species and share a single common origin. Though we look physically different and have different cultural preferences, these differences do not validate the idea of race. Race is a sociopolitical concept created to justify disparate treatment of certain people groups. Further, while some differences indeed correlate very directly to geography in immediately observable ways, others correlate along different factors. In many cases, the differences that actually are significant and meaningful (such as blood type, the pH of certain body fluids, the magnetic permeability of various organ tissue, neural net formation characteristics and chemistry, etc.) show greater variation *within* races than *between* them. But we don't carry around blood monitors or permeability indicators, so we default to what is easy and convenient. We take the lazy way out and practice horrendous and meaningless discrimination against people based on which region of the planet their ancestors hailed from (*after* they left Africa!).

Thus by socializing people based on race, we affect their thinking to such a degree that our self-fulfilling prophecies become true. Tell a child often enough that he will amount to nothing, and very often that's exactly what will happen—fortunately, the opposite is also true. Perhaps nature knew of this tendency and so for years protected against this type of behavior by keeping us separated until we grew out of such foolish thinking. That is, for most of human history, our lack of sophisticated travel technologies resulted in our living primarily in ethno-isolation. If our emotional faculties had developed at approximately the same rate as our intellectual ones, by the time we developed technologies sophisticated enough to put us in constant contact with each other, we would have sufficiently matured to respect and appreciate our differences. Unfortunately, this is not what happened. To this day, we seem to have not grasped the beauty and wonder of differences expressed across the human spectrum.

Our failure to appreciate diversity would not be so tragic if it was merely academic, but it has tremendous implications regarding the safety of our planet and our continued survival as a species. Decisions affecting standards of living worldwide often have a diversity dimension. There was a time when discontentment about such matters could be contained, but as even underdeveloped areas grow in their capacity for lethality, this could become increasing dangerous for all. The methods used to quell discontentment in the past are not foolproof. Estimates of the amount of abuse, deprivation, and ignorance populations from underdeveloped, resource-rich nations can endure might be wrong. Indeed, the same is true concerning developed societies—like ours. We may think we know how much *Lower Ninth Ward* residents are willing to take, but again, the estimates *could* be wrong.

We can keep gambling on others' complacency, hoping to anticipate third-world uprisings and ensuring that puppet masters willing to do our bidding are continually waiting in the wings, but God help us if we guess wrong. Dr. Martin Luther King Jr. once remarked, *"We have allowed our civilization to outrun our culture, so we are in danger now of ending up with guided missiles in the hands of misguided men."* Such are the words of the prescient prophets. However, the inevitable and unthinkable doesn't have to happen. There is a better way. We can choose to evolve our culture in such a way that it catches up to the tremendous capabilities we have obtained technologically. We can learn to solve the diversity problem. We can learn to respect people regardless of their continent of origin. We can learn to accept our obligation to treat one another with dignity and respect. We can even grow to doing it willingly, and we may even grow to doing it lovingly. What unimagined blessings has the universe held in reserve for those who truly appreciate *unity* in *diversity*.

Technology has taken us very far. We can travel multiple times faster than the speed of sound. We can visit distant worlds. We can read the fundamental blueprints of life and are on track to soon be able, on a molecular level, to write sections of those genetic blueprints ourselves. Yet technology will not be able to solve this problem for us. We will not be able to genetically engineer tolerance, sensitivity, and respect into our DNA. As convenient as it would be to relegate this function to science for a solution, its mastery is beyond science's purview. Science can tell us how fundamental universal laws operate, but it cannot teach us how to laugh or how to cry or the meaning of life. Our technologies cannot teach us how to value humanity. Science and technology must play a key role in solving our problems, but it is not the solution.

Some feel that religion is the appropriate venue for challenges such as these. That may be, but my belief is that religion will be frustrated in these attempts until we stop trying to love God *in lieu* of loving man and start loving God *through* loving man. I do not by this statement mean to be irreverent to any religious tradition. My point is simply that there is a vast range in our religious traditions (including atheism), and reaching agreement as to what pleases "God" may be difficult if not impossible. On the other hand, we have a lot better idea about how to please people (especially if they are starving or suffering from debilitating diseases). Religion has great potential for releasing human power and energy—in both positive and negative ways. To date, it has not served to unite the world in spiritual oneness, and the forces that have prevented it from doing so until now are still alive and well today. Clearly, religion has great potential to contribute to healing humanity's divisions, but looking to religion to solve the problem appears to be unjustifiably optimistic.

Where then does our solution lie? With diversity. The principles of diversity are humanity's greatest hope for solving humanity's greatest problem. For every human trait, there is a range of occurrences, a spectrum of existence. Take color for example. Humans can be as fair as Icelanders, as dark as Congolese, and every shade in between. We all are comfortable with dealing with individuals on our preferred region of that spectrum, but uncomfortable outside of that region. But the truth that we simply can't get away from is that people exist outside of our zone of comfort.

The question that each of us must ask is, Are we going to assign people outside of our comfort zone the same value as people we prefer, or will we withhold respect and compassion because they are different? There was a time when we could be smug and make our decisions and live with the consequences. But that time is rapidly coming to a close because the stakes are higher. To return to Dr. King, the choice is simple: *"Now the judgment of God is upon us, and we must either learn to live together as brothers or we are going to die together as fools."*

And that, my brothers and sisters, is why I chose diversity. I will always be part engineer—the part that looks to systematic data analysis, that appreciates scientific methods and accomplishments, and the part that continually strives to make theoretical concepts REAL. I will always be a minister—the part that believes that we are all accountable to a supreme being, and though that being is all powerful, he only wishes to use that power to multiply love among his progeny and that we all are his progeny. And I will always work to promote diversity—because Cindy really is beautiful, and Fernando really is my friend, and we all are capable of pulling each other out of the sand.

As I continue on this journey of life, I am confident that the opportunity for redemption will come. I know I have not met my last Cindy. I will meet others whose unappreciated beauty I can proudly proclaim. I have not met my last Fernando. I will again have the opportunity to defend a friend from the scapegoat-seeking crowd. And most of all, I am certain that, though I might get stuck again, I too will have the opportunity to help pull someone out of the sand. Appreciating, defending, and helping. This is the world I want to live in and the world I want my and our grandchildren to live in and the world that I'm willing to—that I MUST—help build!

# The DiCE Connection

One day out of the blue, I received a call from Sonny Massey inviting me to a meeting he was having at his home in Southern California. The meeting was being cohosted by Mike Vonada—another beautiful soul, diversity champion, and mutual friend. The meeting would be attended by a subset of our friends from the Diversity 2000 community and other like-minded friends of Sonny and Mike. Diversity 2000 (or D2K as we affectionately refer to it) is a group of diversity practitioners principally from the Bay Area but including members from around the country. While I was quite excited about this invitation, I was also somewhat apprehensive about it. As an engineer turned diversity professional, I frequently had a tendency to feel a little like a fish out of water when interacting with other diversity professionals, particularly those who were much more comfortable with its touchy-feely aspects than me. Having been to a few D2K conferences, I knew the potential existed for this to be one of those kinds of meetings in the extreme!

On the other hand, Sonny and Mike were two individuals with whom I deeply resonated on many levels, and I knew that if nothing else worked right, I would appreciate the opportunity to have interacted with these brothers on a deeper level. So I decided to take the plunge. During that first meeting, we listened to one another, shared stories, pondered one another's views, and tried to give voice to the nascent movement that was struggling to be birthed from our collective desire to bring a different order of healing to the world *through*—rather than despite—our differences. After a couple of more meetings that successively helped to define our vision, focus, and approach, the Diversity Community Exchange (DiCE) was born.

I often think back on that initial invite with a sense of wonder at what it eventually led to, and gratitude that I was blessed with the courage to attend it despite my initial hesitations. Most of all, I am overwhelmingly appreciative of the souls my life has now become intertwined with as a result of our decision to make this journey.

My DiCE family is a very special group of people. I am fond of saying that each of us (humanity I mean) is an individual manifestation of God's creative intellect. And while intellectually, I know this to be true of our entire species, I know it is *experientially* true in the case of my DiCE family. They are wonderful, they are thoughtful, they are fearless, they are kind, they are loving, they are hopeful, and most of all, they are *human.* Sonny, Marvin, Simma, Sid, Nadia, Santalynda, Juan, and Joe-Joe. I am continually grateful to God that he has allowed us to share at least a portion of this adventure called life together, and it is my sincere hope and belief that this book that we are birthing in response to this shared experience will bless others in like manner. This group of individuals from different perspectives, races, and walks of life have helped me to see the genius of the Creator in making humanity as diverse as we are. It is my sincere hope that you too, as you read this book, come to recognize and be blessed with the same beauty in those that you have been placed in community with. May you continually be blessed with peace and wonder!

*Dedicated to Cindy, Fernando, Flo, and Marvin.*

# UNTIL I KNOW

Joe-Joe McManus, PhD

OUR PARENTS read to us a lot when we were kids. We were three wide-eyed boys sitting up in our beds, waiting for each night's selection. They would read all kinds of books to us. I remember them all as stories. Stories about history, people, and places. Stories with morals, stories that got our imagination going, and stories that made us want to do something exciting.

I took to telling stories of my own creation to my brothers after Mom or Dad would read to us. I'd tell stories about leprechauns in the woods, heroes that saved the day, or whatever else I could imagine on the spot. Dad used to listen by the door and tell me I should write a book.

When I got a little older and began reading books on my own, the ones I liked best were autobiographies and biographies. I loved reading people's perspectives on their own lives and the lives of folks that they found worthy of writing about. *The Autobiography of Malcolm X* and a biography of Albert Einstein were among my favorites. I loved them, and although my experience was nothing like theirs, I somehow felt connected to them just by learning a small part of their stories as people and not just who they were in history.

At some point in high school, I actually found a poster of Einstein with the quote "Great spirits have always encountered violent opposition from mediocre minds" and a beautiful sketch by Dwight Wilson of Malcolm X, and I hung them side by side on the wall in my room. Today, they are framed and hang together on my office wall. I have always believed that they could have been great friends. They were great spirits, great minds, and I felt connected with them through their stories.

It has been my experience that the more we share our stories with one another, the more connected we become. In a world, in a nation, or in a community as divided as ours, it occurs to me that sharing our stories may be an important way for us to bridge the divides. Once we share our stories and begin developing a shared narrative, it seems to me that it becomes more difficult to judge or stereotype or hate.

Don't get me wrong. I'm not saying that we should all join hands, sing corny songs together, and heal the world with our stories. That's not exactly my style. I'm talking about taking the time to shut up, consider that you don't know everything about everyone, and really listen to other folks' realities—particularly those who you think are significantly different from you. I'm talking about really hearing what someone else has been through and what they think and what's important to them in the world and why.

The divisions between us have been socially constructed and fertilized by those who benefit from our division. I believe there is great strength and dignity in taking that first step toward crossing those divisions by simply shutting off the pundits, getting off the couch, and genuinely connecting with folks on the other sides of those divides. As our connections deepen and we start to work toward common goals, we actually begin to deconstruct the divisions and make strides toward our collective freedom.

From my perspective, this is what has happened for us, the writers who have contributed to this anthology. By consciously crossing the divides and sharing our stories, we have become a part of one another's lives—one another's stories. We are very different people who live very different lives. Without making a conscious effort to come together, it is not likely that we would have connected the way we have. Now that we know one another's stories, we care about one another, and we have become more understanding, more appreciative, more willing to forgive and accept one another for who we really are. In essence, we have become family.

I hope that by sharing our collective experiences through this book, we might inspire you to extend your family across divisions and differences as well. Of course, everyone's story is too complex and intricate to fit into a chapter. For my part, I will share the parts of my story that have led me to become an educator focused on diversity leadership.

\*     \*     \*

"I see the sandpit, I see the sandpit!" That's what Kacey, B-J, and I would holler from the backseat of the Judge (Mom and Dad's 1970 Pontiac GTO Judge) as soon as we could see the sign for the Carver Package Store. That's where my story begins, at least as far back as I can remember. We lived behind the store that my parents owned and operated in the town of Carver, Massachusetts. We called it the sandpit because it was built, well, on a sandpit.

My first memories are of playing with my brother Kacey, chats and playing ball with Dad, and "Fingers McGee" (which meant keep your hands in your pockets) while being out in the world with Mom. I remember the excitement Kacey and I felt as we waited for Mom to come home with our new brother, B-J, whom we thought was the best toy ever! And we loved the trips to Kingston, just a couple towns over, to see Grandma, Grandpa, and other family. Generally, I simply remember a warm and loving family and being happy, spending time together, working, playing, or whatever.

Our family is pretty diverse, and my parents were an interreligious couple—Mom from a Jewish family and Dad's side Christian. When I was a year old, my brother Kacey was adopted. He was five weeks old and African American. A few years later, my brother B-J was born. The three of us couldn't have looked more different from one another as B-J arrived with big blond curls and bright blue eyes like Dad's, and I'm still the spitting image of Mom with dark hair and eyes.

Outside the family, racism became an issue early on because of reactions to Kacey being a Black child in a White family. Later, issues of anti-Semitism came up and classism piled on as we lived in our modest apartment behind the liquor store. There was also a history of interreligious/cross-cultural marriage on Dad's side; Grandpa was Irish Catholic and Grandma English Protestant. None of these differences were particularly acceptable in the White-flight town where we lived outside of Boston, Mass.

I remember everything changing for me and our family's diversity becoming an issue within days of entering Governor John Carver Elementary School. I remember my first day of kindergarten like it was yesterday. Actually, I really only remember the bus ride. Mom had allowed me to pick out my clothes, which in retrospect may not have been the best idea.

If you've seen the movie *Big Daddy*, you'll remember that the character played by Adam Sandler lets the kid he's taking care of dress however he wanted to go to school. He dressed himself in an outfit that included a homemade cape and some huge boots. He didn't look more ridiculous than I did though. I wore purple pants that we found in the girls' department at the local Sears department store, a shiny embroidered purple cowboy shirt that Grandma actually made for me, and a big horse-head belt buckle brought it all together. Yes, there is a picture, and everyone still gets a great laugh whenever Mom digs it out. Anyway, as if that outfit wasn't going to lose me enough cool points with the other kids, Mom rode the bus with me on the first day too. Looking back, I figure she may have felt it necessary to protect me.

The next day on the bus, an older boy decided to make fun of my self-styled ensemble from the previous day. The kid's name was Wayne, and he was bigger than me. I remember getting angry, my brow furling, and my fingers curling into fists. I didn't do anything while Wayne and most of the other kids laughed at me. Just when I thought it was over, Wayne decided to move on to talking about my mother. That was a bad move on his part.

Unfortunately for Wayne, Dad taught his boys how to fight at a very early age. He figured there would be times when we would need to protect ourselves, and he was right. He made it very clear that the only time we were to fight was to protect ourselves or our family. So when I had a natural reaction to Wayne talking about my mom, I knew that this was one of those times when it was OK to fight. Without hesitation, I climbed over the seat between us and went to work on him. It really wasn't a fight as much as it was a beating. Since I'd never fought anyone outside our living room, I didn't know when to stop and ended up doing real damage to my opponent.

Although school was always easy for me academically, it never got any better socially. School was my battlefield, and I had become a little soldier on my second day of kindergarten. I don't remember what Wayne said about Mom, but as the years went on, the comments that brought me to blows always had something to do with race, religion, class, or other diversity issues as they are called today. I always felt that I was simply defending my family's honor.

As we went through our early years in school, Kacey and my friend Joe—both big football players, Joe actually went pro—would tell anyone who started something that I'd be the one to kick their ass. Thanks to a well-established Napoleon complex, I was always willing to take on the challenge. While it felt good to get out my anger, I know now that it is not likely that those fights created much positive change. Even if it had, it certainly wasn't a sustainable strategy. It was ultimately Kacey who convinced me that physical confrontation wasn't the way we could make a difference.

*   *   *

Over the years, nothing was more difficult to cope with than the racism that was directed at Kacey. Most of the time, the anti-Semitism we experienced was more passive, and the classism was simple taunts about where we lived. None of it was good, and it all took a toll, but there was something different when vitriolic racial hatred was directed at my little brother. I was supposed to protect him. I felt an instinctual need to do something. More often than not though, there was nothing I could do that seemed to matter.

Unfortunately, our teachers were among the worst offenders. They taught an overwhelmingly racist and Eurocentric curriculum like most in the United States at the time and many today. It was Christian centered, male dominated, and didn't acknowledge LGBTQI folks at all. It was antiquated and oppressive across the board. It mostly left folks out, which is bad enough, but when it came to race, it was more active. As an obvious example, teachers praised White people who enslaved Africans as great leaders while they actively demeaned leaders of color as supporting violence and by pointing out their personal shortcomings. How they didn't recognize enslaving people as violent or demonstrative of personal shortcomings, I couldn't understand.

Worse still, the teachers and school administrators assumed Kacey was less intelligent and placed him in the lowest possible classes along with the majority of the other Black and Latino kids. Meanwhile, I was placed in advanced classes. We both knew that wasn't right.

The other big thing for us was sports. Kacey played football and ran track, and I was obsessed with basketball. In fact, playing for the school team was the main reason I felt it necessary to continue going to school. My dad was a great coach, and his friends were always there to help as well. Basketball had taken me and my family from the small town of Carver, Massachusetts, to the Washington, DC, area so that I could play in a stronger league in high school. I was actually pretty good, but that's another story, and I don't want to be the Al Bundy of this book, so I'll leave it at that.

My senior year in high school was a blur to me. At some point during the first scrimmage of the year, I jumped, and my legs were taken out from under me. I landed on the back of my head and subsequently had a seizure right there on the court—not that I remember that. What I know from those who were there was that my dad ran onto the court to take care of me, and the team manager called 911. I don't remember the rest of my senior year because of the concussion.

Somehow, I graduated from high school, probably because the school was afraid we'd sue because there was no medical professional on-site during the game as required by law. The next thing I knew, we were in Maine of all places. Maine is not exactly the mecca for basketball. Lobster, yes; basketball, not so much. However, there are a couple of college prep schools there that recruit football and basketball players, for a postgraduate year, who had either been injured or bombed their SATs. There were some great players on my team. One of them went pro—Sam Cassel. Sam was a good friend, and Dad actually helped him improve his shot; again, a story for another time.

So my family was in Maine, and I was trying to get my bearings on and off the court. My brother Kacey was a star of the football team, and B-J was just starting high school. Kacey was very popular, but racism continued to be an issue. Even though there were a number of Black players on the postgraduate basketball and football teams, the postgrads mostly kept to themselves, and the local folks had very limited experience with diversity.

One day, I was sitting in an incredibly boring English class, and Kacey came walking in. He just said, "C'mon." I got up and started walking out with him. Of course, the teacher asked what was going on. Kacey just said, "I need my brother," and we kept it moving.

As we were walking down the hall, I asked Kacey what was up and was everything all right. He said something like, "Yeah, but another idiot just called me a nigger." He said it so calmly. My blood began to boil. He went on to tell me what happened and ended with, "So I think you should make him cry."

Kacey had told the kid to sit in the cafeteria and wait for him to get back. I'm sure there was an implied threat that if he didn't wait, things would get worse for him. Kacey could be intimidating if he wanted to be, add to that the stereotypes that this kid had about young Black men, and simply put, he was scared to move.

As we were walking across the frozen campus toward the cafeteria, Kacey reminded me of an experience we'd had about ten years prior. All he had to say was, "Do you remember the little girl?"

The way we remembered it, we were going to a doctor in Boston for something. When we walked into the doctor's office, Mom told us to sit in the waiting area and wait for her while she went to the reception desk to do some paperwork or something. So we sat down in the waiting area. After a moment, Kacey noticed a little girl playing with some blocks. He was an outgoing and friendly child, unlike his older brother. "Hey, let's go play with the little girl," he said.

The little girl was probably about four years old. She was White with blond hair and blue eyes and a big smile. As Kacey dragged me over, she continued playing, barely noticing us. Kacey said what he always said, "Hi,

I'm Kacey, and this is my brother Joe-Joe." The girl looked up quickly and said, "Hi." Then Kacey said, "Can we play with you?"

The little girl looked up at us, and her smile went away. She looked sad and said, "No, I'm sorry, I can't play with you 'cuz you're a nigger."

I knew three things at that moment: the n-word was the worst thing you could ever call someone, this girl just called my little brother the n-word, and I wasn't supposed to hit a girl. So knowing these things, I did the only thing I could think of—I cursed her out with every bad word I'd ever heard. I probably used half of them wrong, but I was furious and wasn't going to let her get away with calling Kacey the n-word.

The next thing I remember was Mom grabbing me by the arm and pulling me away as the girl cried. I tried to explain to Mom that that little girl was the one that was wrong and that I was doing right by defending Kacey. She wasn't hearing a word I said and made me apologize to the girl and go sit down quietly or Dad was going to hear about this.

As I sat there, bright red I'm sure, wanting to strangle that little girl, I noticed Kacey sitting there quietly next to me. Once he saw that I'd calmed down, Kacey said, "Let's go play with the little girl again." *What?! Are you crazy!?* That's all I could think. "No!"

He said OK, and he just walked over by himself and started to play with her like nothing had happened. I don't know if they talked or what might have been said. I can't even remember if anyone else was around. I only remember sitting there trying to figure out what was going on and at what point my brother had lost his damn mind.

I don't know where the little girl's mother was all this time. But after Kacey and the girl had been playing together for a while and as I sat across the room dumbfounded, I saw her mother stomp over to where they were playing. She grabbed her daughter and pulled her away from Kacey as if he was a lion trying to eat her kid.

Then it happened; her mother called Kacey the n-word. That was it. No one had ever told me I couldn't hit a grown woman. So I proceeded to run over and attack this disgusting woman. I'm sure it looked ridiculous and probably only lasted a couple seconds, but I went to work beating on her leg like I was really doing something.

Again, Mom apologized for her son's terrible behavior and made me apologize, I'm sure. I don't remember anything else except what happened as we were all about to leave. As the girl and her mother began walking out, the little girl pulled away from her mother and ran to Kacey. She jumped into his lap, threw her arms around him, and gave him a big hug and kiss on the cheek. Then she said something I would have never expected: "I love you, Kacey, don't tell my mom."

Kacey was like six years old, and his response was, "Never forget, I love you too."

As we walked out, I was still confused. I looked at Kacey as if to say, what the hell just happened? He said, "I don't know, maybe she learned something" as he shrugged his shoulders in a bit of disbelief.

Years later in Maine, Kacey kick-started my life as an educator by reminding me of the little girl and the idea that he may have taught her something. When he asked me to make that kid cry, he just wanted me to teach him by telling him stories about what racism does to people until he cried. He figured that would be the indicator that he'd understood and that he'd remember and hopefully change.

I sat down at the table across from this kid who'd called my brother the n-word. With Kacey by my side, I proceeded to make the kid cry by simply telling him a few of the, unfortunately, many stories like the one about the little girl. Painful stories, stories that had hurt Kacey and everyone that loved him. The kid apologized to Kacey and promised to never use the word again. Then Kacey actually proceeded to give him a hug and told him that he hoped he meant it. I don't know whatever happened to that kid, but I'll bet he remembers that day, and maybe, just maybe, it changed him.

Later in life, I learned that we were teaching him by creating what the producer and theorist Morris Massey called a significant emotional event. Massey believed that was necessary for changing one's values and behaviors. Jane Elliott, a pioneering antiracist educator, did the same thing in a more sophisticated manner through her well-known brown eyes—blue eyes exercise.

\*   \*   \*

Whether we were in Massachusetts, Maryland, or Maine, the schools that we went to were not segregated per se, but they certainly were internally segregated. The curricula were Eurocentric, the pedagogy was biased, and our peers were often ignorant regarding issues of race and diversity. The resulting experiences distorted how Kacey saw himself. He developed an inferiority complex, particularly when it came to academics. This carried over into how he felt about himself generally and seriously affected his self-esteem. From the outside, it looked like he had it all: star athlete, one of the best-looking guys around, plus he was smart. He had an infectious personality and a smile that lit up the room. All that was undercut by the racism that polluted his youth.

Over the years, our parents fought with the school administrators and teachers, and Kacey and I fought what seemed at times like everyone else. Over time, the prejudice in school, the racism that is everyday America, and the tremendous stresses of being an adolescent became too much. The final straw was when he received poor SAT scores and simultaneously an unrelated rejection letter from a racist college football coach that he'd been warned by one of his players would not want him if he could find a White player for the position he played—middle linebacker.

At the age of seventeen, Kacey became a victim of suicide. I suffered the most profound loss of my young life, and so did everyone in our family and so many of Kacey's friends. It was March 14, 1989, and we were in Pittsfield, Maine. We have never been the same.

Somehow, my parents pulled us together, and our family and friends tried to console us all. I shut down for months. I didn't return to school. I ran miles every day, listening to a few songs over and over that reminded me of Kacey. I spoke at memorial services, wrote poetry expressing my deep sadness, clung to my family and close friends, and spent my time just feeling pain, guilt, and anger.

At some point during the summer, I was contacted by someone at Florida Institute of Technology. I think it was the housing department wanting to know when I was planning to arrive on campus. The truth was that I didn't remember applying. It turns out it was a safety school, one that I was encouraged to apply to in case I was badly injured and couldn't play ball. Anyway, I had decided after Kacey died that I was never going to play basketball again. So why go to college?

There is a scene in the film *Good Will Hunting* where Will and his best friend are standing by a pickup truck having a couple of beers during a break from working at a constructions site. Will was a genius with math and had been offered a few big jobs. He tells his friend that he's not taking any of them, that he's just going to keep working with the same guys and hanging out like everyone else. Even though my parents didn't go to college, they expected me to go, but I felt like Will did. I wanted the safety of home and didn't want to do something different. Anyway, I had a couple of those *Good Will Hunting* conversations with friends Hollis, Elisha, and DeReef and changed my mind. Truth is, if it wasn't for those guys, I probably wouldn't have gone to college.

Years later, when the film actually came out, I was working on my doctorate. Dad called me and said, "Go see *Good Will Hunting.*" That was so unlike Dad that I just got in my car, went to the theater, and waited for the next showing. I cried when Will's therapist, played by Robin Williams, told him, "It's not your fault, son." That was the message from Dad. That was what I struggled with the most, believing that it wasn't my fault. Mom, Dad, and B-J all struggled too. It took me the next nearly twenty years before I was able to push past the guilt, for the most part anyway.

*       *       *

My freshman year in college was miserable. I screwed up my relationship with my high school sweetheart and had already gotten myself into some serious trouble on campus. I don't know how, but somehow I'd become friends with Joya, an amazingly sweet person and strong student. She must have taken pity on the angry miserable guy that I was. Joya was like a little sister, and she kept me from losing it while I was so far away from my family. She listened, and she helped me to channel my emotions into more positive endeavors than getting into fights and otherwise being an idiot.

It was through Joya that I met Fonyea, who brought me to the Grant Street Community Center that Mr. Bennie Hopkins ran. It became my home away from home, and Mr. Bennie and his wife Ms. Audrey treated me like family. To this day, they count me among their children, and like many others who have extended their families to me, my family has embraced them as well. I got involved at Grant Street, coaching a basketball team with Fonyea, and I started a tutoring program that Joya and other students from Florida Tech participated in. I'd found a positive outlet and a sense of belonging far from home.

I eventually made more friends, and spurred on by an incident involving a confederate flag on campus and battles with a racist world philosophies professor, I even started a student organization. It was called the Cultural Awareness Council, and we worked to address the lack of diversity on campus, the Eurocentric core curriculum, and the disrespect for the local community, which was predominantly African American and was referred to during orientation as "Brown Town."

One day toward the end of my sophomore year, I got a call from some professor from Harvard. He said I'd been selected to represent the United States as the first American employee of the Soviet Academy of Science. In my typically graceful way, I said something like, "What the hell are you talking about?" He proceeded to try and explain who he was and that they were impressed with my application. Again, articulate and graceful, I responded, "I didn't apply for anything, and I'm not going to no cold-ass Russia!" Then I hung up.

A few minutes later, I got a call from Russ Blake. Dr. Blake is a mentor, a family friend, and a teacher who had ties to NASA. He went on to tell me that he had applied for me and that he didn't want to get my hopes up, so he hadn't mentioned it to me. He said I was selected to be a People-to-People Ambassador and a junior research scientist at the largest single-mirror telescope in the world. I was a space sciences (astrophysics) major, and all that sounded great except . . . the Soviet Union?

I was finally doing well in my classes—showing up was the secret, by the way. I was making friends, and I was involved in the community and on campus. I had been speaking at schools about racism, and I felt like I was doing something useful. Besides, I just left the cold of Maine, why would I leave sunny Florida for some observatory on top of a mountain in Russia?

Russ responded like the amazing mentor he has always been. He told me that I should just take the free trip to Massachusetts, visit my family, and make my decision after the dinner that the program was sponsoring. So I took the free trip and showed up at the dinner with an uninvited date and no intention on accepting this "honor."

I realized what the good Dr. Blake was really up to shortly after I met the two runners-up. One was from Harvard, the other MIT. They were obnoxious, putting down my college and questioning why I was chosen. Just as I started to raise my voice in response and probably to do something stupid, Russ pulled me aside. He said that I'd have to decide whether I would be taking the opportunity before the announcement was made, and oh, there was one other thing—if I chose not to go, one of those two guys I'd just met would be selected.

Russ had known me since I was in elementary school. So before I even responded, a knowing smile crossed his face as he turned around and made a toast announcing that I couldn't wait to go! All I could do was smile and think about how to tell Mom.

The week I was supposed to leave, there was a coup. It was the fall of the Soviet Union. There were tanks in the streets of Moscow, and the country was in turmoil. I really didn't want to go, so I thought that this might be a reasonable excuse to back out. Then Dad stepped in. We had a chat about how I really needed some time alone. He knew that I was still struggling with Kacey's death and that what I needed was an experience alone; that was even more challenging than being away at college. I knew Mom was worried, but he said he wasn't because I'd faced much worse. He knew I could do it and wanted me to keep a journal because he'd always wanted to go to Russia, and this way, he could read all about it when I got back.

I spent the next year in Russia working at a giant telescope, being an "ambassador," and writing in my journal. It was awesome, and Dad was right, I needed it. Not only did I have the chance to really be alone, especially during the nights at the top of one of the peaks among the Caucasus Mountain Range, but I also learned that my life's purpose wasn't studying multiple star systems. While I loved the science, I didn't love the isolation and disconnection from the people and social issues that I so passionately cared about.

Part of my role as "ambassador" was to speak at events across Russia and the Ukraine. What most people don't know is that I am terrified of speaking in public. That is, unless I care deeply about the subject. If it is something I'm passionate about, somehow I get over the fear and really get into it. Otherwise, I'm what they call a hot mess.

The first few speaking engagements were at schools and universities. The topics were not interesting to me, never mind anything I really cared about. I stumbled through them, hoping that the translator was making me sound better than the sloppy, scared kid I was. Next, I was asked to speak about American holidays at another university. I decided to try and focus on holiday-related social justice issues so that maybe I wouldn't suck this time. I spoke about Thanksgiving, the Fourth of July, Martin Luther King Day, and Juneteenth. I told stories and described the history of these holidays from multiple perspectives. I wanted to show that there was more depth to these stories than they may have heard—and they'd actually never heard of Juneteenth. A highly charged debate ensued with the audience of a few hundred divided between the pro-American and anti-American groups that seemed interested enough in this kid from the States to show up at the event.

It actually went well. We got into a dialogue about capitalism versus communism and about the differences between theoretical democracy and the American brand of representative democracy. We discussed the diverse cultural, religious, and racial realities of the United States and Russia. We debated Angela Davis's writings about Soviet communism and Lenin's revolution in the context of Gandhi, King, and Kennedy. We bonded over shared respect for Einstein and X. It was amazing.

The next day, I told my handlers (that's what we called my official contacts in Russia) that I would prefer only to speak on topics related to diversity, education, and leadership. I was surprised, but they loved the idea. They had seen the previous disasters and the vast difference in how the most recent event turned out. Within a few weeks, I was booked for every moment I had free for the remainder of my year's stay. I met folks who shared their experiences as Soviet ethnic minorities, as Jews, as African students, as widows of fallen WWII soldiers, and so on. I learned what Eurasian means, the many ways that the United States was perceived, and that my voice could keep my brother's spirit alive even on the other side of the world.

I thoroughly enjoyed the rest of my time in Russia, both at the Special Astrophysical Observatory and on the road speaking with students, political figures, activists, and whoever else showed up when I spoke. I made friends that I have to this day. I also had the time and space to get past my anger and learn to live with the pain of losing my brother Kacey. I even published my first papers with the awesome husband-and-wife team of Yuri and Ildiko Balega. They were on the interferometric orbits of stars within binary and multiple star systems based on speckle observations. It is unlikely that you've read them or would want to, but it was exciting for me nonetheless.

I returned home fifty pounds lighter, with a newfound love of tea, and having decided to change my major. Dad wasn't thrilled about that last part. He knew that this unique experience could have helped propel me toward my dream of becoming an astronaut. But I knew that it was more important that I learn how to change the world and to address the issues of poverty, racism, and other forms and manifestations of oppression, which I had learned were not limited to our nation. After Dad saw me teach, he became one of my biggest supporters and understood why I needed to change direction.

Ultimately, I changed my major to psychology but kept a minor in space sciences. I chose psychology because it provided insights into the human mind and behavior. I focused on cross-cultural and organizational psychology. This led me to an internship at the Defense Equal Opportunity Management Institute (DEOMI) where I learned that people actually work professionally on the issues that I had been trying to address. I met educators like Dr. Dansby who led the research department; the godfather of DEOMI, Gene Johnson; and the commandant, Col. Ronald M. Joe. They taught me a great deal not only about the historical realities of racism, sexism, and other forms of discrimination in the military but also about organizational leadership and what a lifetime commitment to social justice looks like.

My next step was to go to graduate school to learn more, particularly about how to change the school systems that were so damaging to my brother but which I also believed were the best hope for change. I studied multicultural education in grad school and went on to do a PhD in educational leadership. As it turned out, I followed in my friend DeReef Jamison's footsteps by going to Florida A&M University (FAMU). He was one of the friends who convinced me to actually go to college, and FAMU is where he had received his master's degree on his way to a doctorate from Temple. FAMU was also Colonel Joe's alma mater, and it turned out he was working there as an administrator in student affairs when I started my doctoral program.

During my years of study, I continued to speak wherever I could and met phenomenal colleagues and mentors. I had worked with Dr. Potter, a great physicist and better person at Florida Tech, and learned from the great Liz Salett, founder and former president of the National Multicultural Institute. I also found ways to meet and learn from many leaders in the field of multicultural education, including those that my cohort of friends in the field refer to as the Big Five—Geneva Gay, Carl Grant, Sonia Nieto, Christine Sleeter, and James Banks. Over time I have partnered closely with outstanding educators like Maya Cameron and Catherine Wong, and developed a cohort of close friends in the field whose counsel and example continue to inform my work.

My doctoral studies experience proved critical in solidifying my passion for teaching. I had the extraordinary opportunity to teach a full load of courses, and then some, while I was working on my PhD. I was given the full responsibilities of an assistant professor and was treated as a colleague by the faculty in the college of education. I continued on for an additional year because I loved FAMU so much and wasn't quite ready to leave.

My studies and my faculty experience helped me to understand the depth of work that had been done in the field of education to promote equity and social justice. Equally important, the FAMU community helped me to understand how great an educational institution could be. Don't get me wrong, no institution is perfect, but FAMU took an approach that was different in my experience. FAMU is also where I became "Dr. Joe-Joe," a moniker I was blessed with by my students and colleagues in the College of Education.

The motto "Excellence with caring" seemed to really mean something at FAMU. I remember hearing President Frederick Humphries sum up the FAMU experience something like this, "We're family, and we're here to help you become brilliant." It's worth noting that I would have missed out on this life changing experience had I been like most White folks and not considered an historically Black college or university (HBCU).

*   *   *

My family, friends, and community had guided me, creating my moral compass and laying the foundation for my understanding of diversity and leadership. Later, my professors, mentors, the Big Five, and other colleagues helped me to develop a professional context for my work in the field of education; they helped me to understand the systems, the realities, and the possibilities in education. I finally found my professional self, meaning that I'd found a professional direction that was in sync with my personal mission and purpose.

After teaching at FAMU, I took on a visiting professorship at Chancellor College at the University of Malaŵi, funded by the International Foundation for Education and Self-Help (IFESH). IFESH was founded by the civil rights leader Leon Sullivan, and I was excited to be connected with his organization and legacy. I also wanted to take the PhD out for a ride, so to speak, to see what doors a doctorate could open. The prospect of having another experience living outside the United States, like I did in Russia, was very exciting.

Shortly after I arrived in Malaŵi came the horrors of September 11, 2001. All the IFESH teachers and professors that had been assigned to Malaŵi were sitting in a meeting about security at the United States Embassy in Lilongwe when we got word of the attacks.

All of a sudden, there was a commotion in the hallway. Officials, including the ambassador who wasn't supposed to be around that day, went running by our door. Obviously, that wasn't normal. Something was seriously wrong. Moments later, we were informed that a plane had hit one of the World Trade Center towers in New York. We were then taken to a room where we were able to watch *CNN*. We watched in shock as the second plane hit the other tower and news came of the Pentagon strike and the plane that went down in Pennsylvania.

We all spent the next days trying to contact family and friends. I was eventually able to contact those friends and family that I was worried about. The one I was most worried about was Joya, my little sister from college. I knew that her father worked at the World Trade Center. He was one of the victims. I considered going home just to be there for Joya, but she convinced me that it was important that I stay in Malaŵi. To this day, I'm not sure I did the right thing.

A few years after I returned from Malaŵi, I sat with Joya as she fought breast cancer. We talked a lot about her dad and how much she missed him. We reminisced about college, and I brought together old friends to come see her. She told me that she was proud of all the amazing work I'd done and how much I'd helped people through my work. That was humbling, but it gave me the opportunity to thank her for all that she had done for me. If it weren't for her friendship and for the fact that she reached across racial and cultural divisions to extend her family to include me, then I wouldn't have even made it through freshman year. After months of suffering physically while rejoicing spiritually and celebrating life with family and friends, Joya went home to her Lord.

Returning to my time in Malaŵi, those first weeks were difficult for us all. Many of the people we met in Malaŵi initially sympathized with Osama bin Laden and the perpetrators of the 9/11 atrocity. People on the streets would actually yell out "bin Laden" when they saw us. There were even Osama T-shirts that we saw for a short time. There were many difficult conversations, and it took a while for folks to understand the magnitude of the attacks and the depth to which this was affecting their visitors from the United States.

Ultimately, our hosts and most of the people we met did their best to empathize and were very kind indeed. It was difficult though, and as I've seen during much of my travels over the years, US Americans are often seen through a lens blurred by the poor behavior of our companies, tourists, our leaders, and our national choices regarding international policies, investments, and military actions. Much like the divided audiences I'd faced a decade before in the former Soviet Union, there were many who loved the idea of America and many who thought of us as the evil empire. As always, it took time to get past those barriers to communication and relationship building.

After that first week of training and meetings, I arrived in Zomba, Malaŵi, to go to work at Chancellor College, the main campus of the University of Malaŵi. Malaŵi is a very small country and one with extreme poverty and real challenges with respect to education. It is a place of great diversity of cultures, languages, and religions. It is also a place of great hope and where educators from primary school through graduate school work tirelessly to improve their nation by educating the next generations.

While in Zomba, I had the opportunities to teach both undergrads and grad students. I took an approach that I would describe as a mix between multicultural education and a positive deviance approach. Together we explored the history, realities, and possibilities of education in Malaŵi as well as examples from around the world. We all brought our best ideas to the table, saw what was working despite great challenges, and ultimately, we developed what we referred to in our classes as a *counter-colonial education* framework.

Again I learned from remarkable educators like Drs. Banda and Kathamalo and dedicated students whom I hope are now teaching. They taught me by example, along with many others in Zomba. There wasn't just a lack of resources like technology and teaching space, there weren't even current resource books, and what there was were all Anglocentric. They made it work because, as I was reminded, it is the teacher that is the most critical resource for the student in the classroom. I learned a great deal about teachers (and professors) as leaders while I was at Chancellor College.

I also spent a great deal of my time with folks who lived in the communities surrounding the campus. I saw similar poverty to what I'd seen in Russia. I also saw the manifestations of colonial oppression, global neglect, and racism. I shared stories with students, community activists, and local friends. We learned about one another and, by spending time together, began to create a shared narrative. Again, my family extended. My closest friend from Three Mile outside Zomba, Sammy Bakali, continues to remind me that what really matters in the world are relationships and community.

\*　　\*　　\*

After my return to the States, there were personal challenges and drama. Dad was struggling with serious health problems and a broken health-care system—again, a topic for another time that includes many injustices. I also had drama around yet another failed relationship. Definitely not worth rehashing, but it did create problems which affected my professional life. After some moving around, I ended up working for Dr. Stuart Lord who at the time was the Dean of the Tucker Foundation at Dartmouth College.

A few years under Dr. Lord's tutelage helped me to understand better how to navigate the politics of higher education and gave me insights into the work of ethical leaders within powerful institutions which often contribute to our social and economic injustices. Stuart also demonstrated compassionate leadership by making it possible for me to be there for my dad when his health was failing. He allowed me to work from home and provided the kind of support that an institutional leader should. My father passed away in September 2008. To this day, I cannot express adequately how profound this loss is to me or how much I miss my dad. I can say that Stuart's act of compassion was another example of someone reaching across lines of division, treating me like family and making a real difference.

During the months after my father passed away, we elected the first African American president of the United States. Dad had seen the campaign and was glad to see that history was about to be changed. As Stuart, my wife, Kecia, and I stood for ten hours in the warm embrace of the massive crowd to watch the presidential inauguration of Barack Obama, I thought a lot of Kacey and Dad and others who had passed away. I wondered what they would think and wished they were there. I also remembered that for years, Dad had been trying to teach me to enjoy the great moments in life. So I did, as I had enjoyed so many great times with him.

Also in the crowd were my great colleagues Kisha Fuentes and the soon-to-be doctors, Christina Joseph and Julie Agosto, and our student fellows from my most recent position as founding executive director of the Ernesto Malave Leadership Academy at the City University of New York (CUNY). Once we thought Dad's health had improved, I had moved to New York and ended up at CUNY. It had been about a year since I'd been brought on-board to build the academy.

I have spent the past few years building the Malave Leadership Academy at CUNY, the largest urban public university in the nation. It has been an opportunity to bring together what I've learned about leadership, diversity, and education and apply it to the education of emerging leaders. It has been a great professional experience and personal privilege. Our small yet productive team, exceptional student fellows, and the programs that we developed to focus on service, advocacy, and leadership have established the academy as a unique leadership education opportunity at the university-system level.

I have always said that my education, any success that I may have, and my life are owed to my family and those who have extended their families to include me. I believe that my work in developing the Leadership Academy has been some of the best work I've done, and I owe it all to them. I am proud of the work we've done and of our outstanding alumni. I learned a great deal from our team, our students, and our partners about leadership. I have also connected with CUNY greats like Michelle Fine and even got to shake Michio Kaku's hand.

On the other hand, I have also learned that cronyism, internal politics, and institutional racism continue to plague great institutions like CUNY as they do so many other institutions that serve underrepresented communities. Unfortunately, these problems severely impede the educational process and lessen the quality of education received by students. It seems obvious to me that this behavior, because it actually does affect the quality of education, wouldn't have been tolerated had the demographics been more like those at a place like Dartmouth. These issues, along with underfunding and other social injustices, continue to block progress in public education from pre-K through terminal degrees.

Today, nowhere in our nation is educational inequity more blatant than in my current home, New York City. The divisions of inequitable schooling ranges from the highly exclusionary independent schools costing more than $35,000 per year, down to the most "savagely" underfunded and ill-equipped public schools serving low-income communities, which are largely communities of color. This same divide is evident in higher education in the city as well. The elite Ivy League Columbia University sets the bar for exclusivity while the public system of the City University of New York represents a continuation of the disparities of the public P-12 system.

The divide in New York, as is true across the nation, is maintained by a class system that is delineated by race and generational wealth. So many wealthy White New Yorkers—including, to my disheartenment, many of my Jewish brothers and sisters—profess progressive politics and a desire for social justice for all while fiercely defending their highly segregated independent schools and elitist universities and the tourist curriculum (a term coined by Louise Derman-Sparks) that they call multicultural. For now, it will suffice to say that Jonathan Kozol's *Savage Inequalities* was written about New York City public schools, and a similar exposé could be written about higher education.

The inequality that is so evident in New York City schools and universities are also obvious when the generational wealth and current income structures of various groups are examined. The most difficult reality, as I sit in a city where the wealthy live atop our buildings or commute from mansions outside while most work check to check or worse, is that this is not terribly unique. Systems of oppression exist as the norm around the world. They do not all look the same or oppress exactly the same people, but there are many similarities, and it is my greatest hope that there may be some collective solutions.

*   *   *

As we witness the revolutionary changes that are occurring in Egypt and other nations around the world today, it is my hope that we recognize the potential that we all have for revolution. I'm not promoting any form of violent takeover, as many tend to read *revolution* as, but any student of history must be concerned that our divide between the haves and have-nots is approaching what Malcolm Gladwell famously called a tipping point.

Not every revolution looks the same. Some happen on camera while others happen outside the public view. And often, they happen gradually over time. The progress that has occurred in our schools includes those made by revolutionary movements to make our schools more inclusive. Revolutionaries such as Miles Horton and Paulo Freire have provided for new literacies and new approaches to public education. The education of girls and women has become the center of educational revolution around the world, from the well-known work of the Oprah Winfrey Leadership Academy to the even more powerful local movements and organizations around the world.

At the same time, we must beware of pseudo revolutionaries. There are many who claim to be working for social justice but who are in effect a part of the problem. There are fashion-level revolutionaries who wear the uniform and occasionally talk the talk when it is politically expedient and safe yet do nothing to support change. There are pop revolutionaries who use revolutionary fields such as diversity and inclusion to build their own personal brand of minor celebrity but do little more than promote ineffectual change because they haven't done the actual work to learn what change is needed. There are even counterrevolutionary hijackers who work against social justice movements by sabotaging from within or by using a public voice to distort a just revolutionary agenda.

Among other related challenges is the constant struggle for funding. The traditional development and advancement efforts focus on those who have benefitted most from the inequitable system that we aim to change. There is an obvious push-pull, even for the most egalitarian of the wealthy individuals, foundations, and government funding sources. This isn't to say that there is no genuine support from folks with access to funding, or that there is no way to fund or otherwise make possible such revolutionary work. It is just to say that it often requires innovation.

Revolution toward social justice is often complex, but as we have seen over and over, it is possible and necessary as we continue to strive toward a more perfect union and a more just world. There are people around the world working to challenge and end social injustice even in the face of what seems like insurmountable odds. Aung San Suu Kyi looks to the successes of Mandela for inspiration. Mandela looked to King. King looked to Gandhi and so on. There is a rich history of revolutionary change toward social justice on local, national, and global levels for us all to look to for inspiration and guidance.

\*   \*   \*

My experiences over the past twenty-five years as a student activist, faculty member, curriculum writer, educational administrator, and leader have all been born out of my family experiences. I am guided by memories as much as by mentors and by life experience even more than all my years of study. And I am inspired by the leaders, both well-known and unknown, that have already changed our world for the better.

Those who know me won't be surprised at all to hear that I learned the most while listening to Grandpa's stories as we worked together and when Grandma shared her reflections on life. I've learned in Mom's embrace and at Dad's knee my entire life. I learned volumes by Kacey's side and in experiencing life with B-J. And now I also learn from my wife, Kecia, and our daughter, Makaila, among many others.

As time goes on, I realize that those times with my family and those that have become family are not only what I cherish the most personally. They are also the source of my understanding of diversity, leadership, and the love that I believe is critical to the work of educators and true leaders. I have seen all this demonstrated through the lives of my loved ones, and I recognize this as an extraordinary blessing.

For many people, the value of diversity is generally an abstract concept that they experience on occasion or when they choose. In contrast, my norm has always been one of diversity. Of course, this doesn't mean by any stretch that I have experienced all the diversity in the world or even in our nation. It just means that I have never lived a monocultural life. In fact, my experiences have taught me that it is important that I not only live a multicultural life but that I actively engage in the struggles against oppression.

I should mention that, at least when I was young, I didn't have any choice in what I was experiencing around diversity. For me, like most who have no choice but to learn about these issues, recognizing the value of the diversity that I thought was normal took experiences of de facto segregation, pain caused by bigotry, and isolation among people who looked like me. These experiences contaminated my childhood, shaped my worldview, and changed my professional trajectory.

Before Kacey died, he and I had tried to make a difference together. We tried everything we could think of—speaking to fellow students, arguing with teachers (that was mostly me as Kacey was very well behaved in school), and taking on anyone that dared make a racist comment. It all seemed in vain when we lost Kacey. To this day, I feel like I failed my brother. I was unable to protect my younger brother from the pain and injustice that eventually made life unbearable. The kicker is that I would have done anything, fought anyone, but it was all just too much.

Years of struggling silently with the loss of my brother Kacey followed, constantly fuming over manifestations of racism that continued to go unchecked. I recognized these things all around me and was frustrated and angry that others just let it go or didn't even see it. That was especially true of many of the people who looked like me, White folks, even my Jewish and Irish sisters and brothers who shared the experience of oppression. That was heartbreaking.

Eventually, remembering what I had learned with Kacey from the little girl and the kid we made cry and encouraged by friends and family, I began to tell our stories. Since childhood, I'd been telling stories to entertain my brothers. Now my stories help me to teach, to connect with people, and to keep the spirits of those I've lost alive.

For many years now, I have shared my stories and what I have learned from them with students, doing my best to encourage them to develop a healthy respect for diversity and to step across social divides. With educators, I have shared my stories to illustrate the necessity for promoting multicultural and actively counter hegemonic education. I have found myself speaking to international audiences at Moscow State University, the University of Cambridge, and other international venues. Back in the States, I have shared my stories at schools, on college campuses, at conferences, in houses of worship, and in community centers. I have even found myself speaking to a packed hall of military personnel at the Defense Equal Opportunity Management Institute (DEOMI).

Of course, as is likely obvious by my work with students and educators, I believe that formal education is important. Our schooling experiences often have a profound impact on our lives—some very positive, and others, like Kacey's, tragic. For me, school is where my anger took root. School was and often still is the primary system of discrimination, laying the groundwork for the modern iteration of divide and conquer. My anger didn't come from this conceptual realization. It came from the very real damage that was done to my brother Kacey, to my friends, and to me on a daily basis by "educators."

Today, children are connecting more and more across color lines; at least that's what we like to believe. However, our schools remain largely segregated, and the social circles of those with access remain, for the most part, exclusive.

Progress does continue, but still millions of children are being miseducated and excluded from the opportunities to compete, which come through access to education, resources, and information. In the most basic terms, educational access in the United States remains segregated by the social constructs built around money and melanin. The resulting disparities are kept alive in part through curricula and pedagogical practices that perpetuate the American oppressive tradition, a tradition that is unfortunately not new or unique in the world.

The effects of societal inequities and institutional biases look different in the halls of the Ivy League than they do among the power brokers in public universities. Manifestations of racism, sexism, and all sorts of other—isms look different in the public schools than in not-for-profit/ NGO environments. In the end, we are all touched by social injustice. Some benefit more, and some suffer more. Our social location, or where we are on those spectra of privilege versus oppression, is most often determined primarily by random circumstances of our birth.

None of these statements about the disparities and inequities in education are anything that you couldn't read in the works of Cornel West or Jonathan Kozol, bell hooks, Paulo Freire, or many others—all of whom are better writers than I am. Even with so many luminaries and intellectuals telling us that these problems persist, change is coming too slowly for so many. The reason I believe that it is important for me to include my observations and what I've learned through experience and study is because it is all part of my story. The more of us who tell our stories and what we've learned from them, the more people might connect, and like the little girl or the kid in the cafeteria, maybe they might learn from our experience and be better for it.

Telling my story, whether in a living room or classroom or speaking to a group or writing a blog, has helped me to overcome the anger that once immobilized me. Over the years, my peers were consistent in the observation that I was angry. In fact, I lost a lot of friends and probably missed out on making even more. Even my family and closest friends thought I was too serious and needed to enjoy life more. They'd remind me that I used to love to play basketball or walk on the beach at night and so on. They tried everything, but it just took time for me to get past my anger enough to appreciate life and the wonderful people that still loved me after all the years when I wasn't exactly fun to be around.

After many failed relationships as the not-so-happy fun guy, I finally got it together. Now that I am married, folks have commented after meeting my wife, Kecia, who is African American, that it was inevitable that I would marry a woman of color. I don't know about all that, but I do know that if I had limited myself to women that share my ethnic background, I would have excluded the woman that I love. And now that we have a daughter, Makaila, I wonder what is in store for her. I hope you will be the friends, teachers, and loved ones that make her life more beautiful and loving than what Kacey, B-J, and I found when we left the safety of the apartment behind the liquor store where Mom and Dad taught us the meanings of family, love, and justice.

Back then, Kacey and I used to talk about our dream world. A big part of it was the idea of a world free from racism and other forms of division and oppression. It was a world we'd never seen, except in our small circles of friends and family, but would refer to often. It was at Kacey's funeral services that I got a larger glimpse of that world. The friends and family who gathered to say good-bye to Kacey crossed nearly every major divide you could think of. From race, class, religion, and gender to those schoolhouse divides of athletes, nerds, cool kids, and outsiders. It seemed everyone was there.

It wasn't the fact that they were all there that made it different though. What made this a dream-world moment was that folks weren't sitting in their usual "assigned" groups. They weren't worried about all the usual divides. They were consoling one another, sharing their stories, and really listening to one another with open minds and hearts. They were crying together and holding one another up. We were all bearing witness to one another's humanity. Tragically, it took the nightmare of losing my brother for this moment to occur.

I'll never see Kacey smash through the line for a sixty-yard touchdown run again. I'll never again hear "I'm Kacey, and this is my brother Joe-Joe." Today, my chats with Dad are only in my head. And my dear DiCE brother Sonny and mentor Marvin will only be with us in spirit as we come together to celebrate the completion of our book and the beginning of a new chapter. I could go on and on about what I miss and what I've lost. The truth is that I have been very lucky. If I wasn't blessed with such an amazing family and wonderful life in many ways, then I wouldn't miss those that have passed away as much as I do, and I wouldn't have so many amazing memories to share with my daughter.

My current aspirations are to contribute the best I have to offer, and in whatever way I am capable, to efforts which promote social and educational justice. I have learned a great deal over the years, particularly about myself, global inequities, and the potential for social change. I couldn't possibly care less whether my name is ever known, but I care deeply that my life's work improves the life of someone enough that they do not consider suicide.

I don't know what happens to us when we die. There are some beautiful theories out there. What I do know is that until I know, until I join my little brother, Kacey, and Dad and Grandma and Grandpa and Joya and Sonny and Marvin in whatever comes next, I will continue to fight in their names for equity and social justice for all our children. I fight with every weapon in my arsenal, not the least of which is the love that has been created by the DiCE group.

I hope that our stories, including how we have extended our families to include one another, will encourage you to want to learn more about us, people like us, and people different than you. I don't know of a more fulfilling or revolutionary act than reaching across differences to extend your family. That is my challenge to the reader.

*Dedicated to my family.*

# FLYING WITH THE ANGELS

Marvin Smith

FOR OVER A decade, I have participated in a myriad of diversity conferences, seminars, workshops, and training sessions. At times, in order not to disrupt or redirect the discussion, I painfully listened as the person conducting the session apologetically declared that this is not affirmative action. The implication was that this disassociation would make it easier for people to participate in a thematic discussion that is potentially less volatile and safer than that of one involving affirmative action. While it is true that diversity is not affirmative action, this disclaimer ignores the fact that diversity is the next logical step in the evolutionary advancement of civil rights and equal opportunity in this country. Accordingly, I strongly believe that it is extremely important to always be mindful that many unique aspects of our society and politics have contributed to the situation that we are facing today. The evolution of civil rights statutes, legislation, executive orders, and regulations—which serve as the foundation upon which diversity work is based—has been, without exception, the result of the government's reaction to crisis rather than in response to an assessed need emanating from sincere moral concern. During this process, there were many people of different ethnicities, genders, and religions who, despite their fears, took the risks that caused some to make the ultimate sacrifice.

Admittedly, patience has not been one of my stronger character traits. However, in recent times, I have become increasingly impatient toward the preoccupation with the notion of establishing safety as an environmental element that is essential for candid and intense discussion about diversity and for affecting social change. In an effort to examine the reasonableness of my annoyance with this concept of safety, I discussed the situation with several trusted colleagues. Consequently, I began to reflect on those circumstances in my life, which shaped and solidified my perspectives about taking risks, avoiding injury, and facing danger.

I was born in Kansas City, Missouri, on February 2, 1941, to Gwendolyn and Marvin Smith. Fifteen months later, my sister Osa was born. In early 1946, after my mother and father had separated and divorced from each other, my mother took my sister and me to Lackawanna, New York (adjacent to Buffalo), where we joined my maternal grandmother, great aunt, and other relatives. In July 1946, my mother married Isaac Richard Mitchell, best known as Dick or Dicky Mitchell. From the beginning of their relationship, my sister and I were instantly connected to him. When he and my mother informed my sister and me that they were going to be married, they asked us what we wanted to call him. In my family, it was prohibitive to address an adult by his or her first name alone. Without hesitation, we responded, "Daddy" and never regretted doing so. We were immediately accepted and adopted by Dick Mitchell as his own.

Early on, I was exposed to the contradictions and dichotomies of discrimination and diversity. Lackawanna was politically and geographically divided into four wards. The first ward in which at that time all people of color (Blacks, Latinos, and most Middle Easterners) resided was separated from the other wards by a bridge and railroad tracks. The majority of African Americans lived in three housing areas: the Village, the Baker Homes, and Albright Court. The biggest employer in Lackawanna was Bethlehem Steel, which was also located in the first ward. The Village was housing that was provided by Bethlehem Steel for its employees and their families. It was a combination of structures—units that were joined together for a block, duplex units, and stand-alone housing. The Baker Homes and Albright Court were public housing projects. In the beginning years of our new family, we lived with my grandparents in the Village and later in a former hotel and restaurant that had operated as a brothel and which was converted into apartments. By the time our family expanded to include my sister Sharon (January 1947), my brother Gordon (April 1948), and my brother Dwight (June 1949), we settled in Albright Court.

My father was an athlete who, while in high school, excelled in football, basketball, and baseball. After high school, he continued to play in semipro leagues. Had he not been an African American, he would have been considered professionally for either of those sports. Accordingly, he was a very popular member of the community. Although we had to live in the segregated areas of the first ward, his popularity crossed the boundaries of the other three wards.

Since my middle name is Richard and my nickname Dicky, in Albright Court and the rest of the African American community, I came to be known as Dicky Mitchell. To my non-Black classmates, I was identified and known by my birth name. Inasmuch as I loved both of my fathers very much, I possessed both identities with equal pride.

During the '50s, the favorite pastime activities particularly of males in the Black community of Lackawanna were drinking, sex, gambling and, to a lesser degree, dope. As I entered my teens, my education in life began to take a very distinctively dual and parallel track. One track in school and another in Albright Court—in the streets. Through my observations and experiential learning, I began to obtain my worldly knowledge. In New York State at that time, the legal drinking age was eighteen years old. When I was fifteen, I was over six feet tall and had a slight mustache. I was also an athlete and excelled in basketball. This combination allowed me great social mobility. Most of my closest friends were older than I and met the legal drinking age. Consequently, by ordering with authority, I began to drink at an early age. In addition, I got to know the prostitutes and their pimps, those who carried numbers and who "banked" them, the location of the most popular gambling places, who smoked marijuana and who was hooked on heroin, and who was sexually involved with another's spouse or significant other. While in high school, I was a college prep major with a focus in language, learning about Latin, Spanish, algebra, geometry, and other courses associated with preparing one for college.

It was as if I lived in two worlds. During the day, my White classmates and I were friends. In the evening, with the exception of those who lived in the first ward outside of the White enclaves, we were estranged.

As the development of my character continued, I learned some determining and lasting lessons from both my father and my mother, who was the disciplinarian in our family. A cardinal rule in our household was that whatever was said within the walls of our house stayed within the walls of our house. One weekend during breakfast, my mother told my father about an experience she had at work with the supervisor the day before. I was taken aback by the candor of her remarks to him, so I asked how she was able to speak to her boss that way. She told me, "If you do your work and you do it well, you can say whatever you want."

My first lessons in politics (New York style) occurred while I sat in the kitchen and overheard the discussions that my father had with some of Lackawanna's principal politicians in the adjacent living room.

My father worked in the steel plant when he married my mother. Shortly after I entered my teens, he became Lackawanna's second African American police officer. Given the lifestyle to which I was exposed and to some extent involved, I had some anxiety about his new job. In his special way, he discussed a variety of things with me and was able to relieve my apprehension.

I was emphatically taught to stand true to my convictions; to maintain respect for myself and others; to judge a person by what they do, not who they are; and to always speak grammatically correctly. My parents also strongly advised me against running away from fights. However, I was told that if given a way out, take it; but if not, come out fighting like hell! In the projects, I learned early on that you do not bluff or allow yourself to be intimidated.

Little did I know at the time that these idioms and teachings would permanently remain in the arsenal of my persona and become automatically activated whenever the circumstances so dictated.

The '50s ushered in the era of civil rights. A critical point in the evolution of civil rights occurred in May 1954 when the US Supreme Court in *Brown v. Board of Education* ruled that racial segregation in the public schools was unconstitutional. Since the schools in New York were already integrated, it didn't mean much to me at the time. However, in August 1955, the horror of the racism that permeated the South was vividly brought to the North by the brutal murder of Emmett Till. The fact that a fourteen-year-old African American boy from Chicago was brutalized and killed for whistling at a White woman in Mississippi and the pictures of him in an open casket displayed in *Jet* magazine had a profound effect on me.

Then on December 1, 1955, Rosa Parks, a black seamstress in Montgomery, Alabama, refused to give up her seat when ordered to do so by a local bus driver. She was arrested for violating a Jim Crow ordinance. Her arrest led to a citywide boycott by Blacks, many of whom walked for miles to work and other destinations, which began on December 5 despite terrorist attacks, including the bombing of the homes of boycott leaders, legal harassment, massive arrests, and civil suits. The boycott continued until December 13, 1956. At that time, the US Supreme Court ruled that segregation on public buses in Montgomery was illegal. Dr. Martin Luther King Jr., who led the boycott, emerged as a national leader.

Although physically removed from the situation, I was deeply affected by the actions, commitment, and determination of Ms. Parks and those who participated in the boycott. I didn't realize the profundity of the act that time. Little did I know that this and subsequent events, such as authoring Lucy's attempt to integrate the University of Alabama in 1956; the gathering of more than fifteen thousand Americans, mostly Black, at the Lincoln monument in support of a Voting Rights Act; and the Little Rock Case of 1957 involving nine children who sought to integrate Central High School would begin to further shape my attitude against injustice. The governor of

Arkansas, Orville Faubus, summoned National Guardsmen to turn away the Black pupils. This represented a direct challenge to the federal government, which had already approved a desegregation plan submitted by the local school board. When the Black students were forced to withdraw from the premises of the school in direct defiance of the Federal District Court, President Dwight Eisenhower, for the first time since reconstruction, sent in federal troops to protect the rights of the beleaguered students.

The nine children entered Central High School on the morning of September 25 with an escort of paratroopers. The soldiers remained on call for the entire school year, inasmuch as Governor Faubus refused to assume the responsibility for maintaining order in the community. Later, Faubus and the forces of segregation failed to get a requested two-and-a-half-year postponement of the integration timetable set up for the school.

Little Rock high schools were then closed for the 1958-'59 school term. But when school closing laws were declared unconstitutional by a federal court, the doors of Central High School swung open once again for the members of all races.

After graduating from high school in 1958, I entered Lincoln University, an HBCU in Jefferson City, Missouri. It was the first time in my life that I was exposed to Black teachers. My first class was English, and an attractive young African American female taught it. As I looked at her, I began to mentally question whether she was competent. I then immediately realized that my concern was based strictly on the basis of my "programming" and the correlation between skin color and competence or lack thereof. At Lincoln University, I became friends with two fellow students, a brother and sister from Little Rock, who were affectionately called Faubus's kids. The discussions that we had were very insightful.

Although I spent only one year at Lincoln University, I developed some lifelong friends. After a dispute with my biological father during the summer, I decided to join the army rather than return to Lincoln University.

At that time, recruits from the northeast and eastern seaboards were sent to Fort Dix in New Jersey for basic training. Since I had a girlfriend in Wilmington, Delaware, and New York City was in close proximity, I thought that this would be an ideal arrangement. A couple of days after I arrived at Fort Dix, a rumor began circulating that some of us would be sent to Fort Benning, Georgia, for our basic training. One evening, shortly thereafter, my unit was assembled in the company streets. A small group of names, not including mine, were read aloud. I breathed a sigh of relief until we were told that this small group of recruits would take their basic training at Main Post in Fort Dix. Then the remaining names, including mine, were read and advised that we would be transported the next day to Fort Benning, Georgia, for basic training.

As the troop train passed the cotton fields in Georgia and the workers waved at us, I realized that I was in the deep South and became very apprehensive about what awaited me at Fort Benning. Other than traveling on a bus from Lincoln University to attend a football game at Tennessee State University in Nashville, I had no direct experience dealing with discrimination in the South.

Basic training was every bit as difficult and challenging as I expected it to be. However, before we were allowed to get a pass to go into Columbus, near where Fort Benning was located, my whole unit had to attend lectures on the Jim Crow laws by the chaplain for four weekends. We were advised that while in town, White and African American soldiers had to maintain separation from each other. At that time, in 1959, if an African American soldier and a White soldier walked down the street together, both would be arrested. The White soldier would be released, and the African American soldier could receive six months in jail and/or a $500 fine.

Needless to say, when I got my first pass, I was very concerned about what I was going to experience. As several of my fellow soldiers and I entered a taxi on post, the White driver asked, "Where do you boys want to go? To the colored part of town?" We looked at one another, and I said, "Yeah, I guess that's where we want to go." After that exchange, silence was maintained until we arrived at what appeared to be the main street of the colored part of town, and the driver stopped and asked us for the fare.

After leaving the taxi, we went to a restaurant. While we were dining, we inquired about the location of the USO (United Services Organization). I was surprised to hear that there were two USOs. Even though in 1948, President Truman issued Executive Order 9981 directing "equality of treatment and opportunity" in the armed forces. The USO, albeit a private organization that was to serve all military personnel, maintained segregated facilities in Georgia. The one designated for African Americans was located in an upstairs dilapidated area of a building that was shared by an African American Veteran of Foreign Wars Post; it received the hand-me-down equipment from the White USO. In contrast, the White USO was located on a major street in downtown Columbus in a larger space at street level with a big picture window through which one could observe the downtown area.

After I completed eight weeks of basic training, I was transported to Fort Gordon, Georgia, for advance training in the Military Police School. Although I didn't relish the notion of spending more time in Georgia, I was anxious to finish my training and get to my permanently assigned post.

During the training at MP school, I learned that some of us might be assigned to a military police field unit located at Fort Gordon. The thought of being permanently assigned in Georgia weighed heavily on my mind. When I completed those eight weeks of training, I received orders of assignment to Fort Richardson, Alaska. Since I don't fish or hunt, hate snow, and don't like cold, I really went into a funk. Two days later, those orders were revoked. I received new orders for a permanent assignment at Fort Mason in San Francisco.

In contrast to my previous two bases, Fort Mason was nestled in the heart of San Francisco between the Marina and Aquatic Park, overlooking the Golden Gate Bridge and Alcatraz. It was dubbed the country club of the army and deservedly so. A small base with open access, Fort Mason was primarily a personnel center for the embarkation and debarkation of military personnel and family members traveling to and from destinations to the east. In addition, there were a limited number of family residences for enlisted personnel and officers, including the commanding general of USATTCP (United States of America Terminal Transportation Corps Pacific). Along with the Oakland Army Terminal, Fort Mason was a part of the USATTCP command. Although rank was always respected and acknowledged, being a military policeman at Fort Mason was like being a member of one big family. I became familiar with resident family members, and they with me.

That familiarization became an important factor in the rescue of the wife of a senior colonel. While on patrol one evening, I received a radio transmission informing me that there was a woman standing along the rocks (now part of a boat harbor) near one of the piers. Upon arrival, I recognized the woman, who was barefoot and dressed only in a negligee, as the colonel's wife. She was standing on jagged wet rocks about twenty-five yards from shore. Since I can't swim and was in full uniform, I worried about maintaining my footage, particularly if she appeared to recognize me. I softly persuaded her to take my hand. She began to relax and allowed me to lead her to shore. I later found out that she had a history of mental problems.

Although Fort Mason was an army base, there were air force personnel stationed there as well. There was also a larger population of civilian workers.

Those of us who were in the army were placed in a headquarters company, which was composed of personnel with a variety of military occupational specialties.

One of the less-than-bright spots during my assignment at Fort Mason was the tension that developed between me and a White sergeant from Georgia named Scroggins. Every month, the command conducted a parade, which alternated between Fort Mason and Oakland Army Terminal. On one occasion, while we were waiting to be assembled at Oakland Army Terminal, a group of my fellow soldiers and I were engaged in a conversation. About twenty yards away, Scroggins was talking to a group of officers, all of whom had their hands in their pockets. Suddenly, Scroggins took his hands out of his pockets and came toward me. When he got near me, he demanded that I take my hands out of my pockets. I told him that I saw him with his hands in his pockets and that I would take my hands out of my pockets when he told those officers to take theirs out of their pockets. On the return bus ride to Fort Mason, Scroggins ranted and raved about how he was going to have me court-martialed.

Late in the afternoon of the next day, I was summoned to the first sergeant's office. He, Sergeant Major, was a "spit and polish," highly respected, no-nonsense, and dedicated but fair career soldier. He discussed the incident that had occurred between Scroggins and me. Early the next morning, Sergeant Major called me into his office again. He informed me that he had talked with the provost marshal (commanding officer of the military police unit), Major Thorpe, who was a stoic, somber, serious person, and they agreed that I should receive a verbal reprimand. Sergeant Major further strongly urged that I should accept the reprimand without comment. Immediately thereafter, I met with Major Thorpe. As I maintained direct eye contact with the major, he proceeded to verbally reprimand me. Afterward, he asked me if I had anything to say. He appeared to be surprised when I replied, "No, sir," and then dismissed me.

On one night when I was asleep in the barracks, I was awakened by the commanding general's cook. At that time, a brigadier general could have a full-time driver and a full-time cook assigned to them. The cook, an African American specialist fifth class (sergeant), lived in the general's residence. He informed me that he was going on leave for thirty days and asked me if I would temporarily fill in for him. I told him that I couldn't cook well enough to do that. He explained that I wouldn't have to cook. I would just have to do some chores around the house and drive the general's wife in their personal vehicle whenever she had to go off base. I thought that it would be good to have a change of pace in my work. So despite the historical connotation of working in the "big house," I agreed to do it. Later, I realized how much of a life-changing decision I had made at that time.

After I had been at Fort Mason for nearly one and a half years, I received orders to be reassigned to San Juan, Puerto Rico. I was worried about the reassignment because my wife at the time was pregnant with our first child. I discussed my situation with a personnel sergeant. He informed me that my orders could not be changed, and I didn't have enough rank or time in my present rank (specialist fourth class) to be able to take my wife to Puerto Rico with me. I thought about the matter for a couple of days and decided that I only had one option. The next day, I walked up to the general's residence and explained my dilemma to the general's wife, who was a wonderful, caring, and compassionate woman. When we finished talking, she telephoned the general. He told her to let me know that I shouldn't worry about a thing. Shortly thereafter, my orders for Puerto Rico were revoked, and I remained at Fort Mason. I was very much aware that I could be questioned about skipping over sixteen steps in the chain of command to gain access to the general. However, I was prepared to meet the challenge by arguing that I went to the general's wife, who was not in the chain of command. The issue was never raised.

As the time of my enlistment in the army was nearing its end, Scroggins decided to take another shot at me. One of the most notable characteristics of a military policeman is a shining appearance. When on duty, one was expected to always display this brilliance from head to toe. In order to meet this standard with the least amount of effort, some MPs wore patent leather, Sam Browne belts, and holsters. We also had chrome or bass whistles with corresponding chains, which were attached to the epaulet on the right shoulder and hung over the breast pocket. For over two years while I was at Fort Mason, some of us had chrome whistles, I included, and some, including Scroggins, had brass whistles. One day, Scroggins declared that we should all have the same kind of whistle and called for a vote. There was a majority vote for chrome whistles. Scroggins didn't like the outcome of the vote and ordered that we all wear brass whistles. Being very mindful of the military's strict adherence to rank and hierarchy, my previous experience with Scroggins, and the short time remaining on my enlistment, I told Scroggins that since I could not afford to buy a new one, I could wear the brass whistle if the army issued it. Scroggins became infuriated and said that I would then have to wear the olive drab plastic whistle that had been issued to me. The whistle was attached to a black shoelace. I wore that whistle with sort of a perverted pride for the rest of my time at Fort Mason.

On June 12, 1962, Fort Mason was besieged by a throng of local and national reporters. The boat that carried prisoners and other residents who lived on Alcatraz Island left from Fort Mason. That morning, guards at Alcatraz Island prison discovered dummy faces in the bunks of three prisoners who had escaped. I and other MPs were detailed to search the area in rowboats around and under the piers at Fort Mason. I fruitlessly searched the area while standing in the rowboat with an M1 .30 caliber carbine in my hands and a .45 caliber pistol on my hip. The choppy waters of the bay heightened my concern about not being able to swim if I should fall.

Although for the most part, my experience at Fort Mason was great, I decided that one enlistment in the army was enough. Therefore, I began looking for civilian employment during the last six months of my enlistment. I applied to the Richmond (California), San Francisco, and Oakland police departments. I was in various stages of the application process when, in July, I was offered a job with the Richmond Police Department. The department wanted to appoint me along with three other persons on August 1, 1962, in order to begin an internal training program. Since my separation date from the army wasn't until September 9, 1962, this presented me with a serious problem. I discussed the matter with a personnel sergeant and was advised that because I had already exhausted my leave, the only way that I could have a leave of absence without pay would be to have it approved by the commanding general. Again, I walked up to the general's residence and shared my dilemma with the general's wife. As before, she called the general and explained the situation. The general told her he would take care of it. On August 1, 1962, I became a Richmond police officer.

Even though I was mindful of the negative opinions relative to the role of Southern police officers in the sit-in movement and the freedom rides, and being supportive of the civil rights activists, I was excited about being a police officer in Richmond. At the time, the Richmond Police Department had about 156 police officers of which, with my appointment, only four were African Americans. This was greatly disproportionate to the sizable percentage of African Americans in Richmond's population. Since I had previous police experience and was not yet known to the African American citizenry, I participated in the training program during the day and worked undercover on gambling and prostitution projects during evening while trying to learn my way around the city.

During the classroom training program, I was repeatedly reminded that police officers were a "minority in blue" and that I was a minority within a minority. Furthermore, I was cautioned that my own people would try to take advantage of me. The first time when on patrol, I encountered an African American who became slightly resistant and I became aggressive, I realized that I was responding to the "programming" and immediately checked myself.

In 1963, I experienced a range of emotions. I was aroused by my progress as a police officer and angered by the scenes on television that showed Commissioner Bull Conner and members of his police force using high-pressured hoses and police dogs to discourage protestors from marching into Birmingham. The protestors were marching for the removal of racial restrictions in stores and restaurants and for the adoption of nonracial hiring practices in certain job areas. Consequently, I vowed that I would do everything that I could to make a positive difference in Richmond.

During the summer of 1963, I was asked by my graveyard shift patrol sergeant if I would consider partnering with another officer to patrol an unincorporated area that the city of Richmond was going to annex on July 1, 1963. At that time, with the exception of two beats, all the beats were patrolled by a single officer in motor vehicles. I told him that I would prefer to work alone. He explained that I would be working with Pat Boyle. I then accepted the assignment. The area was called Parchester Village. It was an older housing development of single-family residences exclusively occupied by African Americans. The sheriff's department had previous responsibility for law enforcement and characterized Parchester Village as a haven for criminals. It was located in the northern side of Richmond and was bonded by the San Pablo Bay on the west and railroad tracks on the east. There was only one way in and out of Parchester Village, and when a train rolled by, it cut off any traffic in or out.

One minute after midnight on July 1, 1963, Pat Boyle, an Irish Catholic originally from San Francisco, and I drove into Parchester Village. The Parchester Village area was combined with the North Richmond beat, which was also almost exclusively African American, to make the most dangerous and toughest area to patrol in the city of Richmond. Soon after we began patrolling Parchester Village, we became known by some as the big guy and the little guy. At six feet and one and a half inches and 225 pounds, I was the little guy. Pat Boyle, at six feet and eight inches and 260-270 pounds, was the big guy. Pat and I had previously developed a friendship, but as partners, we were quickly bonded.

Just before midnight on the evening of September 15, 1963, when Pat and I went on patrol, we stopped at the Doggie Diner, a popular twenty-four-hour hot dog and hamburger stand at the corner of one of the busiest intersections of Richmond. We happened to look at the headline of the paper in the news rack, which announced that four girls had been slain in the bombing of a church in Birmingham. As we stood there in full uniform and in disbelief, tears rolled down our cheeks. We both were taken aback by the senselessness and cowardice of this act. Pat and I had jointly celebrated John F. Kennedy's election to the presidency, we grieved at the bombing of the four little girls, and later, we shared the sorrow of JFK's assassination.

Pat and I worked the North Richmond—Parchester Village beat, known as beat 7, for two years before receiving new assignments. Needless to say, we had more than our share of challenges, which we successfully handled. On several occasions when we were addressing volatile situations, which may have required assistance from other officers, we were cut off by a train.

The 1960s were turbulent times for civil rights and trying times to be an African American police officer. I was bothered by the serious racial disturbances, which occurred in a number of cities across the country in the latter parts of 1964. I was troubled by the discovery of the bodies of Michael Schwerner, Andrew Goodman, and James E. Chaney, three civil rights workers, two White and one Black, who had been active in voter registration efforts and found near Philadelphia, Mississippi. I became greatly disturbed as I viewed the television coverage of protestors being routed by billy clubs, tear gas, whips, and cattle prods as they participated in the march to cross the Edmund Pettis Bridge in Selma, Alabama.

After reflecting on those scenes and the news of the deaths of Mrs. Viola Gregg Liuzzo, a thirty-nine-year-old White civil rights worker from Detroit who operated an auto shuttle service, and her African American passenger who were shot by Ku Klux Klansmen while driving on US Highway 80 near Selma, I experienced an epiphany. I more consciously realized that I had God-given talents that were to be used for the better good. I began to understand why at times I felt directed by a higher authority to take action in certain situations despite the risks. I also committed myself to doing everything that I could to contribute to improving the quality of life for others. Consequently, I immediately increased the extent to which I voluntarily worked with at-risk youths. Moreover, I determined that the time had come for me to make a major decision about injustice and police misconduct. I reasoned that if I didn't take action when I witnessed it, then I would be as guilty as the perpetrator of the abuse and would have to live with that for the rest of my career. If I took action and spoke against it, then I would have to deal with the reactions of my fellow officers and others thereafter. Without further hesitation, I chose the latter.

The period between 1965 and 1968 was marked by bloody and violent riots and disturbances throughout many urban cities across the country. On April 4, 1968, Dr. Martin Luther King Jr. was assassinated. The reaction of the African American communities nationwide was angry, violent, and riotous. Richmond was not an exception. In late 1967, I was assigned to the Community Relations Unit. During Richmond's riot, we were able to avoid causalities either to the rioters or police officers, and only one store was burned. It was an upscale furniture store in a depressed area, which some believed was set on fire by its owners.

Also, in 1967, the Kerner report was released after seven months of investigation by the National Advisory Commission on Civil Disorders. The report took its name from the commission chairman, Governor Otto Kerner of Illinois. President Lyndon B. Johnson appointed the commission on July 28, 1967, and "charged it with analyzing the specific triggers for the riots, the deeper cause of the worsening racial climate of the time, and potential remedies." The report concluded that urban violence reflected the profound frustration of inner-city Blacks and that racism was deeply embedded in American society. The commission collected evidence for a variety of problems that greatly affected African Americans. They involved, but were not limited to, overt discrimination and systematic police bias and brutality. Unfortunately, by 1968, Richard Nixon had become president, and the report—along with its recommendations—were, for the most part, ignored.

In my role as community relations officer, I had enhanced my relationship within the African American and Hispanic communities and was acutely aware of their frustration with police misconduct. After the riot in Richmond had settled down, I reflected on the police interactions that I had observed, some of which I had intervened.

I discussed the situation with my fellow African American officers, and we discussed that we would present the issues of police abuse and brutality to the chief of police. By this time, the person who was chief when I joined the force had retired, and we had a new chief who had come up through the ranks. Moreover, there were now ten African American officers, one of whom was still on probation. I enlisted the pro bono assistance of a friend of mine, a young African American attorney, Henry Ramsey Jr. (now a retired superior court judge, former dean of Howard University Law School, and a prominent jurist). With his guidance, we developed a petition signed by nine of us, the Richmond Nine (we decided not to jeopardize the employment status of our colleague who was still on probation) to present to the chief. In doing so, we were violating the main tenet of police officers by breaking the code of silence. I was selected as the spokesman for our group.

For almost a year, the chief resisted our efforts to meet with him and his command officers (three captains) to resolve our concerns internally. The chief, who was not only unsympathetic but was also angry, reflected his displeasure by saying that he would not meet with a delegation of Black officers. Finally, after almost a year had passed, he agreed to do so. When three other African American officers and I arrived at the appointed time and location for the meeting, which we expected to be with the four members of the command staff, we were told that the location had been changed from the chief's office to the civil defense room. The civil defense room was located in the basement of the Hall of Justice and could accommodate a much larger number of attendees.

I immediately knew that we had been thrown a curve. When we entered the room, all the supervisors from sergeant to chief were already assembled. One of the main reasons that we initially wanted to limit our meeting to the command staff was because we were going to cite documented incidents of abuse and name the responsible parties. Some of them were sergeants, and one had advanced to lieutenant. The change of the attendees and location was obviously an attempt to intimidate us. However, without hesitation, we presented the evidence that we had by directly facing each perpetrator. The group received our assertions without comment or discussion. After we completed our presentation, the meeting was adjourned.

Thereafter, tension between the Black officers and White officers heightened to the extent that I felt if there was to be another riot in Richmond, it would begin in the police department. Many of the White officers only spoke to the Black officers when it was absolutely necessary. In the course of doing the work, some of the White officers on patrol were intentionally slow to cover Black officers when dispatched. Although, much to their credit, some White officers privately approached me and told me they understood what we were doing and why but could not openly vocalize their support. Since we were not able to make any progress with the chief and after "fencing" with him for over a year to no avail, we decided to present our concern to the city council. In doing so, we consciously elected to go around the city manager who had made his support of the chief very clear. The day before we were to appear in front of the city council, the chief had letters hand delivered to each of us. The letters stated that if we went forward to the city council, we could face disciplinary action up to and including termination. Instead of dissuading me, the letter angered me and strengthened my resolve.

## In Memoriam

Our fearless brother, Marvin R. Smith, passed on from this life before he was able to commit the thrilling remainder of this chapter of his story to writing. We know from his widow, Delores, that he and the other eight officers, known as the Richmond Nine, courageously went forward with their grievance and that ultimately, the ruling was in their favor.

Marvin left the Richmond Police Department in 1970 and joined the San Francisco Housing Authority. In 1978, Marvin came to the Lawrence Livermore National Laboratory where he directed the Office of Equal Opportunity. Marvin eventually went on to serve in a management capacity in the laboratory's security organization and ended his laboratory career in 2003 as the business affirmative action officer.

Through all these positions, this larger-than-life man with the ready smile, deep laugh, and powerful soul never ceased to be a tireless champion for an example of the promise and beauty of diversity. We continue to miss him, but we are convinced that his spirit and legacy live on through his words, deeds, and the powerful impact he had on us all.

As an example and expression of how Marvin impacted the lives of so many, we have chosen to include the following poem, which was written in memory of Marvin, to close his chapter:

# Kissing a Cloud (for Marvin)
## Kecia Brown McManus

*His hair reminded me of clouds.*
*Cumulus clouds.*
*Where warmth travels upward.*
*Reminiscent of days of lying on grass,*
*back itching,*
*barrettes missing,*
*and way too exhausted from*
*all that rippin' and runnin'*
*us little wild children do.*
*That's it!*
*He was one of those clouds*
*I saw when I was a child.*
*Rolling slowly, courageously*
*through the sky*
*of my ghetto land.*
*That is why when we met*
*for the first time,*
*I was no stranger.*
*For he remembered me*
*looking up to him.*
*He remembered seeing the*
*innocence in my eyes,*
*and he recalled me telling him*
*my joys & fears about life.*
*He heard my words*
*and fought for me*
*so that when I finally had*
*my chance to*
*wrap my frail arms around*
*the man with*
*the voice of thunder,*
*the impact of lightning,*
*the force of mighty winds,*
*and the renewing power of rain,*
*I would one day understand*
*that such great warmth*
*must always travel upward.*

# EPILOGUE

WE, THE AUTHORS, would like to collectively thank you for the investment of time you've made in reading our stories. We hope that you enjoyed them, and that they stimulated, challenged, or inspired you in some way to action.

Unlike a masterful work of fiction, our stories did not result from a deliberately constructed plot. Instead, the preceding chapters are merely retrospectives on the lives we have lived. Only after taking the time to share them together did their commonality and true power to connect us emerge.

Our differences are in some ways obvious, and in other ways, they are more subtle; but above all, they are undeniable. We would not for a moment attempt to downplay them or suggest that the way to make progress in diversity is by smoothing over differences. As we embrace and celebrate our differences, we also acknowledge that within them all a thread of commonality is present. What we have found is that by sharing our stories and exploring both our similarities and differences, we have allowed for an experiential richness which has created genuine kinship.

We believe that our experience has demonstrated what a deeper process for learning about diversity and connecting across social boundaries can look like. We encourage you to engage in conversation, share your stories, and develop community across social divides as we have.

Again, as Tommy mentioned in the introduction, we also want to stress that the time to do this is now. As we have learned through the losses of our DiCE brothers, Sonny and Marvin, tomorrow is not promised to any of us. We feel grateful that we had the time that we did with these two extraordinary men and that we didn't miss out by waiting too long to come together.

We have been taught by many of society's institutions that our visible differences are significant, meaningful, and valid. And indeed they are. Our physical characteristics very definitely help to define who we are and establish our uniqueness. But there is another and perhaps larger dimension of existence that goes much deeper than our observable traits. The ways we feel, the fears we struggle with, the victories we celebrate can all powerfully shape and mold our inner life; our character. In a very real sense, these aspects of our lives may speak even more completely to who we are, and what gives our lives meaning, purpose, and value. Yet, as meaningful as these dimensions of our lives are, they are typically unknown to others unless we reveal them. Our experience has been that revealing these aspects of our lives to others builds kinship and trust, and encourages others to reciprocate. This mutual exposure, sharing, acceptance, inquiry (and the many other interactions that constitute interpersonal engagement) is the warp and woof of community building: it's how friendships are formed and affinity is built, and it starts from sharing our stories.

The English word "community" has its origin in the Latin word for common. And while the most frequent usage of the term refers to people who reside in the same locale, we submit that community members share a lot more than just a zip code. Today, communities are often developed across thousands of miles. In fact, the DiCE community spans state and national boundaries, and many of us belong to online communities through social media such as Facebook or LinkedIn. There are many other examples such as national alumni associations and professional organizations which develop community without being bound by location. Perhaps this is why stories are so important. Our stories help us to build connections, and can be shared in many ways.

Each of our stories about how we were called to do diversity work are as different as the ways that we do our work, the people we work with, and the professional sectors we work in. Whether it was Tommy's perspective as an engineer that you connected with, or Santalynda's more psychological approach, what we believe is most important is that we have all come to similar conclusions, and an understanding that the next step must involve building deeper connections across the boundaries that most often separate us.

Our hope is that by presenting our stories as we have, that you may have found yourself feeling a connection to one or more of our experiences. Maybe it was Sonny's experience in his father's office, or Sidalia's plan to run away with her sister. Perhaps it was Simma's coming out experience that resonated with you, or maybe you have experienced profound loss and could relate to Juan and Joe-Joe having lost their brothers to suicide. It may have been Nadia's description of feeling like an outsider or how Marvin brought history to life through his own story. No matter which stories touched you or felt familiar, these are the connections that provide the opportunity to build community.

We believe that the connections and bonds formed through sharing stories can allow people to transcend all of the social groupings that divide us to form true community; by both embracing who we are and acknowledging our commonality. Not that we've had the same or even similar experiences, but in the fact that who we are has been shaped in large part by our experiences. Perhaps the most salient lesson that this teaches is that if experiences have played such a powerful role in shaping us to date, they may well continue to play a role in shaping us going forward. Knowing this, we can be a lot more intentional about the experiences we create. What will happen if a group of diverse individuals makes a commitment to hear each others' stories, and use the connections that develop to create a new community? Perhaps that is the question *your* book will answer!

We wish you great joy and success in sharing stories within your own community (however you define it), and sincerely hope that you have a similarly rewarding experience as we have—an experience that extends your family.

*The DiCE Family*

# ABOUT THE AUTHORS

Simma Lieberman is internationally known as "The Inclusionist" because of her ability and passion for bringing people together from across all dimensions of diversity and engage in dialogues that result in dramatic breakthroughs.

She creates inclusive workplaces where people love to do their best work and customers love to do business. Simma has been a consultant, speaker and executive coach for over 20 years.

Her clients include: Kaiser Permanente, Diageo, ABM Industries, Pillsbury Bakeries and Foodservices, Applied Materials, Lockheed Martin, Chevron, National Association of Female Executives, City and County of San Francisco, and Kimpton Hotels and Restaurants.

Her articles and ideas have been featured worldwide in such publications as: The Wall Street Journal, NY Times, Investors Business Daily, Forbes.com, The Economist, Managing Diversity Journal, Forbes.com, Black MBA, Restaurant Hospitality Magazine, National Diversity Workforce Network, Working Mother, Cosmopolitan Newsday, CNN.com and Miami Herald.

Simma is one of the hosts of the popular AM radio show "Swirl Radio," and the co-author of the book "Putting Diversity to Work: how to successfully lead a diverse workforce."

Simma lives in Berkeley, CA with her seventeen year old son, and their dog.

Juan T. Lopez, a third generation Chicano, was born in Pittsburg California and grew up there, in Oakland and Concord. In college, he was a community organizer for youth services for the United Farm Workers and Latino social programs. Upon graduating from UC Berkeley he ran mental health programs for a County Agency.

Mr. Lopez has been involved in Diversity since 1981 and was identified as a Diversity Pioneer by the Profiles in Diversity Journal. Notably, Juan was one of the founders of Diversity 2000 (now Diversity 2020) a unique retreat style conference that brings together diversity leaders each summer. Diversity 2000 is where this group of authors came together to form the Diversity Community Exchange (DiCE) Group.

As an entrepreneur, the call of freedom has allowed Juan to pursue different business endeavors. In 1985 he founded Amistad Associates, an organizational development and management consulting firm, and continues to serve as the President. In addition, Juan has developed a business focused on the cutting edge of energy efficiency with the goal of introducing diverse youth to careers in the sustainability movement.

Juan is married to Giselle Sanchez and they have three children, Jordan, Monique and Maya.

Santalynda Marrero was born and raised as a first generation Puerto Rican in New Jersey, where she received her doctorate at Rutgers University. She now lives in the San Francisco Bay Area in California with her son.

A dynamic coach, organizational consultant, facilitator, and trainer,

Dr. Marrero draws on more than 25 years experience as a counseling psychologist to help individuals, teams and organizations in Diversity, Inclusion and Engagement, Cross-cultural skills enhancement, Team Development, Leadership & Coaching, Conflict Management & Resolution, Keynotes & Retreat Design and Facilitation. Being bilingual and bi-cultural has afforded her the opportunity to work in Brazil, Venuezuela, Mexico and Puerto Rico.

Prior to launching SM Consulting in 1993, Santalynda held several internal consulting positions, at Stanford Hospital and Medical Center, Avantek/Hewlett-Packard, Bell Laboratories, and Rutgers University. (Santa's website: www.santalynda.com)

Floyd "Sonny" Massey III (1946-2009) was the eldest of three sons born in St. Paul, Minnesota to Dr. Floyd and Ethel Massey, Jr. His life was rich with an abundance of loving family, extended family and life-long friendships. He had an audacious confidence that made others seek him out for his opinion and his contagious fun-loving spirit.

Mr. Massey held a Bachelor's degree in Sociology from Macalester College, and completed numerous postgraduate certifications in cross-cultural counseling and training, leadership, and diversity management.

His professional career began in sales and marketing and culminated in the role of Director of Diversity for a major telecommunications company. Later, Sonny founded and served as CEO of SOKAKI & Associates, a diversity management consulting firm based in southern California. Regarded as a leading consultant and trainer on diversity management education, Sonny brought a wide range of business and leadership development experience to organizations ranging from Fortune 500 companies to local community organizations.

In addition to being a skilled educator, Mr. Massey was an extraordinary motivational speaker. He used his humor, passion and warmth to help break down barriers and explore what it means to respect and value our differences.

Sonny is survived by his wife Kathy, their daughter Kia, and is missed dearly his DiCE family.

Joe-Joe McManus was born in Massachusetts, and raised there and in the D.C. metro area of Maryland. Professionally his work focuses on the intersections of diversity, education and leadership.

A passionate educator, his experience has included faculty and administration positions at an HBCU, an Ivy League institution, and an international university. He began his career in higher education teaching at Florida A&M University, where he also earned his PhD, and where his students dubbed him "Dr. Joe-Joe." Also notable, he served as the founding executive director of the Ernesto Malave Leadership Academy at the City University of New York (CUNY).

Dr. Joe-Joe's work has taken him from small town Massachusetts to New York City; to the major cities in Russia and the most rural parts of Malaŵi. He has been an invited speaker at numerous universities including Cambridge, Moscow State, and Syracuse. He has also spoken at the Defense Equal Opportunity Management Institute (DEOMI), served on the Board of Directors of the National Association for Multicultural Education (NAME), presented at national conferences, and worked with students at schools across the U.S. and internationally.

Joe-Joe currently lives in Massachusetts with his wife, author and educator Kecia Brown McManus, and their daughter Makaila. (Joe-Joe's website: www.drjoejoe.com)

Sidalia (Sid) Garrett Reel was born and raised in Berkeley, California as part of a large and nurturing family. College lured her away from home, and upon receiving her B.A. in Sociology from Scripps College and Ed.M. from Harvard University, she entered the professional world of corporate training, consulting and human resources. She worked in local, state and federal agencies, non-profit organizations, consulting services, and large corporations.

In 1993 during her corporate training role at Pacific Bell (now AT&T) she was drawn to the position of Diversity Manager, and then accepted a worldwide position with the Hewlett-Packard Company where she led the global diversity and inclusion organization.

Upon completing her doctorate in Education at USC, Dr. Reel transitioned to academia and returned to her Berkeley roots to become the Director of Staff Diversity Initiatives in the Office of Equity & Inclusion at the University of California, Berkeley.

Sid is a widowed mother of three sons and lives in the San Francisco Bay Area.

Marvin R. Smith (1941-2006) was one of the most well-liked and well-respected Diversity Leaders in the Bay Area and beyond. Marvin was born in Kansas City, Missouri, and grew up near Buffalo, New York. He served in the United States Army, and after leaving the military embarked on a career in law enforcement with the Richmond, California Police Department where he, along with eight other Black officers, made a historical contribution to the Civil Rights Movement by standing up against racism. They became known as "The Richmond Nine."

After leaving the Richmond P.D., Marvin took a management position in the San Francisco office of the Department of Housing and Urban Development. Marvin's interests eventually turned to Diversity work where he made some of his most well-known and lasting contributions.

In 1978 Marvin became the manager of the Office of Equal Opportunity at the Lawrence Livermore national Laboratory. During Marvin's tenure is this position the office realized some of its greatest successes. Marvin also served in a managerial role in the Laboratory's security department, and as the Business Affirmative Action Officer before retiring from the Laboratory in 2003.

Marvin is survived by his wife Delores and his three children, and is sorely missed by his DiCE family.

Tommy Smith was born in Memphis Tennessee, and grew up in Oakland, California. His professional life reflects his varied interests of Diversity, engineering, and spirituality.

Tommy is the Director of Strategic Diversity for the Lawrence Livermore National Laboratory. In this role he helps the Laboratory to acquire a diverse workforce and inclusive workplace. Tommy has worked in this role since 1993.

Prior to working in Diversity, Tommy worked as a mechanical engineer for the Laboratory. This work included the design and analysis of various mechanical systems and components for defense systems, and included his receiving a U.S. patent on a Real-Time Electron Energy Spectrometer. Tommy has also served as associate and interim pastor at churches in the

Bay Area, and is the author of *"In Spirit and in Truth—Rediscovering the Message of Jesus."*

Tommy is married and lives with his wife Sandra in Fremont, CA.

 Nadia Younes has over eighteen years of experience developing and launching strategic cross-cultural, diversity and change initiatives in the financial, biotech, pharmaceutical and non-profit sectors She has also taught cross-cultural and conflict prevention & management communications with various universities and colleges, city governments, and public service departments.

Ms. Younes currently leads the global diversity & inclusion initiatives for Rio Tinto, a global mining and metals company. She is based out of London, England and Basel, Switzerland. In this role she is charged with further integrating cross-cultural competency, equity and fairness into business practices, policies and systems worldwide.

Ms. Younes holds a Bachelor of Arts degree in English Literature from Boston University and a Master of Arts degree in Intercultural Communications from University of Denver.

Personally, Ms. Younes has family in North and South America, Egypt, India and Europe and extended family just about everywhere else. She and her Peruvian husband continue to enjoy an international and cultural fusion lifestyle and the continuous personal growth that this invites.

# INDEX

# Y

Younes, Nadia
  as diversity manager, 122
  experience with Salah, 129
  family of, 113-17
  growing up in Hanover, 117, 119
  living in Switzerland, 132
  relationships of, 126
Young Lords, 70, 77
Young Patriots, 76-77

Edwards Brothers Malloy
Thorofare, NJ USA
May 10, 2012